MEMORANDA

Other Books by
Jeffrey Ford

THE PHYSIOGNOMY
VANITAS

MEMORANDA

JEFFREY FORD

AVON · EOS

AVON BOOKS, INC.
1350 Avenue of the Americas
New York, New York 10019

Copyright © 1999 by Jeffrey Ford
Cover illustration by Phil Singer
Inside back cover author photo by Lynn Gallagher-Ford
Published by arrangement with the author
ISBN: 0-380-80262-7
www.avonbooks.com/eos

Library of Congress Cataloging in Publication Data:
Ford, Jeffrey, 1955–
    Memoranda / Jeffrey Ford.
        p.   cm.
    I. Title.
PS3556.O6997M46   1999   99-30703
813'.54—dc21   CIP

First Avon Eos Printing: October 1999

AVON EOS TRADEMARK REG. U.S. PAT. OFF. AND IN OTHER COUNTRIES, MARCA REGISTRADA, HECHO EN U.S.A.

Printed in the U.S.A.

OPM   10 9 8 7 6 5 4 3 2 1

For
my mother, who taught me to dream
and
my father, who taught me to work

MEMORANDA

1

IN THE YEARS SINCE COMPLETING A WRITTEN ACCOUNT OF the fall of the Well-Built City, which told of my personal transformation from Physiognomist to humble citizen and the inception of this once idyllic settlement of Wenau, I never again thought it would be necessary to put pen to paper, but after what has occurred in the past few weeks, I must warn my unsuspecting neighbors. There is a demon loose in paradise—one that beguiles by resurrecting the past. Its victims grow cold to the world, desiring only yesterday, as their souls dissipate for want of exercise in the here and now. Memories swarm about me, every bit as real as the day, and I will attempt to trap them here in this manuscript, like slapping shut the lid on a box full of bees. Then I'll flee northward in order to lose myself in the vast wilderness of the Beyond. It would be a false assumption to think that because I write this with my own hand, in the past tense, that I came through these adventures in possession of my life. Death, it seems, has many definitions.

It was not long after the settlement was founded that the marketplace at Wenau developed into quite a bustling center of trade. The citizens of our new community no longer merely bartered among themselves but also attracted farmers from Latrobia, which lay a considerable distance to the east. River people from as far south as the villages at Constance occasionally arrived on their barques loaded with handwoven cloth, spices, homemade fishing gear, which they hoped to deal for fresh game and vegetables. Our people became adept at gathering and harvesting food, but the items the outsiders wanted more than any others were those mementos of technology we had taken away with us from the destruction of the Well-Built City.

Something as useless as a single brass gear could be traded for a blanket of the highest quality. The river people wore these remnants as amulets of power on cords around their necks. Little did they know how pleased we were to be rid of them. Everything balanced in the end, though, and there were no squabbles or accusations of thievery. The outsiders, having lived closer to the land for longer, were much rougher than we, but they adopted our peaceful ways. This location we chose for our settlement, nestled between two crisscrossing rivers, engendered its own spell of calm.

I went to the market once a week to trade medicinal herbs, roots, and tree bark I collected from the fields and forests—a practice taught to me by Ea and his son before they left for the Beyond. It was on those days that I also met my neighbors and took appointments to visit the women who were carrying children. Ever since delivering Arla's daughter, word had gotten about that I was an effective midwife, and, because of this, I was in some part responsible for the births of at least fifteen children. My acquired role as that of a healer of sorts pleased me, and I hoped that in the hypothetical ledger of my life it would offset somewhat the harm I had previously done.

A few weeks ago, I carried with me to the market something I never before would have thought of trading—a certain piece of green fabric, the veil left to me by Arla. For years, it remained both a bothersome mystery and a great comfort. On those nights when loneliness surrounded me, I would take it out of the chest beneath my bed and hold it fast for the peace it offered. At other times, I would actually speak to it, as if her face still hid beneath, trying to get an answer as to her reason for having left it with me. I often wondered if it was a sign that she had forgiven me or if it was meant to remind me of my guilt.

The night before my trip to the market, I was called on to deliver a child. All went well as far as the mother's health was concerned, but the baby came forth stillborn. I worked for over an hour to try to revive him, knowing soon after I began that my efforts would probably be hopeless. No one blamed me for this tragedy, and, surprisingly enough, though I felt bad, I could not even blame myself. On my walk home through the night, I stopped to look up at the immensity of the starlit sky and for some reason, I still cannot say why, I suddenly felt released from my responsibility to the past. The thought leaped into my mind, "Cley, you will trade away that green veil. It will not do to simply dispose of it. No matter how meager the material worth of the item you trade it for, you must find someone who wants it."

The market was crowded the following day with haggling traders, children at play, and the old, entertaining with comic and cautionary tales. I carried my sack of medicines thrown over my left shoulder and wove my way amidst the practical confusion of the place, searching out likely patrons.

At first, I went about my business, selling what I could. People knew me well and knew that my medicines were genuine. They described complaints to me, and I would tell them exactly what they might use to alleviate their suffering. After making a few trades for thread and fish-bone needles, salt and powdered orian (a bean from the south that when mixed with boiling water made a beverage that was a dull imitation of shudder), I took out the green veil and began trying to trade it.

Those I approached were as polite as usual, but I could tell they remembered the purpose that it had once served and were reluctant to even gaze at it. Although Arla had been gone for years, she remained a mythical figure to the inhabitants of Wenau. The legendary horror of the face that green cloth once masked, its death-dealing power, was too much for them to overcome. I might just as well have been trying to barter a winding sheet stripped from one of their relatives.

Jensen Watt, the owner of the stills that brewed a form of alcohol that was known as field beer, and a good friend of mine, came over to me and put his arm around my shoulders.

"Cley," he said. "No need to trade such a personal item

as the veil. What do you need? I'll send it over to your place before the sun goes down."

"I need to trade this veil," I said.

"You delivered my daughter, for which you asked no payment, and I still owe you from our last card game, but even I wouldn't take it off your hands. You're spooking the entire marketplace by waving that thing around."

"I can't keep this ghost in my house anymore," I told him.

"Tie a stone in it and toss it in the river," he said.

I shook my head. "I must find someone who wants it."

He took his arm off me, leaned back, and raked his fingers through his beard. "Bring it over to my stall. I have six Latrobians there drinking off the price of a mule I borrowed from them last spring. One of them might be drunk enough to trade a trifle, not knowing the story behind it."

I thought this was a sound suggestion, but we never made it to Watt's makeshift tavern, for as we set out across the marketplace, some slight commotion could be heard among the traders at the different stalls. "Look, look," I heard quite a few of them say. I wondered for a moment if they were reacting to the sight of the veil, which I still held in my left hand, but when I turned around, I saw that they were pointing upward at something overhead.

It came circling down from a great height in an ever-diminishing gyre. The wingspan must have been five feet across, and, though its features bore some resemblance to a giant crow, it shone brightly, reflecting the sun from metallic wings. Silence swept through the marketplace as everyone gathered close to the point where it was evident it would land. With perfect mechanical grace, it glided silently down to perch with chrome talons atop a six-foot flagpole that stood at the center of the market.

My heart sank at the sight of it sitting there, cocking its head from side to side as if taking in the entirety of the crowd through its steel eyes. Accompanying each of its movements was the whisper-whir of gears turning within its tin-feathered body. Those gathered around me were smiling up in wonder at it, but I knew there was only one person who could have given life to the glimmering creature.

My worst fears were confirmed when it finally opened its

beak and words came forth in a mechanized imitation of the voice of Drachton Below. Everything that followed was like a nightmare. My neighbors seemed to have, in the eight years we had been free of him, forgotten the Master's voice. I wanted to warn them, to tell them to run, but my words came forth as pinpricks, and my legs seemed mired.

"Greetings, people of Wenau," said the bird. It flapped its wings, and the children clapped their hands. "You have all been so very busy since last I saw you. Now, it is time to sleep. Watch for me in your dreams."

As the shining crow finished with its message, a sudden look of recognition swept through the adults in the crowd. Then the bird screeched like a machine unable to cope with a sudden surge of power, and their faces gave way to expressions of horror. "Below," Jensen yelled a second before the thing exploded with a deafening roar, spewing gear work, springs, and metal shards amidst a billowing yellow cloud.

I could hear the others screaming and choking. In their attempts to escape, they knocked into each other, trampling the unfortunates who had been felled by the blast. My eyes burned so badly from whatever chemical had composed the cloying mist that all became a watery blur before me. Luckily, I had the veil in my hand, and at the first sign that the yellow fog was more than just the smoke of the explosion, I covered my mouth and nose with it.

Staggering blindly, I made my way to the river, which was just beyond the marketplace. I cleared my eyes well enough to make out the edge of the bank, and when I surmised I was right above the water, I dropped my sack and let myself fall forward. Like a dead man, I sank toward the bottom, and the slow-moving current swept around me, washing the acrid yellow fog from my eyes and clothing. I stayed under as long as I could and then worked my way back to the surface, where I drew in a huge draught of fresh air. When I felt as though I had cleansed myself of the Master's evil, I swam to the bank and crawled out.

I could hear the groans of the wounded back at the market- place, and I knew I had to return to help them, but my head was reeling. "Rest for a moment," I told myself, and collapsed onto my back. Staring up into the empty sky, I breathed deeply in an attempt to calm my nerves. All I could think of was Below and how foolish we had been to believe that he could ever let us live free of his interference. As I worked to compose myself, my memory took me back to the Well-Built City, where I had held the title of Physiognomist, First Class. I had done Below's bidding, deciphering the faces of the populace, bringing my calipers to bear on foreheads, cheekbones, chins in order to determine the moral character of that city's inhabitants. The Master, with his self-assurance, his powerful magic and technological genius, had made me believe that his physiognomical standard would allow me to correctly read all of those *books* by their covers. In the process, I had sent men, women, and children to their doom for no more than the shape of an earlobe, condemned the innocent to prison for the prominence of a brow.

Surface was everything, and at the height of my arrogance, I had even believed I could increase a young woman's virtue by changing her outer appearance with my scalpels. In the end, I had butchered her, the woman I loved, to the point where it was necessary for her to go about with a green veil covering her face. When I realized the ugliness I had created, I finally understood the essence of Below. I then helped to subvert his power and topple his regime. The last I saw of him, he stood amidst the wreckage of the Well-Built City, restraining, by a leash, the pitiful wolf girl, Greta Sykes, while circling high above him was the demon he had brought back from the Beyond. "There is so much work to do," he had said. "Last night, I had another dream, a magnificent vision." That vision had just become reality in the marketplace at Wenau.

The yellow mist cleared by the time I made my way, dripping wet, back to the marketplace. Others, who had fled, were also just returning to help the wounded. Bodies lay everywhere. The sounds of anguish had ceased only to be replaced by an eerie quiet. I found a small child, dead, with the bird's silver beak embedded, like a dagger, in his forehead. A woman's face had been ripped completely off by the blast. Five had actually been killed by the explosion. The others who lay about, eighteen in all, were still alive but had succumbed to the yellow mist. These victims exhibited no obvious signs of distress, but appeared just to have dozed off to a midafternoon nap. The peace with which they slept was almost enviable.

I tended to the minor wounds of those who lay in the fog-induced coma while others cleared away the dead. It was a grim business amidst the groans and curses that came from the relatives of the victims. Although everyone was dazed and scared, we worked together to try to bring the situation under control. Even the outsiders pitched in and did what they could. Jensen, who I was happy to see survived the blast, led his drunken Latrobian patrons to the river, where they fetched water to be used to try to revive those under the spell of the chemical.

I made good use of the herbs and roots in my sack to create poultices that would stave off infection in minor wounds. To the mother of the dead child, I administered a dose of owl's beard, a stringy moss that grows only at the tops of old yew trees. This calmed her for the time being, but I knew, as well as her trembling husband, that there was nothing in nature that could quell the loss forever. We tried everything to revive those trapped in that strange slumber. I broke sticks of ice mint under their noses. Cold water was applied, light slapping followed, and when we grew frustrated, we shouted their names into their ears. They remained wrapped in a deep sleep, each of them wearing the most damnably subtle grin as if they were all dreaming of paradise.

I did not head for home until well after dark, when all of the dead had been buried and the sleeping had been carried safely to their beds. Before taking leave, I borrowed a change of clothes from Jensen and sat with him and some of the others down by the river, where we drowned our anguish with field beer. The conversation was subdued, focusing mainly on the lives of those who had died that day. No one had any answers, but each of us asked at least once what the fog could have been. At the time, it was a better question than, "Will they ever awaken from it?" This was not the only thought unvoiced that night. We all knew that we would have to deal with Below, which would mean returning to the ruins of the Well-Built City. It was clear that we would probably have to kill him.

On my way home through the meadow, I stopped in the

same spot I had the previous night and again looked up at the sky. Reaching into my pocket, I retrieved the green veil and held it out to look at it. Even if I had gotten someone to take it off my hands, I realized that I could never really be rid of it. Besides, it might very well have saved my life.

I spent a sleepless night, the candles burning brightly, unable to face the demons, werewolves, and mechanical exploding birds I might find in my dreams. The stone knife I held in my right hand was for Below, should he appear from out of the darkness; and the veil, which I held in the left, was for me.

2

WHEN THE SUN FINALLY ROSE TO SHOW ME THAT BELOW wasn't lurking in the shadows, I lifted my stiffened body from the chair in which I had kept my vigil and crept over to the bed. I fell into it much the way I had fallen into the river the day before. No sooner did I close my eyes, though, than a knock sounded at the door.

"Cley, are you in there?" said a familiar female voice. It was Semla Hood, a young woman whose child I had delivered and whose husband, Roan, was a fishing companion of mine.

"No," I called out with a heavy sigh, and rolled myself to a sitting position.

"Please, Cley, you must come. Something terrible has happened."

I stood slowly and shuffled to the door. My only solace was that I did not have to change, since I had spent the night fully dressed, supposedly ready for action. I opened the door.

"Cley," she said. "Roan has fallen asleep."

"Most enviable," I said as I reached up to block the sunlight from my eyes.

"No, I mean he won't wake up," she said, and I could now read the distress on her face.

Then through my fatigue the ordeal of the previous day came back to me. "Did he breathe much of the yellow fog yesterday at the market?" I asked.

"He wasn't at the market yesterday," she said. "He never went to the market. But last night, he sat with one of the neighbor's children who had been sent to sleep by the fog. The girl's parents were worn-out and didn't want to leave her unattended, so he volunteered to stay beside her till dawn."

"What have you done to try to wake him?" I asked.

"Everything," she said. "I even drove a needle into the palm of his hand, and he didn't so much as stir."

She begged me to accompany her back to their home so that I might take a look at him. I went along with her, in order to ease her worry.

"Do you think it's bad?" she asked.

It was very bad, but I didn't tell her that. At first I had thought that the fog had somehow affected the nervous systems of those who had been put to sleep by it, but now I realized that what we were dealing with was a disease and a virulent one at that. The incubation period in Roan's case had been a mere matter of hours. My training had not been in germs, but I knew a smattering about them from my basic biology classes at the university. I knew it was not beyond Below's powers to have either discovered or engineered a parasite that would cause these symptoms.

At the Hoods' home, I took one look at Roan, who was now laid out in his bed, and, seeing that smile on his lips, I counted him among the victims.

"What can we do?" asked his wife.

I shook my head. "Keep him comfortable," I said. "Try to force some water into him, but be careful not to drown him in the process."

"Isn't there anything else?" she asked. "I thought you might know of some plant of the forest that could bring him back to me."

"Herbs are useless here, Semla," I told her. "There is something else I've got to try." With that I turned and left the house. The minute I was outside, I started running.

I did not stop until I reached the marketplace, which was utterly abandoned. At its northern entrance is a bell that can be rung to bring the people of Wenau together for a meeting. The only other time we had faced a crisis in our history was three years earlier when the rivers had, after torrential rains, breached their banks and flooded part of the settlement. Now I hoped that there was still someone left awake to hear the call. I pulled its rope and sent out my alarm. Then I paced back and forth for a quarter of an hour, waiting.

Slowly, those who had not succumbed to the disease began to show, and by each of them I was told of at least one person they knew who had caught the sleep through the night and could not be awakened. When a good number of them had gathered, and it seemed there were no more coming, I raised my voice and begged for silence.

"By now," I said, "I think it is evident that Below has sent us more than an explosion. He means for us all to sleep to death. We could take the chance and hope that our loved ones will awaken, but knowing the Master, I would not count on that."

Both men and women began to shed tears, and the children gazed up at their parents with faces filled with confusion. It was these looks that gave me the courage to go on and make my proposal.

"Time is so crucial now. We must leave today for the Well-Built City. Our only hope is to find Below and somehow force him to divulge an antidote for this illness he has sent. All we can do is pray there is some cure for it."

"And how do you expect to get him to cooperate," yelled Miley Mac from the middle of the crowd. "We all remember him. We suffered as much as you did."

"I don't know," I said, "but if we do nothing, I'm afraid that both we and our settlement are finished."

"I'd rather wrestle the Devil, himself," said Jensen.

"Agreed," I said.

"It could pass," said Hester Lon but with so little conviction that the very tone of her words proved my point.

"We haven't time to debate. I'm going. Will anyone else come?" My request was met with silence. The good citizens of Wenau had lost their nerve in the face of tragedy. None of them looked me in the eye.

"I need a horse and a gun," I said, not quite believing the madness I was suggesting.

"I've got a horse you can take," said a voice from the crowd.

Someone else made an offer of weapons and another volunteered his hunting dog.

"Now, who will go with me?" I asked.

Not one of them spoke or stepped forward.

I waited for some time, thinking the silence might draw a
few of them out. My spirits lifted as I saw Jensen take a step
forward. But as he moved toward me, I noticed his eyes rolling
back into his head. His lids closed, he uttered a low grunt and
fell to the ground. Some ran from him, knowing he had the
disease, while others gathered around to try to help. By the
time I got to his side, he was lightly snoring.

From those who had offered provisions for my journey to
the ruins, I secured a promise that they would deliver them
to my home at dusk. My plan was to travel by cover of night
in case Below had spies or assassins watching us. Paranoia, a
constant companion from our days in the Well-Built City,
moved freely among us again, draping a friendly arm over
the shoulders.

On my walk home, I watched the sky for a glint of metal
and constantly scanned the underbrush and tree line for sudden movement. Whereas Below had sent the citizens of Wenau
to sleep, he had also infected the place with a disease of oppos-
ing symptoms that transformed its usual repose into an atmosphere of nervous, jangling tension. I spoke aloud to myself
for a sense of company, saying, "If you think you are scared
now, Cley, wait until you are out on the plains and in the
forests by yourself at night, riding toward the heart of this
evil."

A wild turkey broke through some tall grass to my left
just then, and I leaped to the side and gave a short scream.
The bird stood there for a moment and looked quizzically at
me before retreating. That stare with which the creature sized
me up, as if to say, "Cley, you are a ridiculous specimen,"
made me laugh out loud. Here I was, the self-appointed cham-
pion of Wenau, about to start on a quest to slay the *dragon*. I
pushed on toward home, while in my mind I looked forward
to the day when I could again sit with Jensen by the side of
the river, drinking field beer.

You can imagine my reluctance to sleep that afternoon,
but, having had none through the night, I knew I would need

to rest. At first, I was overtired and found it difficult to relax. The uncertainty of the future came to me in a variety of morbid and terrifying thoughts, not the least of which was my failure to succeed. Eventually, though, I fell warily into a dream of the green veil. In it, Drachton Below stood in the center of the marketplace, surrounded by the supine forms of all the inhabitants of Wenau. All were fast asleep and their faces were covered by scraps of a green material. A yellow mist curled around him as he beckoned to me.

"Your turn, Cley," he said, and flung a handful of sparkling dust in my direction. The cloud moved like a swarm, and I was amazed to see that it was composed of tiny metallic birds. They swept into my eyes, blinding me. I fought as best I could against the weariness that descended. As I fell to the ground, I heard the Master's voice.

"Come to me," he said, and I could feel the veil lightly landing on my face. I panicked in my sleep within a sleep, thinking, "I have caught the disease," and then suddenly came awake to the sound of a dog barking.

I scrabbled out of bed, dressed quickly, and went to the door. Upon opening it, I was greeted by a most unpromising sight. The oldest, saddest-looking gray horse I had ever seen was tied up to the crank handle of my well. The beast's spine was concave, its tail was a ragged whisk broom, and it kept its head bowed as if in humiliation at the physical state its years had visited upon it. Circling nervously between the well and the tree line was an underfed black dog, whose skeletal anatomy was completely evident through a thin scrim of hide. I had seen likenesses of him in allegorical paintings by the artists of antiquity. He was often depicted with a blind beggar, and was meant to represent Want.

To round out this embarrassment of riches, I discovered a crossbow along with a quiver of twelve arrows lying next to it. A thirteenth arrow was stuck in the ground, spearing a scrap of blue paper with writing on it. I pulled the shaft from the dirt and retrieved the message.

Cley,
  Here are the things you requested. The horse, Quismal, is not swift but he is strong. The dog, Wood, has been known

*to be ferocious on certain occasions. Feed it a scrap of meat
and it will follow you for two days. Give it more and it
will do your bidding. We would have liked to have given
you a rifle, but those who had them thought it would be
better to keep them on hand in case of an attack. The crossbow is a well-seasoned weapon. It can kill accurately at one
hundred yards. Good luck, Cley. We will never forget you.*

Your friends,
The Citizens of Wenau

This note gave me a clear understanding as to my neighbors' assessment of the potential success of my mission. Perhaps I should have taken this warning, given in to fear with
the rest of them, and waited to see what would happen. The
unkindest item in the entire inventory had to be the crossbow.
How effective could it really be at a hundred yards against
the charging wolf girl, Greta Sykes, or one of the Master's
mechanical monstrosities?

"I might just as well spit in self-defense as fire this old
log," I thought as I leaned over and lifted the weapon. It was
more firepower than I possessed, though, so I made the decision to pack it on the horse. I strapped it to the saddlebag
along with the quiver, thinking that if things got too horrifying, I could at least impale myself on one of the arrows.

I went back in the house and gathered my supplies: a sack
of herbs, the bone knife Ea had given me, some dried meat, a
blanket, and, of course, the green veil. Before I closed the door
to leave, I took one more look around my small rooms and
was filled with a melancholy sense of longing that I might one
day return to live out the rest of my life in peace and comfort.

Outside, I called to the dog to come. It continued moving
erratically around me in wide circles, its tongue lolling, its
eyes suggesting madness. Reaching into my pack, I retrieved
a scrap of dried meat and held it out.

"Wood," I called. "Come, boy."

The instant the creature saw the meat, it bolted out of its
meandering orbit and made straight for me. I had only a second to turn to the side as it leaped into the air to snatch the
morsel and nearly two of my fingers. He took his prize a

few feet away and began devouring it, making all manner of
unnatural noises. I approached slowly, my hand out.

"Good, boy," I said. "Wood, Wood, Wood," I sang softly.

The ungrateful wretch growled and lunged for me. At the
last moment, I jumped back, and as it passed, I gave it a
mighty kick in the rear end. It yelped and ran away into the
undergrowth.

By the time I was able to get onto the horse, which took
a good measure of struggle, the sun had nearly set. There was
still a mere wisp of red light on the western horizon above
the treetops. It was going to be a beautiful night, warm enough
but with a nice breeze beginning to blow. A few stars had
already appeared in the sky directly overhead, and I prayed
for a moon so it would not be too dark in the forest.

I had been on a horse maybe once or twice before in my
life, and that was as a boy when I lived along the Chottle
River. Now it seemed a long way to the ground from where
I sat. The poor thing buckled somewhat under my weight,
and it stank like death had already taken up residence in its
swollen belly.

"Go," I said, but it didn't move.

"Charge," I said, and drove my heels into its flanks. It
passed gas in a long, loud, gurgling stream and then lurched
forward like a drunken man put off-balance by the planet's
rotation.

My quest was begun. As we inched our way toward the
tree line, the black dog came dashing out of the undergrowth
in pursuit as if aware he was an allegory who could not be
separated from his blind beggar. I did not consider my chances
of success or the insidious ways I might die. Instead, I contem-
plated Below and his terrible need for control.

3

I TRAVELED ALL NIGHT ON THAT LUMBERING NAG, COW-ering at every dark form that rustled the fallen leaves or swooped low beneath the canopy overhead. Meanwhile, the black dog disappeared for a half hour at a time and then, all of a sudden, broke from the undergrowth to my right or left and ran between the slow-moving legs of my mount. Quismal was confused by this and immediately halted in his tracks. I tried driving my heels into his sides to get him going again, but I might as well have been kicking myself. Finally, I discovered that a few kind words whispered into his ear did the job better than any violence. "Onward, noble steed," I said, or some such nonsense, and sure enough he lurched forward.

The voices of crickets in the breeze became conspiratorial whispers. Even the full moon, which I had been so happy at the start to have as a companion for the journey, began to take on a sinister aspect. We broke into a clearing, and I looked up to stare its milky brilliance full in the face. The features of its physiognomy were exceptionally clear and struck me as closely resembling Below's. I thought about the Master, standing atop a high tower, spinning on the heels of his boots to take in the entirety of the puny lives of Wenau. It would have been no surprise to see a giant thumb descending to squash me.

I breathed deeply in an attempt to suppress my fugitive imagination, and it was then that the scents of the forest broke through to calm my fears. From that one inhalation, I was able to distill the aromas of trailing serpent vine, fantail blossom, and the oozing root of tarasthis fern. These were all familiar to me from my daily forays into the woods to search for medicines. Each of them, when dried and ground, was a cure for a different illness—gout, river blindness, acute melancholy—and now just their fragrances were enough to cure me.

I kept to the trail that had been forged in recent years by merchants from Latrobia, but with the first light of morning, I coaxed Quismal into the underbrush, and we headed northwest for the fields of Harakun. I hadn't seen or heard Wood for over two hours before changing direction and was resigned to the fact that he had most likely found a rabbit to torment instead of myself.

By the time the sun was high in the sky, I was exhausted from having traveled all night. Quismal was damp with perspiration, spluttering and frothing from both ends, and obviously as much in need of rest as myself. When we finally broke clear of the forest and forged the creek that defined the southern boundary of the plain, I found a huge, spreading Shemel tree overhanging the water. It was here that I decided to stop for a spell. I tied the horse to a low-hanging branch where he would have access to both water and grass. Retrieving the crossbow and quiver of arrows from the saddle, I chose a spot in the shade for myself and sat down.

I was saddle sore, bleary-eyed, and altogether overjoyed once again to touch down on solid ground. The day was warm, and the ever-present breeze of the plains moved around me, lulling me into a temporary amnesia. I had wanted to try the crossbow at least once before reaching the city, but instead, I lay back and stared up at the sunbeams that found their way through the swaying clusters of star-shaped leaves. The thought of sleep still frightened me, considering the fact that I might have carried the disease away from Weanu with me, but I finally closed my eyes.

I woke sometime later to the sound of barking, and even in my half cognizance felt a surge of disappointment to think that the dog had found me. Sitting up quickly, I turned around to check on the horse. The faithful Quismal was still where I had docked him, munching grass and swatting jade flies. I cleared my eyes and turned around, trying to get a bead on where the dog was. When I finally spotted him, he had crossed the creek and was standing on the bank some twenty yards away from me, shaking water from his coat. With nose wrinkled back and teeth exposed, he crouched down in front while the hair along the ridge of his back spiked up. His curled tail straightened as he began growling.

If he had seemed mad before, he now looked positively deranged. I reached slowly down next to me and grabbed the crossbow. "Good boy," I called to him. He continued growling and barking. I'd had quite enough of the benefit of his presence. He would be nothing but a liability to me when I tried stealthily to navigate the ruins of the city. My hands shaking, I lifted the bow and then grabbed an arrow from the quiver. Continuously speaking to him in as soothing a voice possible, I tried to pull the weapon's cord back. I moved the string about three inches and it would go no farther. My knowledge of the operation of crossbows was less than shallow, and having lived a life of relative ease, I didn't posses half the arm strength of a well-trained soldier. Quickly improvising, I brought my feet up to hold the cross of the bow in place and then, still gripping the string, leaned back. With this technique, I barely managed to hook the cord up over the firing mechanism.

Then Quismal whinnied and snorted, and I looked up to see Wood charging, his teeth bared, his tongue lolling, his eyes fierce. "Harrow's hindquarters," I yelled, and reached for an arrow. I had half a mind to forget the ancient weapon and scramble up a tree. He was five feet from me as I fitted the shaft into place along the barrel of the bow. I curled my finger around the trigger, lifted the stock to my shoulder, but as I aimed, I could see that he had already leaped. I gave a very unsoldierlike yelp of fear and, instead of firing, dropped the weapon and fell facefirst to the ground, covering my head with my hands. To my astonishment, he sailed right over me, snarling like some demonic creature of the Beyond. Before I could grab the bow and spin around, I heard another beastly voice join his with a sharp cry of pain.

In seconds, I was on my feet, the bow up against my shoulder, aiming at two forms that struggled on the ground only a few feet from me. Before I could clearly see what it was Wood had by the neck, I smelled the depraved bile scent of the Latrobian werewolf. Then the silver-gray coat, the half-human haunches and claws came clear to me. Gathering its strength, it stood on its hind legs, lifting Wood with it. With a cry of agony, it spun ferociously back and forth, whipping the dog free of its neck, a piece of which came away in a shower of yellow blood.

I pulled the trigger and the arrow shot out with a force I hadn't anticipated. The weapon fell from my grip, but still, I was able to follow the progress of the shaft as it caught the monstrosity square in the underside of its chest. There was more yellow liquid, more horrendous bellowing, and though I was frightened beyond measure, I actually cheered and gave a slight jump like a child who has just won a round of split the muggen. It was a momentary victory, for the instant the creature hit the ground, it began loping toward me on all fours.

Wood again came to my rescue, charging from where he had landed in the grass, and leaped onto the werewolf's back, burying his fangs in the top of its spine. They both went down again, rolling and slashing in the dirt. This gave me the time I needed to lift the bow, pull the string back while holding the cross down with my feet, and affix another arrow.

"Get off, Wood," I cried as I took aim again. The creature threw the dog down in front of it, struggled to its hind legs where it reached back a massive hand-paw studded with four-inch claws, and took a swing at my protector's head. That dog was insane, but he wasn't stupid—he slipped between the werewolf's legs, free of the blow. I aimed quickly for the chest again, fired, and the jolt of the bow lifted the arrow in its course, sending it directly into the thing's forehead. The werewolf stumbled forward a few steps on its hind legs and stopped suddenly. It stared at me momentarily with a pitiful gaze, as if recalling its lost humanity, and then its eyes crossed as it fell forward onto the ground. It continued to writhe, growl, spit, and chew the earth until I gathered my wits and bashed the remaining life out of it with the butt of the crossbow.

As soon as I was sure it was dead, I dropped the weapon and walked to the creek where I plunged my own head into the water. When my adrenaline had finally stopped pumping and my heart lost its hummingbird flutter, the real terror set in. I was elated to have come through the encounter with my life, but the face of the vanquished monster told me in no uncertain terms that this was only the beginning. The creature Wood and I had killed was not Greta Sykes, Below's original beast. It had moved somewhat more clumsily than she. On closer inspection it proved to be a male and had no headbolts as Greta had. Given Below's propensity for carrying all projects across the boundary of absurdity, I realized there could be an entire pack of these things guarding the perimeter of the city.

I was shaken, but the discovery of a second werewolf was an undeniable argument that the Master had to be stopped as soon as possible. Before moving on, I went to the saddlebag on Quismal's back and retrieved a handful of dried meat. I called Wood to me. He came quietly enough and sat at my feet. Kneeling down, I expressed my thanks to him, petting his head, scratching his chest, while I fed him the strips of meat. He panted and ate and made a face with his teeth showing as though he were smiling. When he had finished the meal, and there was nothing else I could say, I stood and went to fetch the bow and quiver of remaining arrows. I bent over to lift the weapon, and he ran by behind me and bit me on the rear end, pulling my trousers down. I turned to kick him, but he was off like a shot, streaking across the plain.

"Idiot," I yelled after him, and then turned to see that Quismal, savant of horses, had somehow undone his reins from the tree and was standing in the middle of the creek.

I spent a half hour fishing my mount out of the water before I was on my way again. We crossed the open expanse of the fields of Harakun, where so many historic battles of oppression had been waged by the forces of the Well-Built City against the farmers of Latrobia. Thousands were buried in mass graves beneath the ground I traversed, their lives cut short by the Master's will and whim. There was an eerie sadness to the desolate plain, which, as I had read in school, had once been fertile ground. Now nothing grew there but a tawny-colored saw grass and an occasional gnarled tree, as if the deaths of all those souls had also killed the very earth on which they had battled. I was equally tense for the fact that there was little cover with which to block my approach to the walls of the City.

Quismal could obviously feel the spirit of the place, for he overcame his usual lethargy and was actually skittish at times, prancing to this side or that, whinnying at the sight of birds and rabbits. I stayed low on his back, trying to present as slight a spectacle as possible to anyone or anything that might be watching. When we would move across a clearing that held no grass, I more than once saw paw tracks in the soft dry dirt that I knew were too large to be Wood's. In the late afternoon, I saw something moving through tall grass about a quarter of a mile to the west and was almost certain it had a silver-gray coat. As I continued deeper into the heart of the plain, I had the sickening realization that they were probably encircling me, waiting for nightfall.

It was twilight when I first caught sight of the City's jagged silhouette in the distance. The few remaining spires, the blasted outer wall, and crumbled buildings appeared all together like the fossil of an ancient behemoth that had fallen from the sky. The shaft of the crystal tower that had been the Top of the City glimmered like a diamond eye in the setting sun. I could not help but think that it could see me returning. For a moment, I forgot about the horrors that had been perpetrated there and experienced a brief wave of nostalgia. I had spent my youth there, had risen to power, learned my gravest lesson there. I reached into my coat and retrieved the green veil. I could not deceive myself that I had come solely to save my neighbors.

As I gauged by the position of the sun how long I had until nightfall, I noticed three birds moving through the sky from the direction of the ruins. At first, I took them to be crows or hawks, but then the last of the sun touched them and they glistened like splinters thrown off from the remains of the crystal tower. I needed no more of an indication than those brief sparks of light to know exactly what breed of bird they were. I reached back and brought up the crossbow. As soon as I had the quiver of arrows slung across my back, I leaned forward and pleaded for Quismal to run. He must have felt my fear, because, to my astonishment, he actually began to canter.

By the time he achieved a gallop, the first of the metallic birds had begun to spiral down toward us. I pulled hard on the reins from left to right, directing the horse in a zigzag pattern while all the time watching the deadly mechanism in its descent. As if it had intelligence, it stayed with us as we fled erratically across the plain. When it was no more than a hundred yards above, it hovered for a second and then simply plummeted like a stone dropped from a cliff. It missed us by less than ten yards and upon impact with the ground exploded with an intensity that threw earth and rock high into the air, nearly knocking me out of the saddle. We had narrowly escaped, but the blast frightened Quismal back into his usual apathy. He hobbled a few more steps and came to an abrupt stop.

The second and third of the flying bombs began to circle downward toward us as I pleaded for the horse to move. In the space of ten seconds, I had called him everything from the noblest creature that had ever lived to the essence of equine genius, but it was clear he had become a living statue. I had no choice but to abandon him and run. When I leaped to the ground, Below's chrome messengers of death had begun their free fall. I sprinted fifty yards in little more than the time it might have taken to sign my name and then dived onto the earth. Shielding my eyes, I looked back just in time to see poor Quismal come apart at the seams like a bursting flagon of wine. The roar and shock wave rolled over me as hooves and entrails showered down in a twenty-yard radius from where he had once stood.

The fear I had worked so hard to keep in abeyance now spread through me—an ice that formed with the speed of fire. I thought nothing as I ran headlong toward the ruins. When I finally stopped to catch my breath, I realized that night had fallen. I immediately set about arming the crossbow, but before I could engage an arrow, something came bounding out of the dark. There was not even time to be startled. Never did I think I would be so happy to see the black dog. He trotted over and sat at my feet.

4

I MOVED CAUTIOUSLY FORWARD, THE BOW LOADED, ITS stock against my shoulder, my finger on the trigger. It was impossible to see more than a few yards in any direction, and I had lost sight of the remains of the City. Wood stayed mercifully close to me, and this took a fraction of the edge off.

The sky was overcast, offering no moon or starlight, and I wasn't sure this was to my benefit or not. We managed to cover what I surmised to be about half the distance to the wall before the howling started. Until then, I thought we might have a chance of making it undetected. These creatures made a noise like angels in mourning. Their voices came from all over the plain, and it was clear to me very quickly that they were communicating our position. My arms and legs began to tremble, and I found I was paralyzed with fear.

Wood trotted over to where I stood, grabbed the top of my right boot with his teeth, and began tugging. This had the same affect as someone nudging me awake. I shook off the fear as best I could and tried to concentrate. Even though I started walking again, I couldn't put together a rational thought. My mind was simply blank, and I felt a great weariness in my limbs. Then the howling abruptly ceased, giving way to a silence that was even worse.

"They're coming," I said to the dog, and

stopped in my tracks. I turned around in a full circle, aiming
the bow from the level of my chest. Wood began to quietly
growl. My eyes had adjusted somewhat to the darkness, and
I was able to peer a few feet ahead of me. I stood still for
some time, listening as hard as I could. At first I could only
hear the blood pulsing in my head. A few moments later, I
detected the slight sound of the breeze moving through the
grass, and a short time after that came what seemed the subtle
patter of paws scampering in the soft dirt some distance behind us.

Knowing I probably wouldn't be getting much older, I
decided to hell with caution, and we both broke into a frantic
dash at the same instant. My adrenaline was pumping again,
which was the only reason I was able to keep pace with the
dog. I'd never moved so fast in my life until we heard their
howls right behind us, and I managed to increase my speed
even more. They were charging hard, and from the sounds of
their yelps and snapping jaws, they were closing on us.

My lungs were heaving, tears were streaming from my
eyes, when I foolishly looked back to see how close they actually were. That is when one leaped out of the shadows to my
right, its head ramming hard into my shoulder and loosening
my grip on the bow. The weapon flew out of my hands as I
lost my balance and went over facefirst in the dirt. The creature
was on me in a second, those deadly fangs miraculously mis-
judging the distance to my neck and instead snagging the col-
lar of my coat. I was too scared to think, but immediately
reached down into my boot, where I kept Ea's stone knife. As
the werewolf disengaged from the cloth, I plunged the razor-
sharp blade into its underside and sliced up toward the head
as if unfastening a huge zipper, trying to sever as many major
organs as possible. Even as its putrid insides spilled out onto
me, it took hold of my shoulder with its teeth and began
applying pressure. Wood rammed the dying monster in the
side with his snout, and flung it off of me as another appeared
out of thin air and landed on his back.

I didn't bother standing but rolled over to where the bow
lay with the arrow still engaged. As I aimed, I lifted myself
to my knees, jostling the weapon in the process. I should have
taken more care, for fear of hitting the dog, but my finger

seemed to pull the trigger of its own volition. The arrow merely grazed the left shoulder of the new attacker, but it was enough to get its attention. It left Wood on the ground and charged me. As it lunged, I dropped the bow, and reached back to pull an arrow out of the quiver. Holding it angled up with two hands, I skewered the odious wretch right through the chest as it descended. Of course, it wasn't dead, so I lifted the bow and swung it like a club. The head of the creature caved in with a hollow crunch, but at the same time the weapon splintered and split in half.

I began running again, stumbling forward, and the wounded dog hobbled along at my side. Only now did I begin to feel where the first werewolf had lacerated my left forearm with its claws. The pack was still a little distance behind us, but I knew it was over. I felt there was no sense in torturing myself any longer. In that moment, Wood peeled away from me and took off in the opposite direction, heading straight back toward our pursuers. I didn't know how badly he was wounded, but I knew that he meant to buy me a minute or two. My mind was in a state of utter confusion, but still, I managed to think, "All this for a few scraps of meat?" Then I heard his vicious growl as he met the pack, and I forced him out of my mind.

The noises that came from behind me sounded like a hundred death cries at once. I ran on a few more yards until I simply collapsed from exhaustion. The pressure in my heart and lungs made me feel as if I were going to explode like Quismal. I welcomed this prospect in light of the alternative. Looking up, I saw the shadowy outline of the crumbling, circular wall and the jagged silhouette of the Top of the City. It was a mere fifty yards off, but I didn't have enough strength to get to my knees. In the midst of my distress, I did not miss the irony that those things my neighbors had given me to help in my journey, which I had judged so paltry at first, had actually almost carried me to my destination.

As I heard the pack approaching, I began to lose consciousness. Groping in my coat pocket, I searched for the green veil and gathered it into my fist. Something then pounced on my back. I waited for those fangs to rip through my flesh and crack my spine. Instead, I was lifted bodily off the ground and ascended into the empty sky. "This is death," I thought. The terror of it made me close my eyes, and I fell into myself like an ember into an ocean.

Imagine my surprise when I woke sometime later, lying on a cot with a blanket pulled up around me. My body was still tense with fear, and every strained muscle and pulled ligament ached unmercifully without me even moving. Pushing back the covers, I propped myself up on my right elbow and discovered then that someone had bandaged the claw wounds on my forearm.

The room I was in was very dimly lit, only one candle burning on a table a few feet from where I lay. Everything beyond the circle of its glow appeared murky, but I could at least see that the ceiling was very high above, vaulting up fifteen feet or so. Some distance beyond the table, I barely made out a wall with a closed door. I turned over and peered into the shadows and saw row upon row of bookshelves. The aisles between them led off for a long way and disappeared into the darkness like tunnels.

There was something familiar to me in the location. I knew I had been here before. It was most definitely a site within the City. I had made it to my destination at least, but neither my existence nor the success of my mission were any less tenuous. Just then, I discovered that I was still holding the green veil balled up in my fist. I unclenched my fingers and looked at it for a moment's comfort, thinking it might help me to make a decision as to what to do next. My choices were either to flee or stay and hope that it had been Below who had found me. I thought that if I only had a chance to speak with him, I might be able to convince him to help me reverse the effects of the sleep. It turned out that a choice was unnecessary since I heard someone approaching from the other side of the door. I quickly shoved the veil into my coat pocket and lay back down on the pillow, pulling the covers up over my shoulders.

I was in place and feigning sleep only a moment before I heard them enter. Whoever it was closed the door, and then I knew they were lighting the spire lamps mounted on the walls from the aroma of the gas. The sounds of the flames igniting were like birds whooshing by. A set of boots tapped against the coral floor as they approached me. The steps halted right next to my cot, and I tried to, very slowly, without fluttering my lashes, open my eyes a mere razor slit in order to see the face of my savior. A shadow came across my eyes, and I could tell that the person was leaning over me. I snuck a brief glance, but then his hand touched my hair to smooth it back, and I gave up trying to see. All I had caught in the split second I looked was the reflected glint of a pair of round spectacles. None of the face's features had been clear to me. Luckily, the person moved over to the table. I heard a chair being dragged back and the sound of him taking a seat.

I was almost certain that this was not Below. In the time I had known him he had never worn spectacles, and unless he had gone senile in recent years, the last thing he ever would have done is run his hand over my hair in such a caring manner. I decided to bide my time and do some slit-lid spying before abandoning the mask of sleep.

I turned onto my side, grumbling like one caught in the throes of an unpleasant dream, so as to get a better look at the table and its occupant. In waiting a short while before attempting to open my eyes, it came to me where I must be. The long rows of bookshelves, the high ceiling, made it evident that I was in the basement of the Ministry of Information, where I had once done research in order to try to discover the blueprints for the false paradise.

When I thought enough time had passed, I opened my eyes a quarter of the way and saw the silhouette of what appeared to be a man, a large cumbersome cape draped over his back, leaning forward, reading a book. At half aperture, the man became clearer and was not a man at all. My eyes shot open wide and a cold sweat broke out across my back, for sitting there, wearing a pair of round-rimmed spectacles like any scholar in the world, was the demon. That cumbersome cape I thought I had seen became his pointed wings, and that sound of boots on the coral floor had really been the sound of hooves. His barbed tail danced rhythmically behind him as he turned the page and began silently moving his lips.

I wanted to scream but tried not to, and the result was like a dog barking. He turned his horned head to look at me, his yellow eyes magnified behind thick lenses. Ripping the covers off, I rolled out of bed and ran, limping down the nearest aisle between the rows of books. I screamed as I ran. In between my yells, I could hear his wings beating above as he pursued me.

Eventually, the shelves ended, and I was facing a wall. I backed up against it and watched as he descended, his wings kicking up clouds of dust from the old books. My trip to the Beyond had shown me what these demons could do to human flesh. As he approached, I cautioned him not to come any closer or I would take action. He did not heed my warning. I have no idea why I did it, but I reached into my coat, pulled out the green veil, and threw it at him. Though it had been wadded into a ball, it immediately opened up in midair inches from my hand and fluttered to the ground like a feather. The demon grimaced and a strange sound welled up from his chest.

I stood there, shaking, waiting for him to pounce, and then, after a long time had passed, I realized that he was laughing. He bent over, picked up the veil and handed it toward me. When I reached out and took it from him, he said, "Physiognomist Cley?"

I was astonished at his use of human language and could do no more than nod.

"I am Misrix," he said. Then he bowed slightly and brought his hairy, clawed hand up to shake.

Perhaps it was the ridiculous nature of a demon wearing spectacles that told me finally that I had nothing to fear. I reached out and clasped hands with him. As we shook, his wings opened and closed slightly. Then he turned and started back down the aisle. Motioning to me with his tail as though it were an arm, he called over his shoulder, "Come, I'll make us some tea."

5

"SUGAR?" ASKED THE DEMON.

I came suddenly to attention and nodded without realizing what he was asking. From the time I had taken a seat at the library table, and he had gone through the door to fetch the tea, I was unaware of both my surroundings and the passage of time. In my mind I kept replaying the scene of me throwing the balled up veil at him. The memory of his laughter had left me reeling.

"One lump or two?" he asked, lifting the lid off a silver sugar bowl that was part of the service he had brought in on a lacquered tray.

"Yes," I answered.

He bowed his horned head and reached daintily into the bowl with two of his claws, like pincers, to pull out one cube at a time. Putting two in my cup, he lifted a spoon and stirred five times, his wings rising slightly with each orbit.

"We haven't had lemon for a long time," he said, averting his glance.

I said nothing but continued to stare in disbelief at his cordiality. "A shy beast of prey?" I said to myself. It might even have been easier had I come to my senses and found Greta Sykes chewing my leg. All I could think of was having seen my friend, Bataldo, the Mayor of Anamasobia, attacked by demons in the Beyond.

While preparing his own, he looked up every so often, showing enough fang to make me uncomfortable. He brought the cup to his lips when he was done and tested the mixture. The steam rose from the tea and fogged his spectacles, so he took them off and cleared them against the reddish brown fur of his stomach. His eyes intrigued me with their vertical serpent slits instead of irises, but at the same time they stirred some primal fear in me, and I could not look for long.

"You saved me tonight," I said.

He nodded. "I was out for some air, and I saw you running."

"The werewolves," I said.

"I'm sorry," he told me. "I have no control over them. I'm as frightened of them as you are. If I landed outside the walls and stayed on the ground, they would as soon rip me apart as you."

"Thank you," I said.

"You are welcome, Cley."

"How do you know me?" I asked, lifting my tea.

"My father," he said.

"Who is your father?" I asked.

"Master Below is my father. He showed me you," said Misrix.

"Drachton Below?" I asked.

"He birthed me into the world of men. He gave me language and understanding," he said.

"Is he here, in the ruins of the city?" I asked.

"He is here," said Misrix.

"I've got to speak to him," I said.

"I will take you to him soon."

"How were you birthed into the world of men?" I asked.

"It was like a great wind blowing out a candle in my head. With the brightness of the Beyond extinguished from me, I could concentrate. I began to think as humans do."

"Tell me about it."

"Very well, Cley," he said, and with this reached back into the folds of his leathery wings and brought forth a pack of cigarettes and a small box of matches.

"You smoke?" I asked.

"From what I have read, it is most appropriate that a

demon should smoke," he said with a bashful grin. "But you won't tell my father, will you?"

"Not if you give me one," I said.

He reached the pack across to me.

"Where did you get these?" I asked.

"In the ruins. I can find almost anything in the ruins if I look long enough. These spectacles, do you like them?" he asked, leaning his head down and peering over the top of them. "I found them on a dead one. My father says they do not help my sight, but I like them. When I look at myself in the glass, I see 'intelligent.' "

As he lit his cigarette and inhaled, his hooves clicked a rhythm against the stone floor. He passed me the matches and coughed profusely, like the muffled roar of a lion. The smoke wreathed his head, and if not for the spectacles, I saw before me an illustration from the catechism of my childhood. He flapped his wings to clear the air, took another drag, and began.

"I still vaguely remember when I was a beast, gliding through the forest, sniffing at the breeze of the Beyond for a trace of living flesh. Then I was captured and brought to the city. All I remember from that time is rage and fear. I escaped from my captors. Food was easy to find, though, and rarely put up much of a fight. Once I battled a powerful man in the underground, and he cracked off one of my horns. The horn grew back, and I went on to hunt again. Finally, there were explosions everywhere, and I flew up out of the City and circled in the air until they ended. After that, it was difficult to find food. I could not eat the dead even though there were so many. To eat the dead is to die. I lived on stray cats and dogs who survived the end of the City. Sometimes I would swoop down on pigeons, but this was meager food, and I was beginning to starve.

"One day I saw a man, it was my father, before I knew he was my father, standing out in the open. I flew down on him to take his living flesh, but as my claws ripped into him, he was not there. He had vanished like smoke, and what I knew next was a net dropping over me. Then he was there, and he stuck a long sharp thing into my arm. I was awake and dreaming all at once for a very long time. Through that time I heard his voice always speaking to me. The words seeped into me and twisted around my inside, grew like vines and flowers, blossomed in my skull. It was painful, but the pain was far away.

"*Sheer beauty* were the first words I came to understand, and I knew they meant the bite of the needle. When I awoke, I no longer desired living flesh. Father fed me plant meat. I no longer knew every moment what I would do in the next moment, but instead sat for long moments thinking. This thinking was a curious thing at first. It was a clock ticking, a music I did not want to hear the end of. Finally, I was released from my waking dream, and I knew before I stood up and took my first step that I was Misrix. I cried to know that I was born then. My father put his arms around me. 'You have much to learn,' he said."

Here the demon motioned for me to return the pack of cigarettes. He took another and this time reached up and struck the match head into flame against his left horn. As he brought the light down, he looked out of the corner of his eye to make sure I had caught his performance.

"So," I said, "Below dragged you into humanity."

"Birthed me," he said. "He showed me many things. Told me many things. And then one day, we discovered that I had a special way of learning. I used to be his assistant in the laboratory. I watched him make his inventions and experiments, as he called them. At the time, he was turning men into the wolf things that surround the ruins. A group of men from somewhere came to the City. They had weapons and were hunting through the debris for treasures. We captured them, he and I and Greta. He told me that he was going to help them to return to their true forms. What they were really searching for was to be turned into wolves. We put them all alive in cages and then one at a time, he would take them out and work on them. Their screams upset me. He told me it was not easy for them to become what they needed to become.

"One day when he was sleeping, I heard one of them screaming in the laboratory. I went in there, although I was not supposed to without him. The man begged me to let him go. I tried telling him he needed to become a wolf, but he cried most pitifully. He told me he would be all right if I would just let him loose to take a walk for a few minutes. I hurt inside for him and undid the straps, letting him up. He ran away. Father was furious with me. He yelled and even struck me in the face. I was told to stand in the corner, and he sent Greta out to find the man. She returned an hour later, but I guess she never found him.

"Later, he came to me and told me never to do anything in the laboratory without his permission. I told him I was sorry, and he said I was good then. I wanted to put my arms around him, but his face was still frowning. Instead, I reached out and laid my hand on top of his head. That is when the learning came in a great storm through my hand and arm and into me. It was like his life was in my mind. I saw him as a boy and a young man. I saw him doing a thousand things and speaking a million words. 'Remarkable,' he said as he lifted my hand from his head. He had felt it too and said it was a part of my animal nature that I had not lost—that it would be a valuable tool. From then on, we learned to contain the storm, we birthed it into a human thing, and this is how he taught me so much in the few years I have been alive."

"And what did he teach you about me?" I asked.

"He told me you were one of his children and showed me you in his thoughts."

"Did he tell you he once tried to have me killed?"

"No," he said, and pushed his chair back. He stood and his wings lifted, his tail danced.

"What kind of father tries to kill his children?" I asked.

The demon took off his spectacles and stood quietly for a long time, pulling at his pigtail of a beard.

"I know," he said in a quiet voice. "That first time the storm came through my hand and into me, before we learned to contain it, I saw everything."

"It bothers you, doesn't it?"

Misrix shook his head. "Why did he do that to the woman with the green cloth? Why did he shoot the man? Why did he make the soldiers scream with pain to become wolves? The knowledge came to me through him, but also there came a small stinging insect, always buzzing through my thoughts. Everything I have come to know is poisoned by the sting of this creature. At night I cannot sleep for wondering."

"Why do you stay here?" I asked.

"He is my father."

I told him what had happened at Wenau—about the exploding bird and the sleeping disease.

"Yes," he said, "I know."

"Please. I must help those people," I said. "Take me to him. Let me reason with him."

"Come, Cley," he said.

He waited for me to get out of my chair, then led me through the door, holding it open as I passed. We walked in silence down a long, door-lined corridor, and I marveled at this beast with a conscience. What struck me was that as depraved as Below was, he was somehow capable of raising a "child" who had a sense of morality. I thought I might be able to enlist the son as an ally.

At the end of the corridor there was another door. As we approached it, Misrix reached out and put a hand on my shoulder, the claws curving down to point at my heart.

"You must promise that you will not hurt him," he said.

"Me, hurt Below?" I said. "I was hoping that you would protect me from his anger."

"That won't be necessary," he said as he turned the knob and pulled back the door.

The room was small and dimly lit by one candle. It took me a moment for my eyes to adjust, and in that time Misrix had entered and was standing beside me. The candle sat in a holder on a small table next to a large bed with an ornate headboard. Lying in the bed was Drachton Below, his eyes closed. His head was propped up on cream-colored pillows as though resting on a cloud bank, and he was dressed in blue silken pajamas. In the time since I had last seen him, he had grown a long mustache and beard, the same color as the pillows. His face was remarkably clear of wrinkles for one as old as he, but the thick hair that he had once worn in an impressive wave was now all but gone.

Misrix walked over to the side of the bed and reached out to pat him lightly on the head. I approached and asked if I could awaken him.

"I wish you could," said the demon.

"What do you mean?" I asked. Before he could answer,

though, I noticed the expression on Below's face. He wore a subtle grin, the same I had seen back in Wenau on Roan and Jensen and the others who had succumb to the disease.

I turned to Misrix, and he simply nodded. "We were in the laboratory three days ago, and he was preparing one of his metal birds. He told me, 'Another gift for my children at Wenau.' There was a small beaker of steaming yellow liquid in his hand that he was preparing to pour into the mouth of the bird. He began to tell me something, and when he did, the beaker slipped from his fingers and crashed against the floor. I was on the other side of the laboratory, and I began to rush to his aid. By then a thick yellow smoke was rising around him. He spoke excrementally, and motioned for me not to come near him. I stayed at a distance, because he kept his finger pointed at me to remain. Then his eyes rolled back in his head. He said, 'Good night,' and fell onto the floor. I have not been able to wake him since."

I felt a tightening in my stomach. "Is there an antidote? Do you remember him mentioning or working on a cure for the yellow smoke?" I asked.

The demon nodded his head sadly. "Yes. When he first created the smoke, he made an experiment using one of the werewolves. He put the creature to sleep and then after two days awakened it with a needle full of something."

"What was it?" I asked.

"I never knew," said Misrix, and I saw him begin to get upset.

"That's fine," I told him. "It's not your fault." I put my hand on his arm. "Do you know where he keeps it?"

"Yes," he said.

"Where is it?" I asked.

With the tip of a claw, he touched Below's temple. "In there," he said.

6

I ASKED MISRIX TO TAKE ME TO THE LABORATORY, BUT HE said it would be impossible until daybreak, when the werewolves would be sleeping. It was situated on the main floor of a partially intact building all the way on the opposite side of the ruins, and the path to it led through some treacherously narrow spots that were havens for ambush. The lab itself was unprotected, and the creatures knew how to get in.

"They could trap us there, and we'd never get out," said the demon as he took one last look at Below before shutting the door.

"Why did your father keep a laboratory so far away from your living quarters?"

"Two reasons," he said. "In case one of the experiments escaped while we were sleeping, and he used the daily journey to it as a way to get physical exercise."

"Can you carry me through the air?" I asked, as we walked the long hallway.

"During daylight, the metallic birds guard the sky. They will not strike us on the ground, but flying is too dangerous while the sun is up. They are set to intercept anything that crawls or walks outside the City walls and anything that flies over it. My father was particularly frightened of an attack by military balloons or rockets.

"This is my room," he said, and opened it for me. He set about lighting the spire lamps as I looked around. The place was enormous, well lit, and spotlessly clean. It was divided into a small living area and the rest was more rows of library shelves. He beckoned me over toward the shelves, and I followed.

"I've gotten rid of the books in here and begun my 'Museum of the Ruins.' These shelves are lined with the most interesting items I have salvaged from the Well-Built City."

I looked to the shelves and saw row upon row of artifacts—bullets and skulls and huge shards of soap-bubble crystal, obviously scraps from the false paradise. As I moved along the aisles, staring at the remains and reading the hand-printed cards that went with each small display, the ghost of the City came over me, and I remembered so clearly. In my memory, I rode the crystal-enclosed elevator to the Top of the City, while in actuality I walked past squashed shudder cups, a demon horn, bracelets, dolls, teeth, mummified toes, and a severed head from one of Below's gladiators—gear work showing through empty sockets.

"Remarkable," I said to him, as he followed, hands clasped as if in prayer to his accumulations.

"What did your father think of this?" I asked.

" 'Abhorrent' was the term he used, but he never demanded that I dismantle it."

"What made you start?" I asked, turning to watch him.

"I had the feeling that there was a story in all of this," he said. "If I just put the right pieces together it should all become clear to me—the story of the Well-Built City."

"You've done a fine job here," I said. "But what do you make of this story?"

"A love story, I'm sure of that much, but after that I lose the thread in a small object I cannot make out the meaning of. It's down here," he said and walked past me, leading me deeper into the aisles of shelves.

He finally stopped in the last row, at the very corner of the far-flung room. "Here," he said as I caught up to him. He pointed at the shelf and stared.

There, in a display between an empty Schrimley's bottle

and the blue hand of a hardened hero, sat a white fruit at the moment of ripeness.

I reached toward it, but was quick to bring my arm up short, landing my index finger on the paper card that held the message: UNKNOWN FRUIT—plucked from tree growing among the ruins.

"What is it?" he asked.

"This is the fruit of the Earthly Paradise," I said. "A kind of miracle engine. I've seen people poisoned by it, and I've seen it bring back the dead."

"Interesting," he said.

"What does this do to your story?" I asked.

"It's too early to tell. It's got to be important, though."

"Why?"

"Otherwise, I wouldn't have found it," he said.

He led me back to his living quarters, which included a writing desk, a lamp, a small shelf of books.

"Do you sleep?" I asked, not seeing a bed or couch.

"Sleep is my return to the Beyond, for I still dream like a demon. Occasionally I will dream human, and these are always nightmares. But here," he said, and his wings swept out. He gave a slight jump and lifted into the air, the papers on the desk flying off in all directions. I followed his course upward to where there was a metal bar affixed to the ceiling. He wrapped his fingers around this and then brought his feet up beneath him, bending his knees and resting the soles against the bar between his hands. Crouched upside down like this, he folded his wings closed and hung, motionless, like some prodigious fruit of the Beyond.

". . . is where I sleep," he said, his voice muffled by the cocoon of his wings.

Without thought, I applauded.

"Rest now, Cley," he said. "There is only an hour or so till dawn."

A moment later he was snoring. After retrieving the green veil from my coat, I took it off, sat down against the wall by the door, and closed my eyes. I was exhausted, hungry, and completely confused. There was no sense in fighting the course of events. Like one of the artifacts in the Museum of the Ruins, I was a mere fragment of debris from a far-reaching story. I tried to think of what I should be looking for in the laboratory the next morning, but the words on the list in my mind began to drip off the page, and I nodded forward into a dream of Wenau. I found myself walking silently through my own darkened house. Outside, in the moonlit yard, a dog was barking.

I opened my eyes a few hours later and saw Misrix sitting at his writing desk, plunging, into the crook of his arm, a hypodermic of what I was sure was sheer beauty. When he finished, he grimaced and slid the needle out.

"What are you doing?" I asked.

He turned quickly and stared into my eyes. At first his look conveyed guilt, but I could sense the beauty wrapping around his mind, and guilt soon became innocence.

"The beauty," he said, smiling.

"Do you need to take it?" I asked.

"I need to take it when I am going out into the ruins without my father. It makes me lighter and gives me ideas where to hide if I have to."

"Don't we need to concentrate on getting to the lab?"

"Certainly, certainly . . ." he said and took to staring at the wall.

I got up from where I had slept and walked over to him. "Misrix," I said.

He gave no reply.

"Misrix," I said, and touched his wing. He turned his head slowly, and said, "Yes, Cley, I know, the lab." He pushed back his chair and stood. "No resting," he said. "When we get out into the ruins, we must move quickly."

I nodded, letting him know I understood, but he had already brushed past me and was heading out the door. I followed him down the hallway almost to Below's room when he abruptly stopped and put his hand to his head.

"Wrong way," he said, turned around, and went past me in the opposite direction. Imagine yellow eyes, bloodshot, and hands that were slightly trembling. Just the very mention of the beauty was bad business as far as I was concerned. This drug had been the leash that Below had used to restrain us all in the days when the City was still whole. Its powerful hallucinogenic effects left one in a rictus of paranoia, totally suggestable, the Master's favorite environment through which to govern. I had spent many years wrapped in its hellish nightmare and quite a few more trying to forget its insistent tug. Misrix was using it, much as I had in the old days, as an antidote for his fear of being human.

We went through another door which opened onto another long hallway. At the next door, Misrix let me catch up to him. "Cley," he said, and smiled foolishly. "When we go out this door, I will lock it behind me. We will have entered the remains of the public baths. Through these we will get to the street."

"What are you thinking about right now?" I asked him.

"About the white fruit."

"Let's think about werewolves instead," I said.

He laughed and put his arm on my shoulder. "You think about them," he said, and pushed the door open.

I followed him out quickly. He turned around, and with a long key I had not noticed him holding before, locked the door. Then he straightened up, and we made our way amidst the still-bubbling cisterns. Great chunks of the roof had fallen into the pools, letting the daylight stream into the water that had remained crystal clear. When I looked down, I could see frogs and fish darting about, and down deeper yet, I could make out the remains of a human rib cage.

Although the baths had sustained less damage than many other sites in the City, broken tile lay everywhere, and there was one spot where we had to leap over a fissure in the floor through which a swift stream of purified water now ran. The real problem came when we reached the entrance. That once grand archway that had led to the street was choked almost to the top with an enormous hill of shattered coral masonry. Misrix began the climb toward the sliver of daylight that shone in at the very peak. I took to the hill and made my way up the uneven slope, twisting my ankle and cutting my forearm in the process. Misrix reached a hand down and dragged me up the last few feet. We had to lie on our stomachs in order to slip through the opening into daylight.

The sky was clear and the sun had already lifted away from the horizon. For the first time, I could see the extent to which the City had been decimated. Entire ministries that at one time had held hundreds of workers on any given day were completely leveled. The pink coral that Below had used for the structures lay in boulders, slabs, and jagged toppled columns everywhere. Reaching from beneath these weighty fragments were the skeletal arms and hands of the citizens of the City. In the crevices, I could make out the glint of brass gears and the twisted belongings of Below's children. A fine pink powder swirled in the street when the breeze blew.

I followed Misrix down the gently sloping hill of debris, taking care as to where I placed my feet. As I leaped off the last boulder and onto the street next to the demon, I could tell there was something wrong. Misrix held his head back as if he were looking at the sun and sniffed the air.

"What is it?" I asked.

"I'm not sure. It might be the wolves, but it would be very unusual for them to be awake so early. It might just be the beauty, playing tricks on me."

"Wonderful," I said.

The demon looked nervously over each shoulder, but didn't move forward. I knew that he was panicking as I had out on the fields of Harakun.

"Come on," I said. "Your father will die without the antidote. Everyone will die."

"There's something out there," he said.

"It's your fear," I told him.

"This way," he whispered. Then he pointed down the street to where the road was blocked by the fallen facade of the Ministry of Education. "Through there," he said, and began to run, using his wings to propel him.

"Wait," I yelled, and sprinted to catch up.

I followed the demon through a chaotic maze designed by explosion, leaping from rock to rock, squeezing through tunnels, sprinting down powdered streets. Misrix used his wings and legs together in a way that made his every move fluid and weightless. I was a crooked shadow, stumbling merely at the thought of his ease.

When we finally came to a long stretch of clear street,

Misrix slowed down and waited for me. I caught up to him and stopped to get my breath.

"It looks like we will make it there, Cley," he said.

"I'm glad you think so," I said, still heaving.

"A quarter of a mile up this street," he said.

"One of the old munitions factories?" I asked.

"Where they used to make the shells?"

I nodded.

"Very good, Cley," he said, and the tip of his barbed tail came up and tapped me on the shoulder.

He started walking more slowly then, and I easily moved along at his side. From his dazed expression, I could tell he was lost in a daydream of the beauty.

"Stay with me," I said to him.

"I was thinking," he said.

"I know."

"I was thinking about my father telling me that you were a great Physiognomist. No, not great . . . the best, he said. He told me that no one read a face like you did. It makes sense to me, the Physiognomy, as he described it."

"It's one of those things that sounds like it's got to make sense, but it never does," I told him.

"Read me," he said, and stopped walking.

"Here?" I asked.

"I know you have no instruments, but give me an estimated reading," he said putting his enormous horned head down in front of me. "What do you see?"

Behind Misrix on the side of the street was a grim tableau—a mother, cradling an infant's skull in a splayed web of finger bone. I preferred to stare at that than to stare into his face and apply the bogus science that had in the past made both a fool and a butcher of me.

"I see, 'intelligent,' " I said, and quickly began walking.

"Intelligent," the demon said. He followed behind me.

"Perhaps it is merely the spectacles," he said.

"It's the wings," I told him.

"What about the horns?"

"A nice touch," I said.

"What do you say to the way my forehead bulges and to

the prominence of my cheekbones. They must say something to you."

He continued to beg for my approval the rest of the way to the laboratory. It became difficult thinking up accolades that would be subtle enough to make them convincing. I won't describe to you what the Physiognomy really told me about him. If I'd believed it, I would have fled.

7

"THEY KNOW HE IS SLEEPING," SAID MISRIX AS WE SUR-veyed the damage to the lab. Not one beaker or test tube was left unbroken. Brightly colored liquids had spilled out, painting the floor like a dream. There was a horrific stench of chemicals and werewolf excrement.

"How do they know?"

"You don't understand; the wolves know things that we can't know. They have been waiting for this for a long time. Once, when I hid above them in a dark nave of rubble among the ruins, I heard them whispering of revolt. I told my father about it. He called them to him from the plain and the ruins the next evening and served them large platters of a green, raw meat. They ate ravenously and when they were satiated and lying on the ground in a daze, he put a pistol to the heads of two of them and blew out their brains. The others cowered. He kicked one in the side and put a few bullets into the ground near Greta. Later that night, I was awak-ened by them howling out on the fields of Harakun."

"They've done a thorough job, here," I said, stepping over a pile of shit. "Still, we might find something."

"They've marked this place as their territory," he said. "I think they knew we would come here."

"Take anything that appears remotely interesting," I told him. "See if there are any vials of the antidote, any written notes." I moved farther into the lab, pushing aside nets of wire, glass shards grinding beneath my boots. The stench was blinding.

I followed a row of wooden tables along the back wall. Gingerly picking through the remains of beakers, I searched for a shred of Below's thoughts. Instead, I uncovered a dozen palm-sized creatures that mixed the attributes of man and fish. The heads were bulbous and gilled. Although there were legs with feet, there were also tails. I stared far longer than I should have.

It was slow going, and the discoveries were all wondrous but unsettling. I found gears made of bone, and bones grafted from metal. These lay in a patch of grass that grew out of the top of a table as if it were dirt instead of wood. Next to this was a collection of female heads of a lime complexion. They lay drenched in a clear viscous solution beneath the shattered remains of the huge jars in which they had once floated. There were racks of instruments, none which I could identify, and springs and gears scattered amidst the glass.

Every few minutes a machine in the shape of a diminutive lighthouse at the center of the lab would begin to glow and project three-dimensional images of colorful, long-tailed birds flying through the air. Their different songs filled the lab. As abruptly as the device turned on it would suddenly go dark, and the sounds and images would fade. It was during one of the flights of the birds that I found a scrap of paper on the floor. On the shred of rumpled parchment, rendered in ink were two objects, an hourglass and an eye, with an equal sign between them.

"Come here, Cley," Misrix called. I put the paper into my pocket and carefully made my way past an operating table rigged with wires and tubes and around a chair made of metal. When I reached him, he was pulling a case out from beneath a worktable.

"What do an hourglass and an eye have in common?" I asked him as he hefted the object up onto the table.

"The past has run through both of them?" said the demon, then flipped the latches on the sides of the case and opened it to reveal a blue-velvet lining and five vials of some liquid arranged in a star-shaped pattern, their corked tops almost touching at the center.

"What is it?" I asked.

"This isn't it," he said, and shook his head. "I remember Father telling me that he called this mixture Holy Venom. What it does, I can only remember is not good."

"Have you seen any other cases like this one?" I asked.

"None that haven't been broken into and the vials shattered."

"Let's keep looking," I said, but just then Misrix held his hand up, motioning for me to stay quiet. He leaned his head back as he had done earlier and sniffed at the air. I could see his ears actually twitch slightly as if tracking some vague sound.

"They are coming, Cley."

"We haven't had a chance to find anything."

"There's nothing to find. Everything is destroyed, and Father never committed his ideas to paper. We've got to leave now."

I looked around one more time to see if there was anything promising I had missed. The sight of the place in ruins saddened me, for I would have liked to have seen all of the products of the Master's obtuse mind. It was the thought of the werewolves approaching that brought me to my senses. "It's better off that all of this is destroyed," I said.

We made quietly and cautiously for the door. Misrix leaned over my shoulder, and whispered to me, "When we leave the building, don't stop running." He had us wait what seemed an incredibly long time before he broke into the daylight and took off down the street. I followed close behind, running away from the stench of the lab as fast as I could. I knew there was nothing more I could do to save my neighbors.

If the werewolves were there, I didn't see any and began to get suspicious as to whether Misrix had merely panicked again. I slowed down to a walk when we reached the boundary where the rubble began, mounds of treacherous wreckage sloping toward a distant ridge formed by the southern wall of the Ministry of the Territory.

"Hurry, Cley," the demon called back. "They're coming."

"I don't see them," I said, climbing onto the first boulder.

"You won't see them until it is too late."

"Where are they?" I asked. Just as I said this, I looked over my shoulder and saw ten sleek forms charge out of the laboratory door and head up the street in our direction. I scrabbled to the next rock and from there kept climbing, leaping with a precision that seemed unnatural. I could see Misrix ahead of me, spinning and tumbling in his leaps from spot to spot while behind me the baying grew louder.

When I saw the demon scrabble down into the rubble, I went to my stomach and followed him through a tight passage which led to a fall through darkness and an abrupt landing in the underground network. As I fell I heard the wolves pass overhead like a distant wave, their claws tapping on the coral.

Misrix helped me to my feet. "The beauty showed me this escape a long time ago," he said.

He motioned for me to follow him, and we began walking down the winding tunnel. "I want to show you a secret," he said, and put his tail around my shoulders.

The instant we left the tunnel, I knew where we were. In the center of the huge underground expanse sat the shattered crystal egg that had at one time been the false paradise.

"This is part of the story," he said.

I nodded.

"I named this place Paradise," he said.

I looked through the jagged remains of the crystal shell and saw beneath barren trees the skeletons of exotic beasts scattered in the dirt. The fresh water that had at one time run through the center of the transplanted territory had dried up.

"Why that?" I asked.

"A strange thing," he said. "The first time I discovered this place, I found, lying on the ground out there, the head to one of my father's gladiators. I'd seen them before among the ruins, but this one caught my interest because it had belonged to the man that I, myself, had fought here in the underground. It was the man who had snapped off my horn.

"I picked up the head and considered taking it home for my collection. The moment I lifted it, I could feel a light vibration coming from inside. I looked down to where I had it cradled in my arm, and I saw the lips move. The gear work inside the head began to whine as the eye lids fluttered open. The mouth moved, and it whispered the word *Paradise*. I dropped the head and kicked it away from me. But ever since then, I call this Paradise," he said, pointing to where a cold, floating ash had replaced the once brilliant sun.

I said nothing.

We continued on through another tunnel that finally opened onto the street across from the entrance to the public baths. I looked toward the dark opening we would have to enter, but halfway up the mound I saw six of our pursuers sitting on the rocks, staring down.

"Not good," said Misrix, and I saw the werewolves turn in our direction. They began to growl and slowly descend.

"Back underground," I said.

"No," said the demon. "Run for the hill and climb as fast as you can, straight at them."

"What should this accomplish?" I asked.

"I can't explain; go," he said and pushed me with all his might.

I ran forward and began climbing. The werewolves snarled, and I snarled back at them as we drew closer. Misrix climbed behind me, yelling for me to keep going. When they were within ten yards of me, I felt a breeze begin to blow at my back. I heard the wing thrusts just as I felt Misrix's hands grabbing me beneath the arms. He lifted us up, away from the gathering danger, straight into the sky. We remained there for a moment, treading air, and Misrix said, "Where are the birds?"

"There," I said, pointing off to the east.

"That's them," he said, and stopped beating his wings. We dived headfirst, then glided along an arc that swept us down over the leaping beasts and suddenly up toward the top of the hill. Misrix put me down beside the opening into the baths. The werewolves had reversed direction and were now climbing toward us.

"Let's go," I said, but the demon waited until he made certain that the metallic birds had fixed on our position. When they dropped in altitude to exactly the height at which we were standing, he called over his shoulder, "Now."

I slid through the hole and Misrix followed close behind, his wings snagging for a moment on the top of the entrance. Carefully pushing down on the dark flaps, I was able to free him. As he got to his feet, I crouched down and looked back through the opening. The birds were less than fifty yards away, and I could hear the growling of the werewolves directly below us. Again, he lifted me beneath the arms and leaped off the top of the inside mound. We flew low over the debris and dived into one of the cisterns. The water was freezing, and I had only had a second to hold my breath. I tried to struggle free of the demon's grasp, but he would not let me go.

He placed his hand atop my head, and I instantly felt my thoughts swirling through a storm that spun my consciousness into a globe. I became like a tornado in a paperweight and flew upward through a tunnel whose walls rippled with orange energy. The demon flapped his wings behind my eyes, and suddenly I found myself deep in the Beyond, staring down from a tree branch. I flew off the tree, now a demon myself, out across the inland ocean. When I wheeled around and headed back toward the shore, I saw the outline of a fantastic walled city, the buildings, huge dripping mounds riddled with holes. I knew it was the Palishize, that deserted city that had been described in Arla's recollections of her grandfather's journey through the territory.

Then there was the muffled sound of an explosion, and I came to beneath the water. Bits of rock and debris pelted the surface and fell slowly around us. Misrix pulled his hand off of me and let me float to the top.

The next thing I knew, he was dragging me out of the pool and standing me on my feet. "I don't know how many of them the birds destroyed, so we have to hurry," he said.

We made for the door and reached it without a moment to spare. As Misrix turned the key in the lock, one of the creatures leaped the width of a pool and came bounding straight at us. The door opened, I was pulled inside, and it was shut.

"We made it," I said, leaning back against the wall.

"Yes," he said, catching his breath, "but now they know where we are."

I dried off and was given an old suit of Below's to wear. The fit was unsettling in its perfection. In the room that had served father and son as a kitchen, Misrix made me a salad. I sat down at the table with my bowl of food and bread. The demon sat across from me with a cup of real shudder. I asked him if he could make me a cup, and he pushed his across the table to me. Then I asked him for a cigarette. Again he accommodated me, and together we smoked. The taste of the shudder almost brought tears to my eyes. I reached into my pocket and pulled out the scrap of paper I had taken from the lab. Spreading it out with one hand on the table, I took a quick look at the symbols and handed it to him.

The demon blew smoke and brought the scrap in line with his spectacles. "This is what I was looking for," he said. "This is a torn corner from a handwritten book—the only book my father always kept nearby. It was written by his mentor, Scarfinati, and it described the secrets of an ingenious memory system. Now the werewolves have it, and Greta is quite capable of reading."

"Below had mentioned it to me once in the old days, but my recollection is vague," I said.

"Father would talk to me about it at great length. The idea of it is this," and as he paused to inhale I could see that he relished the role of teacher. "The adept creates a palace in his memory. He envisions this palace with a clear mind and total concentration. Once it takes root in his memory, he fills it with objects—a vase of yellow roses, a mirror, a white fruit. Each of the objects he places around the palace stands for something he wants to be able to remember. For instance, the vase of flowers might represent a concept like a mathematical formula. If the adept wishes to regain that formula, he travels through the memory palace, and upon seeing the vase, instantly remembers it."

"Everything in the palace is symbolic," I said.

He nodded. "My father designed the Well-Built City with this method. Once it was rebuilt in coral and steel, every portion of the architecture was, for him, the physical representation of a concept, a theory, an experience, worth remembering. Out there," he said, pointing behind him, "those ruins are the devastation of his memory. Every now and then, as we wandered among them he would come across a broken gargoyle or a fallen column, and I could tell he was momentarily recovering a lost fragment of himself. He found a piece of a pressed-tin ceiling that held the likeness of a pelican, and this made him weep."

"The white fruit exploded that memory palace from his mind, and, through some strange property, also destroyed its representation in the real world."

"I love to think of that white fruit," said the demon with a smile.

I stubbed out my cigarette and cut into the salad as if it were a steak.

"He's built another one," said Misrix.

"Another what?" I asked.

"Another palace. He's built one in his mind. It is magnificent, and in addition to the objects carrying symbolic meaning there are even people in this one who stand for certain ideas."

"How do you know?"

"I've been there," he said.

8

WE STOOD NEXT TO BELOW'S BED, STARING DOWN AT HIM. the candle's glow illuminated his head, and its dance created the illusion that he was about to awaken.

"It's all in there," said Misrix, pointing.

"In his memory?"

The demon nodded. "I can put you in there," he said.

"How does that work?" I asked.

"You felt it in the cistern when we were hiding from the explosion. I put my hand on top of your head."

"It was like a dreaming wind," I said.

"I can put a hand upon your head and the other upon Father's, and you can travel through me into him. You will appear in his new memory palace in your present form. It will have all the reality of this world," said the demon.

"All the reality of this world?" I said, and laughed.

"The antidote is there," he said.

"I have been trying to forget about the antidote," I told him.

"It's there in a symbolic form in the memory palace."

"Maybe I could find it."

"But how would you be certain you have found it? You don't know the symbolic meanings of the

52

objects. How do you decipher the secret language that is the center of that world?" said Misrix.

"What about you? Why don't you just enter into his memory? It would seem more direct that way," I said.

"I was there once," said the demon, "and because I appeared in my form, the inhabitants of the place were frightened of me and tried to kill me. I was forced to flee after only a short time. I know in my deepest self that if you were to go in there and some tragedy were to befall you, you would also die, here, in this world."

"There's a solid recommendation," I said.

"Yes, but you look like the other inhabitants. You could use your intelligence to decipher the symbolic system," said Misrix, putting his hand on my shoulder.

"But that could take forever."

"In the world of the memory palace time runs at a different pace. Seconds here are minutes there," he said.

"What did you see when you were there?" I asked.

"A small island that floats among the clouds a mile above a silver ocean of liquid mercury."

"He's really basting the shank with this one," I said.

"He's limited only by the boundaries of his imagination," said the demon. "On the island there is a tower called the Panopticon. It sits at the center of everything and from a series of portals issues a flying female head with streaming hair and bright, searching eyes. It moves through the village at the base of the tower, watching the lives of the inhabitants. When I was there, I was chased by it. It bit my back and neck."

"Very appealing," I said.

"For the antidote, I would guess you would have to get inside the tower, but there is no telling where he has hidden it."

"It could be an ant I unknowingly step on while hurrying after a clue," I said.

"Possibly," he said. "But remember, Father has to be able to readily find the object in order for the memory system to be worth his while. Now, would you like to take a journey?"

"I'd thought I already had," I said.

"You must go farther."

Given I was able to elude the werewolves, I could return empty-handed to a sleeping Wenau, or I could enter into a world whose atomic structure was Below and grope for the antidote. I told Misrix that I needed to take a short walk in order to clear my head. He said that he would need a few minutes to get two chairs set up.

I left Below's room and walked down the hallway. My thoughts were still adrift, and I kept returning to the image of the demon standing beside the remains of the false paradise. There was only one thing I could do to increase my chances. When I came to Misrix's door, I found it open and went in.

As I passed countless rows of objects in the Museum of the Ruins, memories went off behind my eyes like strings of firecrackers. Misrix had told me that all of his artifacts should add up to a love story, but I was beginning to think he had missed the mark. Instead, I foresaw peril and strangeness without resolution. For that reason, I took the white fruit.

It felt almost like a ball of smooth flesh in my hand. The aroma of Paradise swirled around me, and my mouth began to water. I tried to think noble thoughts, knowing the fruit's disposition to reward and punish. The taste was sweet dripping energy, and I felt it in my blood. I couldn't stop eating it. The salad Misrix had served me had left me hungry, but now I felt as if I would never have to eat again. Upon taking the last bite, I saw the mental image of my neighbors at Wenau before it flapped once and folded into a green veil as the demon's hand touched down upon my shoulder.

"Misrix," I said, turning quickly.

"What have you done, Cley?"

I held the core of the fruit out to him, and said, "You see, the story isn't over yet."

He shook his head sadly and took the core out of my hand. "I have the chairs ready," he said, bringing the remains of the fruit to his nose. He breathed deeply.

"*That's* Paradise," I said.

Back in Below's room, we sat in our respective chairs. Misrix had been kind enough to also bring me a foot bench, so that I would be comfortable. The demon sat next to Below, within arm's reach of the Master's head. I sat last in line, in the shadows, waiting to feel the effects of the fruit of Paradise. There was no sensation except fear.

"Sit back and close your eyes, Cley," he said.

I took a last look at him in the wavering candlelight, and he smiled at me, but this did little to relieve the doubt I was feeling. I finally closed my eyes and rested back in the chair, putting my feet up.

"You will feel my hand upon your head," said Misrix, "and then you will feel the dreaming wind you spoke of. If all goes well, you will go where I direct you."

I pictured him laying one of his enormous hands upon Below's bald scalp. Then I felt him drape one gently over my own head.

"Think of it this way, Cley. To decipher the symbols, you need only read the Physiognomy of Father's memory," he said. "Hold on tight. While you were eating the fruit, I indulged in the beauty." His laughter became a strong breeze behind my eyes, which grew into a twister of dreams that lifted upward, taking me with it.

I found myself draped across the demon's arms, flying through a starlit sky. It was freezing cold but everything was perfectly clear.

"Look, Cley," he said, "we are passing over the Beyond."

"Am I in your memory now?" I asked, looking down. We passed low over the top of the forest, and it seemed to stretch forever in all directions. An occasional scream vaulted up from beneath the trees, barely audible above the constant beating of his wings.

"Yes," he said.

We flew on through the night for quite some time, and I was just becoming accustomed to the strange experience when I heard Misrix groan. His face was quite close to mine, and I could hear that his breathing had become labored.

"Cley," he said.

"Are you all right?" I asked, feeling his grip on my legs loosen slightly.

"I'm having a bad reaction to the beauty."

With this, he began to shiver and suddenly moved the arm behind my back to clutch at his chest. I reached up and grabbed on to his right horn like a stirrup.

"Let go of me," he yelled. "I can't see."

"Do you have me?" I asked.

"Yes," he said, and although his grip was again firm, I could tell that we were losing altitude.

"I've got to land," he said.

"In the forest?" I asked.

"We'll head for the Palishize."

By the time the dripping mounds of the ancient city came into view, the demon's hooves were clipping branches from the tops of trees. I caught only a glimpse of the ocean beneath a newly risen moon, before he dived through a clearing and landed at the entrance to a place I had visited in my dreams.

Misrix had his arms wrapped around himself, fangs chattering like icicles. "It was foolish to have taken the beauty before attempting this," he said.

"I have practiced such foolishness," I said, distracted by the height of the crude mud walls that surrounded the city.

"Cley, you've got to wait in there for me," he said.

"Where are you going?" I asked.

"I'm going to leave you in my memory here for a short time, while I return and have a cup of shudder to offset the beauty."

"Out of the question," I said.

"You'll be safer in there," he said, pointing through the entrance. "I'll hurry."

"It's dark out," I said.

"Go, quickly," he said, still pointing, "there are demons about."

I stared down the shell-cobbled path that led inside and split around the melting sand castles. The moon revealed peaks riddled with crude openings. When I turned back, Misrix was gone.

The Palishize was deathly quiet, even the wind made no sound there. I ran as lightly as I could, for each footfall echoed like a gunshot. I did not want to get lost in the winding maze of the structures, but I wanted less for the demons to find me.

When I had to stop running, I chose one of the holes punched as if by a giant finger into the base of the closest mound. Inside the shadows of the tunnel, I felt somewhat safer. As soon as my breathing returned to normal, I began listening.

I don't think I moved for a full five minutes, but then I heard a sound in the distance, and my head turned sharply to the right. It was the merest echo of a footstep. This was followed by another and another, each growing more distinct as did the beating of my heart. Then a voice shouted something. I moved closer to the opening in order to hear more clearly. "Perhaps, it is Misrix," I thought.

"Cley," the voice called, but I knew it wasn't the demon.

A shadowy figure strode in front of the opening where I hid, and I moved back farther into the dark. From his outline, I could tell he was wearing a broad-brimmed hat. He turned in a way that told me he knew I was in the tunnel.

"Cley, I know you are in there. Come out and say hello to an old friend."

Though I could not place it, the voice was familiar to me. I walked forward and stepped clear of the opening.

"Come here, Cley. It's good to see you," he said.

"Who are you?" I asked, trying to catch a glimpse of the face.

"It's me, Bataldo," he said.

It was Bataldo's voice, and I remembered that he would sometimes wear a broad-brimmed hat. "Is it really you?" I asked.

He took a step forward, and now I could see that it was the rotund Mayor of Anamasobia, himself, smiling fruitlessly as always. I walked cautiously toward him, and he laughed and put his hand out to shake.

"How have you been, Cley?" he asked.

"I'm well," I said.

"I heard you would be coming, so I crawled out of my hole and came by to visit."

"Are you dead?" I asked him.

"Your delicacy is appreciated," he said.

"I'm sorry."

He laughed. "I was devoured by a demon in the Beyond, do you remember?" he asked. "Calloo shot me, but I was still alive when the creature sank his teeth into my flesh."

I shook my head, unwilling to picture what he described.

"This demon of yours, Misrix, was the one who took me. He was later captured by Below and brought to the Well-Built City. When you are devoured by demons, they steal your energy, and you live on as long as they do somewhere in their memory."

"So you are always here in this memory of the Palishize?" I asked.

"I wander here among the mounds always at night. Sometimes I go down to the side of the ocean in hopes of seeing a ship I could hail to rescue me. There's some regularity to it."

"What do you eat?" I asked.

"Nothing," he said."

We began to walk, and he asked me about Arla.

"She's married and has two children," I told him.

He pulled a handkerchief from his breast pocket and blew his nose. Then he stopped suddenly and turned. "What was that?" he said.

I too turned and listened.

He pointed at me and started laughing.

"You have a good memory," I told him.

"That's what I do while I wander through the tunnels here, I remember everything," he said. "We have to move a little faster; I have an appointment I can't miss."

We quickened our pace. "With the exception of you, Cley, the visits have been limited. But I can tell you about an interesting one before I have to leave you."

"Where are you going?" I asked.

"I bet you didn't know that your demon's first female was that wolf girl."

"What do you mean?"

"Greta Sykes," he said. "I'm talking about love."

"Harrow's hindquarters," I said.

"And then some . . . I heard he was flapping his wings so hard, he had her rump three feet off the ground. His member is barbed for the give and take."

"Please," I said.

"Well, when the two of them came together, I got to see my wife. It was Greta Sykes who devoured my wife. Lilith's energy is captured in the memory of the wolf girl. But during sex, a merging of memories takes place."

"What did you say to her?" I asked.

"I told her I loved her and that I missed her. We couldn't actually touch. When we hugged, we went through each other. With air between us, we danced on the shore of the inland ocean. It was a night like this," he said, pointing up at the stars. "Later on she disrobed for me, and I for her, since we knew it might be an eternity before we saw each other again.

She slid her tongue through my chest and heart. Mine curled through her skull, and then she dissipated into a brown powder that carried the scent of cremat."

I looked up and he took me by the arm and began to walk briskly. "I can't be late," he said. "I'm due to be torn to shreds and devoured."

"You're making fun of me again," I said.

"Each and every night. There's nothing fun about it," he said all the humor gone from his face. He turned and walked away from me.

When I looked up to watch him, I realized that he had led me back to the entrance. Bataldo headed out of the city toward the tree line of the forest, and I could hear him weeping. As he disappeared into the darkness at the edge of the wood, Misrix instantly appeared from the very same spot. He walked toward me, his wings outstretched.

"I'm better now, Cley. We must continue," called the demon as he approached.

"Is my body doing well?" I asked.

"You are sleeping like a pup," he said. "Come now." With this, he moved behind me and clutched me beneath the arms. A cry of agony cut through the forest as we lifted off the ground, dried dirt billowing around us from the action of his wings. We hovered above the city, and for a moment I could make out the entirety of its spiral design.

"I feel strong now," said the demon, as we flew at top speed through the cold night again.

"I met one of your victims from the Beyond," I said, as he changed direction straight upward toward the now fully risen moon.

"Regrettable in hindsight," he said. "But back then he served me well."

"And will I serve you also?" I asked.

The demon stopped flying, laughed, then plunged head-long out of the sky. The sudden rush of the wind was a roar that stole my scream. He put his mouth to my ear, and shouted, "You will serve us all."

9

I FOUND MYSELF SITTING IN A GREEN-CUSHIONED CHAIR in the corner of a large parlor. There were windows without glass, bookshelves, a chandelier, a thick pink rug with an interwoven design of flowering tendrils. The warm night breeze drifted in over the four figures sitting at a table in the center of the room. They were drinking cocktails and conversing about the disintegration of something. There was a woman and three men, and when one of them noticed me and pointed, they all turned and stared.

"Your specimen has arrived, Anotine," said the man who first saw me.

The woman smiled and waved her hand for me to join them. "Come over," she said.

"Have a drink," said the thin man to the right of her.

My head was still spinning from the fall, but I got out of the chair and walked unsteadily toward the table.

"What is your name?" asked the woman, adjusting the strap of her yellow dress.

"Cley," I said.

"Anotine," she said, and put her hand out to me. Her hair and eyes were dark. She was smooth-skinned, perhaps a year or two younger than myself.

I did not touch her for fear that my palm might pass through hers, but I nodded and smiled.

She pointed to the man across the table who had first seen me. "Doctor Hellman," she said. A small, bearded fellow with spectacles and prominent ears shrugged, and said, "Welcome," as if he were asking a question.

"This is Brisden," she said, laying a hand on the shoulder of the man to her right.

"Are you light-headed, Mr. Cley? Sometimes when the specimens arrive, they complain of light-headedness," he said. His suit was wrinkled where it wasn't stretched by his obesity. The watery eyes, the weary measure of his speech told me he had already had quite a few sips from the dark pint bottle he held.

"I'm fine," I lied, as the third man handed me a drink.

"Nunnly," he said, pulling out the chair that sat between the doctor and himself. "Good of you to come."

I sat down warily at the table and took a sip. The instant I brought the glass to my mouth, I smelled the warm floral scent of Rose Ear Sweet. It was the first taste of it I'd had in years, and it flooded my senses.

"Rose Ear Sweet," I said aloud, not meaning to.

"Have as much as you like," said Nunnly, pushing the bottle closer to me.

I took another drink, and Anotine said, "Where are you from, Cley?" She moved her dark hair behind her ears and leaned back in the chair, folding her arms.

"Wenau," I said.

"Never heard of it," said Doctor Hellman, and the others agreed.

"You'll be helping me with my discoveries," she said. "Occasionally, your duties will include assisting the gentlemen here in their own pursuits. The term of your service is one year. Do you have any questions?"

"Is it common for people to simply appear before you?" I asked.

They smiled and looked at each other.

"How else?" said Nunnly. "When one of us orders a specimen, like yourself, the subject usually coalesces in that chair over there."

The aplomb with which my strange entrance was greeted silenced me. I worked on my drink as well as my composure while the others continued with their discussion. The Sweet was just what I needed to calm myself. "Now, if I only had a cigarette," I thought, "things might almost be tolerable." My mind was still swimming upstream through the implications of my meeting with Bataldo amidst the mounds of the Palishize. The conversation of my hosts seemed intriguing and serious, but when I tried to follow it, my head began to throb. I let their words pass over me.

At one point, after my third Sweet, I came to my senses and heard Anotine say, "It's all in the moment."

"No," said Doctor Hellman. "In the memory of the moment."

Brisden cleared his throat and cut in on the Doctor. "The present is a doorway—a randomly located aperture assigned its location by ourselves, arbitrarily, contradicting the totality of the void."

By some sleight of hand, Nunnly lit a cigarette without my noticing. "The three of you," he said, "your words are like the mechanisms I design—purposeless. Your theories are desperately searching for a reason to exist. And Brisden, someday I'll have a vague clue as to what you are getting at. My god, your drivel is a crime against humanity."

They laughed, Brisden hardest of all.

"Well, let's not let it ruin the day," said Doctor Hellman, pushing his chair back and rising.

They all stood and I followed their lead. Each of the men stepped up and shook my hand. I was not sure if it was a good thing that I did not pass through them. "Good night," they said as they left.

Anotine turned to me, and said, "Come, Cley, it's late. There is a lot to do in the morning." We followed the men down a corridor lined with arched window openings that led to a terrace. Once there, in the moonlight, they all went off in different directions.

I followed like a shadow behind Anotine, weaving somewhat from the effects of the Rose Ear Sweet. It felt good to be outside. The air was clear and filled with the mixing scents of various night blossoms that grew everywhere from planters built directly into the architecture.

We went down a wide stairway to another level, then turned left and passed an open-air hall of columns to the right of which was a pool, perfectly still, reflecting unfamiliar constellations. She walked slowly, stopping from time to time and staring up.

The place was an unraveling mystery, a series of terraces built at all different levels with rooms and halls and courtyards of every conceivable shape connected by long and short stairways. There were fountains and sculpture at different locations. I passed dozens of entrances without doors, windows without glass. Everything was open, dark, and perfectly quiet.

"Where is everyone?" I asked, as Anotine stopped beside a fountain to watch the arc of water falling from the breast of a stone pelican.

"Everyone?" she asked.

"The rest of the people who live in all of these rooms," I said.

"It's just the four of us you met tonight, Cley," she said.

"No others?" I asked.

"We are fairly sure there is someone in the tower, but I've never seen him," she said, pointing over my shoulder.

I turned around and looked up. The height of it made me take a step back, and I came near to losing my balance. It rose more than a hundred feet above the terraced village that surrounded its base. The glass dome at the top of the brick structure glowed like a lighthouse beacon.

"The Panopticon," she said. "The term implies that we are being watched."

"Are we?" I asked.

"Most definitely," she said. "I only wonder if what is being seen makes any difference."

She began walking and said no more to me. We climbed a last set of steps and came to a series of lighted rooms. She led me through an open portico and an arched entrance.

The smooth walls of the room were whitewashed. It was furnished with only a bed, situated in a corner beneath a window opening, a brown rug, a small table, and a chair. A hall-

way led off from the middle of the left wall of the room, and
at the back there was another, larger window opening.

"You may sleep on the rug if you wish," said Anotine as
she turned down the spire lamps so that their light was the
equivalent of a single candle.

I walked to the back of the room and sat in the chair next
to the table. From the shadows, I watched as she sat on the
bed and removed her shoes. When she stood and unhooked
the straps of her dress, I realized that she was going to disrobe.

I coughed weakly to remind her of my presence.

She let the dress slip off her onto the floor, then turned
and asked me if I had said something.

Her breasts were exposed, and I studied them closely as
she leaned over to remove her underwear.

"No," I replied, as she turned around and bent over to
pick up the dress.

She tossed her garments down the hallway and turned to
face me one more time. I took in her entire figure. Anotine
smiled and said good night before lying down on her bed.

She slept atop the covers on her stomach with her legs
apart, and the candle glow of the spire lamps dissolved the
dark enough for me to see everything. I was somewhat beyond
the perpendicular as I sat there staring. There were two things
I repeated in my thoughts: "Nothing is real here," and "Everything means something."

I finally tore myself away from the sight of Anotine by
standing and staring out the back window. With the help of
the moon and the dome of the Panopticon, I was able to see
out across a field that lay below the window. The grassy expanse was bounded by a wood which seemed to encircle the
village as the village appeared to encircle the tower. I was
exhausted, but I decided to take a walk and think through the
complications of my quest. There was a moment of trepidation
in which I wondered if I should ask permission of my host to
go out, but I reasoned that it would be a shame to wake her.
Besides, there was a limit to how far I could wander, seeing
as we were on an island.

It took me the better part of an hour to traverse the maze
of stairways that led to that field, but I was glad for the puzzle,
hoping the concentration might clear my thoughts of Anotine's

body. Finally, I ascended a long set of steps and, upon reaching the top, strode onto the grass. Although I should have been sleeping, I needed to see if Misrix's description of the island had been accurate.

The trees were almost perfectly straight, and the entire forest seemed so strategically laid out in a crisscrossing, geometric pattern, I was sure it must have been planted. Leaves fell around me in great numbers as I kept to a crude path that snaked through the shadows. I walked quickly, thinking that each one of the trees, even the leaves, could be a symbolic representation of one of Below's grand schemes. But when I touched the rough bark and smelled the sap, I could only think of them as devoid of anything but reality.

"Cley," said a voice from within the dark outline of a tree.

I turned quickly, half-expecting to see the Mayor again. "Who's there?" I said.

Nunnly, the engineer of useless machines, stepped forward so that his lean face and frame emerged from the shadows.

"Out for a walk?" he asked.

"Yes," I said, unsure if I was supposed to be on my own.

"You are curious about the edge of the island, no doubt," he said.

"I am," I told him.

"How did you hear of it?" he asked.

"I can't recall."

"Follow me, Cley," he said, and started off ahead of me.

"You are lucky that you are Anotine's specimen and not Brisden's," he said. "The last one that old gasser had, he literally talked into a coma. We had to send the poor fellow back and request another one. By the time we took him to the chair in the parlor, he was extraordinarily dull, as if Brisden's babble had eaten his wits. Anotine, on the other hand, will do anything for her specimens."

"She already has," I said.

"That's the spirit," he said.

We walked a few more paces, then Nunnly held up his arm, preventing me from going on.

"Do you hear it?" he asked.

Behind him, I could hear a strong wind and beneath that a very distant sound of waves.

I nodded.

"Don't get too close to the edge," he said. "It's very dangerous now." Then he lifted his hand and let me continue.

I walked up a small hill, and when I reached the top, I found myself staring out over the end of the island. There was a fallen tree next to me, which I leaned against as I tried to encompass the entirety of nothingness beneath us. Far below, through the trails of passing clouds, I could see the liquid-mercury ocean, shining a distant silver where the moon and the tower's brightness touched its surface. I felt a great rush of my blood as I stood there staring and wondered how glorious the fall would be from that height.

"Look down there," said Nunnly, who, I just then noticed, had stepped up and was standing next to me. He was pointing to the very outline of the island.

"What is it?" I asked, searching for his meaning.

"The edge of the island," he said. "Brisden discovered a few weeks ago that it is slowly disintegrating. Close your eyes and listen carefully."

I did as he said and tried to listen at a point between the wind and the far-off waves. "I think I hear it," I said.

"Now, look again," he instructed.

Concentrating my sight on a jutting root just at the rim, I noticed, the way one might notice, with the proper focus, the hour hand of a clock moving, that it was almost imperceptibly diminishing in thickness. It seemed to come apart into tiny crumbs that did not fall but instead crackled into nothing.

"Is that bad?" I asked.

"Well," said Nunnly, tapping a cigarette against the back of his wrist and leaning almost elegantly against the fallen tree, "when you are on a disintegrating island, a mile above a sea of liquid mercury, I would consider that cause for a modicum of concern."

"Do any of you know why it is happening?" I asked.

"No," he said, striking a match, "but Anotine has calculated that in a matter of a few weeks or so, we will have to worry about it while we are falling."

"How long have you been here for?" I asked.

"Forever, it seems," he said. "We were all hired some time ago by a fellow none of us had actually met by the name of

Drachton Below. Everything was done through correspondence which offered handsome payment for us to come here and do research in our particular fields. Since we have arrived, we haven't seen him. We keep working in good faith, but, my god, I wouldn't mind leaving at this point."

"Where are you from?" I asked.

"I tell you, my head is so full of designs for machinery, I can hardly think of it. I vaguely recall having had a family before I arrived here, but I can no longer see their faces. That's why I come out into the wood at night, to try to remember. I experience all of the loneliness and loss, but for whom or what remains a mystery. I am beginning to wonder if I ever really knew."

We left the edge of the island and walked back through the trees toward the village. Nunnly asked me about my own life and how I had been chosen to serve as a specimen. I told him I had been chosen for my good looks.

"You too," he said, and laughed. "You'll be interested to know that Doctor Hellman believes that neither we nor the island exists. Everything to him is dreams."

"What do you say to that?"

"What can I say? I'm an engineer. My work is with matter, not with mental indigestion."

We walked on across the field, and then Nunnly showed me a shortcut back to Anotine's rooms. Before leaving me, he shook my hand again, and said, "Cley, for a specimen, you are a bright fellow. Be diligent at your work. It would be pleasant to have you around for a while."

I lay down on the brown rug in the middle of the room and stared at Anotine's back as it rose and fell with her breathing.

"The Master, asleep in the clutches of the disease, is wasting toward death," I thought. "His memory is evaporating with his life, and that is why the island is disintegrating."

As my eyes shut, and I began to doze, I remembered the drawing of the hourglass on that scrap of paper I had discovered. Particles of light passed through the neck of the figure eight.

10

I CAME AWAKE TO THE GLARE OF SUNLIGHT FLOODING
the room reflecting off the smooth whitewashed
walls. There was an unreal, immaculate clarity to it,
a vitality that offered perfect warmth and submerged me in a sense of well-being that ignored the
countless dilemmas I faced. After rubbing my eyes
and reminding myself as to who and where I was,
I looked around and saw that Anotine was no
longer lying on her bed.

"Hello?" I called as I stood up and stretched.

As if in answer, a shrill, steady note, like the
cry of a thin-throated pig, sounded from down the
hall. There was no modulation to the tone at all,
and its relentless nature forced me to cover my ears.
In this manner, I proceeded to search out its source.
I passed a room to the left, also sparsely furnished
and brimming with sunlight. Somewhat smaller
than the bedroom, it appeared to be a dining area,
for there was a large wooden table, surrounded by
four chairs.

A few paces farther along on the other side of
the hall was a small, windowless space, almost a
closet. I could make out that its walls were lined
with shelves and that they were filled with shadowy
objects, but by then I realized that the sound was
coming from the room at the end of the hall. From
my limited vantage point, it appeared to be a much

larger space than the others. I moved up to the opening, my hands still protecting my ears, and leaned forward to peer inside.

This room was also bathed in the clear light of morning, and, to my wonder, filled with all manner of strange-looking equipment that demanded my immediate attention. All of it, though, receded out of view as my eyes came to rest on perhaps the strangest scene I had ever witnessed.

Standing by a large window opening at the far right of the room was Anotine. Her face was lifted slightly so that she could make direct eye contact with, of all things, a human, female head that floated in the air of its own volition. The sight of this caused my hands to drop to my sides, and the maddening noise that issued from the open mouth of the bodiless woman passed unimpeded into my ears, drilling my mind. The intensity of it made my head swim as I focused on the twin beacons of green light that connected one woman's gaze to the other's. Both the pain of the din and the utter madness of what I witnessed made me gasp. I fell against the side of the entrance for support.

Anotine's tormentor shut her mouth, and the noise suddenly ceased. The green rays of light appeared to retract into the eyes of the floating head, and the moment they disengaged from Anotine's, she let out a deep breath and doubled over.

Then, like a hummingbird flitting from one flower to another, the head flew across the room and hovered in the air three feet from my face. I thought of running, but instead I simply slid down the side of the entrance until I was kneeling on the floor. The horrid thing floated there in front of me, and I was hypnotized by the way its black hair writhed behind like a nest of angry snakes. The face was drawn and appeared perfectly cruel in its pale green complexion. Its lips were deep red, its sharp teeth and irisless eyes, pure white. A growl sounded from somewhere within it, obviously not its throat, for it had none. Even in my state of panic, I understood that it was admonishing me for having interfered. I was certain for a moment that it was going to lunge at me, but as quickly as it had come, it circled once around the room, hair streaming behind it, then flew out the window.

Anotine looked over at me and smiled. "You're shaking," she said.

I got to my feet, somewhat put out by her offhand reaction to my fear. "I'm glad you are amused," I said.

With this she began to laugh out loud. "There, there," she said, and she walked over and put her arms around me.

This was almost as surprising to me as the sight of the flying head. All I could think in the brief time that the embrace lasted was how fortunate I was that she was now dressed. As she released me, I suddenly realized that the act was not one of affection but merely that of a researcher comforting a frightened lab animal. It would be dangerous for me to assume that I was anything more than Cley, the specimen.

"We call that the Fetch," she said as she backed away.

"It's an atrocity," I said.

"Not very pretty," she conceded, "but an amazing device."

"You mean it is a machine?" I asked.

"Not a machine in the sense of gears and motors, but an organic entity that works as a tool. It swoops down from the tower and, we believe, like a dog retrieving a stick, fetches back information to whoever or whatever is up there. Doctor Hellman named it. It seems to gather our discoveries into itself through the beams emitted from its eyes. We have all been scrutinized by it many times, and we have all witnessed it probing inanimate objects in the same manner."

"Does it hurt when it studies you?" I asked.

"It's an odd experience. The only unpleasantness comes from the fact that you stop breathing while it does its work," she said.

I shook my head and grimaced.

"I suppose it's better than having to write reports constantly," she said with a forced smile.

"How does it fly?" I asked.

She shrugged. "How does the island fly? What ocean is this beneath us made of liquid mercury? What are we all doing here? These questions have become rather useless. We do our work and live in hope that someday we will be returned to the lives we have traded away for this commission."

I had a thousand questions, but I thought it better not to bother asking them. It was clear to me, as Misrix had warned, that Below was only limited by his imagination in this mnemonic world he had built. Flying heads and islands were probably only the beginning of it. What was pitiful to me was the belief that both Anotine and Nunnly had expressed, namely that they had real lives and loves elsewhere that they longed to return to.

"Come, Cley, let's eat breakfast," she said.

I could only nod, for my mind was preoccupied with an awareness of the tyranny we exercise over the creations of our imaginations. In waking from a dream, we obliterate worlds, and in calling up a memory, we return the dead to life again and again only to bring them face-to-face with annihilation as our attention shifts to something else.

Anotine led me down the hall to the room I suspected was for dining. There, on the long table, two meals had been served, the steam rising off of them as if they had come that moment from the oven.

"Oh, you're in luck, Cley," she said as she took the seat beneath the window. "We have caribou steak."

How it all had gotten there—the vase of flowers, the pitcher of lemon water with ice, the baby carrots and threaded dumplings, was a phenomenon that should have floored me, but at which I hardly blinked. I sat down, lifted my knife and fork, and set to work on the meat, which was, of course, cooked to perfection.

"Delicious," I said after my first bite, and I could see in Anotine's eyes her relief that my utterance was a statement rather than another question.

We ate in silence for some time. I wasn't particularly hungry, and as I continued to eat I never really felt full. It was as if we had been preordained to finish the meal. Even the fleeting realization that what I was ingesting were Below's thoughts didn't put me off from slicing away at the sizable piece of meat.

I was just discovering the cheese vein in a threaded dumpling when she looked up, and said, "I study the moment."

"The moment?" I asked.

"That near nonexistent instant between the past and the future. The state we are always in but that we never recognize. When we stop to experience it, it flies away into the past and then we wait for the next one, but by the time we recognize its arrival, it too has gone."

"Why does it interest you?" I asked.

"Because there is a whole undiscovered country there. In my experiments, I try to pry a hole in the seam between past and future in order to get a look at that exotic place," she said.

"Interesting," I said, and stared as if caught up in her ideas, when in reality I was caught up in the depth of her eyes.

"Thinking makes us forget the instant," she said. "The present is not a function of thought. It is the absence of it."

"Good steak," I said, having lost her meaning early on.

She smiled, and I forgot not to stare. "God is there in that country," she said. "When you are finished eating, please take off your clothes."

A half hour later I was in the room at the end of the hall, naked, strapped into a metallic chair, feeling very much like Cley, the specimen. Anotine sat at a table in front of me, holding a small black box with buttons. Laid out before her were a notebook and a pen.

"You may feel a little discomfort during this experiment," she said, lifting the pen and writing something in the book. "But don't worry, this will cause no irreparable damage."

I was embarrassed and scared, and truly knew for the first time how my physiognomical subjects must have felt when I had called them forth to be examined.

"I will be recording your responses, so please be as candid as possible. Take your time and search for the proper words to describe your experience," she said.

Then she put the hand holding the black box beneath the table where I could not see it. "Now, I want you to look out the window behind me. Concentrate on the sunlight. It is warm and beautiful. Try to recall something pleasant," she said.

I tried to do as she said, but the only image that came to my thoughts was that of Bataldo, weeping as he walked off through the dark tree line of the Beyond. I shook my head and forced myself to remember the faces of Ea and Arla and their children. Then I settled on a memory of Jarek. I had taken the boy fishing one balmy summer day on the outskirts of

Wenau. There was nothing special about that particular day, only that he had caught a huge river smad with bright orange spots. He unhooked the fish and laid it on the bank. I watched as he performed a ritual his father had taught him, wherein he thanked the fish for the food it would offer him. He passed his hand over its scales to calm it as it drowned in the air, and I remembered that on that idyllic day, a soft breeze blowing, how lovely and unusual I thought the sentiment that he expressed.

Then it came like a bolt of lightning, shattering my daydream—a sharp pain in my left buttock, as if it were being burned and bitten at the same time. The sudden force of it nearly made my eyes leap from my head. I cried out.

"Can you describe what just happened to you?" asked Anotine.

Tears had formed in the corners of my eyes. "A sharp pain in my rear end," I yelled.

"Did you experience anything else?" she asked.

"Like what?" I asked unable to hide my anger.

"The moment, perhaps?" she said.

"It hurt like hell," I told her, and she jotted all of it down.

"Did you see anything?" she asked.

I shook my head.

"Did you feel the presence of the almighty?" she asked.

"If the almighty is a searing pain in the ass, I felt it," I said.

"Good," she said, and silently mouthed the words *pain in the ass* as she wrote them.

I tested the straps to see if I could break free but found them immovable. "What are you doing to me?" I yelled.

"Relax, Cley," she said. "Now I want you to calculate the sum of 765 and 890."

I didn't even get through five plus zero before the next shock blasted me in the right shoulder blade. The torture proceeded in this manner. I cursed and yelled and begged to be released, but she simply smiled and told me always that it was almost over. I don't recall how many times she pressed the buttons on the black box, but near the end I merely fell into silence. It was then that I actually saw the almighty. The room faded from view, and I had a vision of Below, laughing uncontrollably at me. Through my desperate condition, I wondered if, within the depth of his diseased sleep, the Master knew I was there in his memory.

My return to consciousness was a slow and painful experience, and before I was fully awake, I had determined to leave the floating island and abandon my mission. All I needed to do was let Misrix know by thought that I wanted to return. But when I sat up and opened my eyes, I found that it was night. The spire lamps in the bedroom had been reduced to the glow of a candle again, but I was not on the brown rug. Instead, I was in Anotine's bed and she was asleep next to me. This night, she lay on her back, and one glance wilted my rage toward her, replacing it with awe.

I lay down and turned onto my side, resting my head on my hand so that I could see her. Through the window came the scent of the night blossoms and the murmur of the ocean. I reached out my free hand and cautiously passed it an inch above her body, tracing the topography of her face and breasts and stomach and thighs. I thought again of Bataldo and how he had danced with his wife without touching by the shores of the inland ocean. I remained in that position for over an hour, trapped in the moment.

11

THE NEXT MORNING I AGAIN WOKE TO FIND ANOTINE gone. I recovered my clothes from where I had left them the day before in the room at the end of the hall. As I dressed, I stared at the metallic chair and shuddered at the memory of the pain it had inflicted.

A series of tables lined the perimeter of the room in the same manner they had back in the laboratory that Below kept in the ruins of the Well-Built City. Now that I considered it, the room seemed almost a scaled-down version of that place. In keeping with the original, the tables were cluttered with strange-looking equipment, sprouting wires and needlelike appendages. Mirrors, candles, bowls of powder, and huge jars of colored liquid were scattered amidst the collection of exotic hardware. The very thought of how Anotine might make use of these in discovering the present sent me quickly down the hall to the dining room.

There I found, as I knew I would, a breakfast of eggs, sausage, and, to my delight, a steaming cup of shudder. None of this had been there, when, only a few moments earlier, I had passed the room on my way to retrieve my clothes. I smiled at the perfection of how it all looked and smelled as I took a seat. When I brought the cup of shudder to my lips and sipped it, I was swamped by a wave of nostalgia similar to when I had tasted the Rose Ear Sweet two nights earlier. It came to me as I took a bite of the sausage that I had dreamt of this very meal through the night. The implications of this phenomenon abounded, but I had no interest in considering them. I ate, as before, not so much to quell any hunger, but simply to fulfill a mysterious sense of obligation.

When I was finished eating, I pushed the plate away and took the last few sips of shudder. The drink gave me that same rush of energy I had come to rely on back when I was a busy servant of the realm, and the taste made me long for a cigarette. I made a mental note to try to appropriate one from Nunnly at our next encounter. As I was considering how I might approach him on the subject, it came to me that I was wasting valuable time. It took some effort to remember my neighbors in Wenau and the dire predicament they were in. "Don't forget," I told myself.

I left the dining room and walked down the hall to the laboratory. Perusing the tables that lined the room, I wondered what mathematical formulas, philosophical secrets, personal memories might be contained in the souls of the objects that lay before me. "This could very well be the chemical code of the antidote," I whispered as I lifted a gold, three-pronged fork with a diadem at the opposite end of the stem. I put it back down, and reached for a steel ball the size of a fist that perched upon a small stand. Lifting the sphere, I found that, although it appeared solid, it was lighter than a crumpled piece of paper. I decided that it was as good an object for study as anything. Taking it with me, I left the laboratory.

In passing the dining room, I looked in to find that the dishes had vanished, and now only radiant sunlight lay atop the table. Back out in the bedroom, I sat down cross-legged on the brown rug and brought the shiny ball up close to my eyes. Its smooth surface reflected my face and, with the distortion of its shape, spread my features out, making my nose enormous.

I tried with all my will to see past myself, as if I might find some image beneath my own that would offer a clue to the thing's essential nature. What I saw were my own eyes, and mirrored in them, twin steel orbs each bearing miniatures of my face. Of course, if I could have seen with the power of a microscope, I would have been witness to the same optical trick ad infinitum. Long after I knew this technique to be useless, I continued with it till my eyes crossed and the squinting gave me a slight headache.

The next procedure I tried was to bring the ball up to my ear. I closed my eyes and listened with the concentration I employed when listening for the weak heartbeat of a newborn child. What came to me were the myriad sounds of the island—the breeze, the distant ocean, the call of some mnemonic bird off in the wood. These gave way to the sound of my own blood pulsing in my temples. I focused so intently that I heard everything but the ball, which revealed itself to be a large marble of complete silence.

I rolled the object around in my hands, rolled it along my forearms and my face. I rested it atop my head, thinking that its symbolic meaning might penetrate my skull through some kind of osmosis. Occasionally, an image would jump into my mind, and I would see the black dog, Wood, or the jagged column that was the remains of the Top of the City, but there was no feeling of certainty accompanying any of these mental pictures. I thought for a moment of Misrix and wondered if I would ever escape the reality of Below's memory.

I spent a good hour and a half there on the floor of Anotine's bedroom with the ball, rolling it, dropping it, whispering and shouting at it, tapping it with my knuckle and banging it against my forehead. My growing frustration finally got the better of me, and I threw it against the wall. In my desperation, I thought this might jolt the meaning out of it, but it didn't. It merely struck the smooth plaster with a dull thud and fell to roll some way back to me along the floor.

I stood up and stretched in an attempt to disperse my anger. "I'll clear my head," I thought and walked over to the window opening at the back of the room that gave a view of the field below and the boundary of the wood just beyond. I spent some time staring out at the peaceful, sunlit scene, and the sight of it relaxed me. Eventually, I turned away from the hypnotic tranquillity of the view and took a seat at the table that stood just to my right.

"Come on, Cley," I admonished myself. "You must . . ." But I never finished the thought, because lying now on the table in front of me was a pack of Hundred-To-Ones, my brand of cigarettes from the days of the Well-Built City. Next to them was a box of matches and an ashtray. My hand shot out instinctually to the cigarettes, and I lifted them to make sure they were real. On the front of the green package was the usual red insignia of the wheel of fortune. I flipped it over and on the back was the expected image of Dame Destiny, wearing a blindfold. In her right hand she held a revolver, and in the left, a flower.

I opened the pack, retrieved one of the cigarettes, and immediately lit it. That first blast of smoke against the back of my throat was a great relief. With this aid to concentration, I turned my attention again on the steel ball. As I stared at it now, from a distance, my mind wandered and I came up with a theory about the sudden materializations of food and cigarettes.

These, it seemed to me, were incidentals. The mnemonic world was very convincing in its important detail, but one could never plan for all of the contingencies of logic, so things that weren't really necessary were created extemporaneously, so to speak. The memory filled in the gaps when the reality of the island was found wanting. Food, cigarettes, probably alcohol, were unimportant. That is why when I ate, it was not because I felt hungry. I realized then that since I had arrived on the island, I had yet to use a bathroom. There probably were no bathrooms, which was just as well, since I felt no urge in that direction at all. Hard, fast rules and definite limits abounded, pain and probably true death among them, but then there was a gray area where the memory created as fast as the need arose.

With my second cigarette, I began laughing at myself, picturing my crude attempts to break through the shell of symbolic representation. While I was puffing away, an indescribable urge began to take hold of me. This feeling increased until, upon stubbing out the cigarette in the ashtray, I rose and approached the shiny sphere of frustration. Then, I lifted my foot and brought the heel of my boot down on the thing with as much force as I could muster. To my surprise, the ball collapsed, splitting open in three places and crushing down into a flattened, ragged disk of steel. I stepped back and inspected my work. There had been a degree of satisfaction in the act, but in all I was no wiser than before.

"What are you doing, Cley?" asked Anotine.

The voice momentarily frightened me. I looked up to see her standing in the entrance, wearing a puzzled expression.

"Looking for the moment," I said, and forced a smile.

She shook her head. "Leave the experiments to me."

I nodded and looked away, embarrassed at the thought of how I had gawked at her body through the night.

"Come, we have work to do," she said.

Imagine my relief when instead of heading down the hallway to the laboratory, she turned and went back through the entrance into the sunlight. I hurried after her.

She walked quickly, leading me up and down stairways, across terraces, through a labyrinth of winding alleys lined with flowering vines drooping down from planters situated high above. It was the first time I had been outside in the sunlight since arriving, and now I could see just how beautiful and complex the village was.

I looked ahead to where Anotine waited for me at the bottom of a short set of steps. She wore a loosely fitted, white-muslin dress that the breeze had its way with and the sunlight had no difficulty penetrating. Her hair was tied back and woven together in an intricate braid.

As I caught up to her, she said, "You had a difficult time with the experiment yesterday."

"I apologize for not being more help to you," I said.

"There was a period after I took you from the chair that I thought you might expire on me," she said. "The other specimens never exhibited such a dire reaction to it."

"Why do you think that was?" I asked.

She began walking again, and I could see that we were now heading for the field that lay between the wood and the terraced village.

"There seems to be something quite different about you," she said. "You are more like my colleagues and I than the other specimens that were sent. You are more . . . I suppose I would say *substantial*."

"Are you saying I am thick?"

She laughed and placed her hand on my shoulder for a

moment. "No. I can't quite put my finger on it, but you have a kind of aura about you. You actually seem to have feelings."

"I do," I said.

"Yes. After having to lie with you last night in order to make sure your heart rate and breathing returned to normal, I determined that it would not be right to subject you to the chair again. I'm not looking to discover death, only the present."

I could not help but smile.

"I dreamt about you after I fell asleep," she said. "I'll have you know I never dream. As long as I have known Doctor Hellman, he has always spoken to me about his dream theories. I understood the concepts, but I always doubted their validity because I had never had the experience. Quite startling, it is."

We reached the wood and entered it along a dirt path. I could see now what I had missed in the darkness the night I had arrived. The leaves that fell everywhere around us, twirling slowly in the breeze, covering the ground, were not brown and dead, heralding the approach of autumn. They came from the branches with the deepest green.

Anotine saw me stop to watch their descent. I stooped over and picked one up. "They began falling only last week," she said. "Something is seriously wrong with the island."

"Nunnly told me it was disintegrating," I said.

"I'd rather not think about it," she told me, and began walking again.

"Can you tell me what your dream was then?" I asked.

"I saw you wrestling a monster," she said. "You were fighting for your life. It was very troubling."

"A monster?" I asked.

"Yes, a creature with horns and fur, great flapping wings, and sharp teeth. It was much like the one that visited the island years ago."

"The creature had actually been here?" I asked.

"A foul beast—it flew in from out of the clouds one afternoon. We were all quite frightened. Nunnly and Brisden threw rocks at it. The Fetch was beside itself, flying about it, biting at its back and arms."

"What came of it?" I asked.

"They managed to chase it off, but for weeks afterward we lived in fear that it would return."

"And how did I fare in the dream?" I asked.

"I think you lost," she said quietly.

It was obvious that the experience had upset her, so I did not ask for more details. After rounding a turn in the path, we came to a grassy clearing in the wood near the rim of the island. Doctor Hellman stood there, dressed in a black suit and coat, staring up as if studying the wispy clouds that moved slowly across the sun. His right hand rested on his beard, and in his left, he held the handle of a small leather bag the same color as his attire.

Behind him stood an enormous wooden contraption, resembling a catapult of old, which at its base contained a large flywheel full of rope, like a giant's fishing reel. This rope threaded through metal rings embedded sequentially along a thick beam that jutted up at a forty-five-degree angle and out over the edge. Attached to the end of the beam was a large pulley through which the rope was fitted. At the end of the rope was a wicker basket, like a gondola for a balloon, big enough to hold a horse. There was also a crank handle and gear train affixed to the farside of the machine.

"Good day," he said to us when he noticed our approach.

"Are you ready, Doctor?" asked Anotine.

"The question is," said Hellman, "is Mr. Cley ready?"

I felt a seed of nausea begin to sprout in my stomach. "An experiment?" I asked.

Anotine laughed.

"Nothing to be afraid of Cley," said the Doctor.

"Will it cause irreparable damage?" I asked.

"Only to your sense of self-importance," he said.

"Don't worry," said Anotine. "The Doctor only needs you to help him with his instruments."

"Let's go," said Hellman. "Anotine, you will work the crank. Try not to drop us in the ocean."

"I'll do my best," she said.

"Your assurance is underwhelming," he said as he stepped toward the basket, which dangled a foot off the edge. Leaning over carefully, he opened a small door in the side of the waist-high compartment. "You first, Cley," he said, and swept his hand in front of him, motioning for me to climb into the basket.

I stepped forward and then hesitated.

"Don't look," called Anotine.

"Where are we going?" I asked, my legs beginning to feel weak.

"Where else," he said, "but down, of course."

I closed my eyes and reached out to grab the edge of the basket. The Doctor took my arm and guided me into the gondola. Once I was inside on the pliant, unsteady floor, I heard him step in and the door close behind him.

"All right, my dear," he said. "Off we go."

There was a high-pitched whine followed by the rhythmic metallic click of gears engaging. The basket lurched slightly forward, and, for a panicked moment, I thought I was going to be flung out. Still with eyes closed, I seized the Doctor by the sleeve of his coat.

"What are we doing?" I yelled.

"A little daydreaming," he said.

12

I COULD HEAR THE TIMBER SHAFT OF THE WINCH ABOVE us creaking with the strain of our weight. The pulley squealed and its cry traveled along the taut rope as we were slowly lowered in fits and starts. Increasing my grip on the Doctor's coat, I worked at trying to balance myself.

"You can look now, Cley," he said. "I'm afraid we're still alive."

I slowly opened my eyes as we passed the bottom of the floating island. I don't know exactly what I expected to see, but I never guessed that it would be a gigantic wedge of earth like the clump of dirt that trails the stem of a weed pulled from the ground. Tree roots jutted out the bottom and interlaced in a mesh that, though it was impossible, held the entire thing together. There was no rational explanation for how something so immense might stay aloft in midair. Only the imagination could so completely cancel the effects of gravity.

"Quite a marvel," said Doctor Hellman, smiling at the sight of the foundation as we descended beyond it.

I nodded, but could not hide my terror of feeling like an ant on a string.

"I am never more alive than when I am dangling out over nothing," he said.

"I can't say I share the sentiment," I told him.

"It takes some getting used to," he said. "If you can muster the courage to stare down over the edge of the basket, it will literally frighten the fear out of you, and I think you'll feel much better."

I inched my way across the wicker compartment and grabbed the rim of the waist-high wall. Cautiously, I leaned out a few inches and stared down. A blast of wind came up from below and blew my hair back as I took in a view of the silver ocean, stretching out endlessly to all points of the compass. The sight was so awesome, I could feel my anxiety rapidly shrinking in the face of it.

After a few minutes of this, I turned back to the Doctor, feeling much better. "I think it worked," I said.

"Fear will always fall to wonder in those who are capable of it," he said.

"What should I do now?" I asked.

"We have to wait until Anotine has finished lowering us close enough so that we can get a good look at the surface of the ocean."

He sat down on the floor of the compartment, and I did the same. I thought that he might question me as Nunnly had, but instead he closed his eyes and rested against the wall. I looked up to see how far we had descended from the island, and as I craned my head back, my vision was obscured by an airy white substance that seemed suddenly to be everywhere.

"Doctor," I shouted.

Hellman never opened his eyes. He simply smiled, and said, "A cloud, Cley, a cloud."

The white vapor passed over us, leaving my clothes damp. When the last wisps of it had cleared, I looked up again, and there was the island, flying at a great distance like a kite on a string. For some reason, I cannot say why, that sight made me reach up and touch the breast pocket of my coat. Since the beginning of my mnemonic journey, I had forgotten about the green veil. Never really expecting it to be there, I patted the pocket and, to my surprise, found a thickness to it. I reached in and pulled out the scrap of cloth. The feel of the material against my fingers offered some solace as though it were a kind of rope itself, connecting me to my own place and time.

As the novelty of the adventure began to diminish, I realized that the thick, rolling sound of the ocean grew more distinct. The force of the wind also increased, causing the gondola to sway to and fro with a pleasant rhythm. Just as I was about to rise and check our progress, the basket came to a jarring halt. The Doctor's eyes opened; he reached up to get a hold on the edge of the basket and pulled himself to a standing position.

"Cley," he called over his shoulder, "you'll never see anything like this in Wenau."

I stood up, adjusted my balance to the rocking of the basket, and inched my way across the wicker floor to stand next to him. The initial sight of it made me slightly dizzy, for as we moved the sea had its own motion, and the whole world seemed, for a moment, a silver spinning top. We dangled no more than fifteen feet above the crests of the largest waves. I stared in awe at the lazy creation of thick, liquid mountains that curled at their peaks back into themselves and diminished. The swells in between were as deep as canyons, and the sight of them worked like a magnet, drawing my leaning body farther over the side.

Hellman laughed and clutched me by my shirt. "This pool is closed to bathers," he said, pulling me back. "How does it make you feel?"

"Insignificant," I said, "but not in a negative way."

"I know what you mean," he said, shouting over a particularly fierce gale.

"Why are we here?" I asked.

"You've got to get over the majesty of it," he said. "Only then will you notice the phenomenon. Keep staring for a minute or two and it will become clear to you. Look closely at the moment when the wave, in its descent, reaches a certain flatness."

I could not help but continue to stare. Then, slowly, my perception of the ocean began to change. I started to notice that everywhere, not only when it passed through an instant of flatness, there appeared to be designs that swirled across the surface of the mercury. I covered my eyes for a second and looked more intently, only to see that these were not merely designs but actual scenes involving people and places. When the scope of what I was witnessing struck me, I stepped back away from the edge of the basket. The entire ocean was an ever-changing collage of animated tableaux that mixed into each other, then separated out into fresh revelations.

The Doctor turned and looked at me. "Dreams," he said. "The ocean is dreaming."

I moved back to the edge and looked down again to see a clear image of Below, sitting in his office back in the Well-Built City, injecting himself in the neck with a syringe of sheer beauty. The sight of this made me realize that the Doctor had been close in his diagnosis. What we witnessed, though, was not an ocean of dreams, but instead, true memories from the Master's life.

"I am convinced there is meaning to all of this," said Hellman. "All I need do is interpret it. The same characters keep appearing as if it is a vast, continuous story, that I, unfortunately, have come to in the middle of its telling."

"What do you think it means?" I asked.

"All I can tell you is that I am certain it is a love story. Recently, something about it has been nagging me. It is as if there is a connection I am missing that lies right before my eyes, but I cannot put it together."

"When you have interpreted the entire thing, what do you hope to discover?" I asked.

"It's what we all want, Cley. I want to know why I am here," he said.

The Doctor had somehow come very close to the truth, and I was torn between explaining to him what I knew and saving my secret knowledge as an advantage that might be useful later. I nearly spoke, but then I realized that he would never believe me, and if he did, what would my truths say to him about his existence?

"Snap out of it, man," he said.

When I looked up, I saw that he had gone to the black bag he had brought with him. From within, he pulled a long glass cylinder with a glass jar attached to the end.

"Nunnly designed this for me," he said. "You see, it's retractable. He began pulling concentric cylindrical stems out of the main unit until he had an exceptionally long glass rod at the end of which was the jar. The contraption extended out over the sides of the basket on either end.

"This process would be much easier if I could use wire or string, but the nature of the liquid mercury is such that it would eat right through them. I've discovered glass will hold the stuff. Not even Nunnly could spin thread from glass."

"I think you are going to be short a foot or two," I said, seeing that the long-handled jar was no more than ten or eleven feet.

"Well, this is as big as he could make it without danger of it snapping under the weight of the sample I bring up."

"But what good is it?" I asked. "You will still be two or three feet short."

"That, Cley, is where you come in. You will hold me firmly by the ankles and lower me over the side of the basket, where I will scoop up a portion of the ocean."

"That's mad," I said.

"Quite," he replied. "Let's get on with it." Holding the unwieldy rod in one hand, he struggled up onto the edge of the basket, placing his free hand on the rope that connected us to the island above. He stood there unsteadily, balancing.

"What if I drop you?" I said.

"That would be unfortunate, but if you do, I want you to watch and notice if I appear as part of the story." Just then a huge gust of wind blasted the side of the basket. The Doctor began to lose his balance, and I lunged forward and grabbed him by the ankles.

Luckily he was a small man; otherwise, I never would have been able to hold his weight back. He hung down under our carriage where I could not see what was going on.

"The view is even better down here," he yelled.

I was grunting and straining merely trying to hold him in place, and wasn't about to start a conversation.

Just when I thought I was going to lose him, he finally called, "Heave ho, Cley. Don't jostle me too much, or we'll have to do it again."

I began to back up across the basket as slowly and steadily as I could. When his waist was even with the edge, the Doctor straightened his body, bringing the jar end of the glass device up in both hands, taking great care not to spill a drop. As his feet touched down on the floor, he said, "Cley, come quickly now and unscrew the arm."

The glass rod had threads in the end that attached it to the jar. I worked quickly to remove it and release the Doctor from its drag.

"Just let it fall into the ocean," he said. "This is my last expedition. The rim of the island will soon be too unsteady to support the winch."

I did as he said, and after watching it fall away into a growing wave, I turned to see him affixing a fitted glass lid on the jar. He held his specimen up in front of him, where it gleamed in the brightness of the sun.

"I think we've got something here, Cley," he said, smiling. "I should have thought of this sooner." He stepped over and handed me the jar.

I grasped the glass container tightly for fear of dropping it, and discovered that it radiated a subtle warmth. Doctor Hellman moved back over to the black bag and pulled out a wide-barreled pistol. Aiming straight up, he pulled the trigger and the gun discharged. There was no explosion, only a loud pop followed by blue smoke. A projectile sped out of the end and rocketed toward the island. I followed its course for a moment, then lost it.

"Look now," he said.

I tilted back my head and witnessed a red splotch, like a bleeding wound, spreading out across the resilient blue. It was not long after that we began to ascend in the same uneven manner as we had been lowered.

"Where does Anotine get the strength to lift us?" I asked.

"Nunnly's gears make the job easy. Turning the crank is no harder than reeling a bucket of water out of a well. Still, it would be a mistake to underestimate Anotine's strength," said the Doctor with a laugh.

I handed him back his small portion of the mercury sea and went to the side to get one last look. We were almost too far away for me to perceive the detail of the etched surface, but I managed to make out one final scene. A prodigious curl carried on its back a tableau of the Master and his demon son wrapped in an embrace. Then the wave fell into itself, devouring the portrait, and, with two more upward tugs on the rope, I could no longer make out any details.

Doctor Hellman and I again took up our positions resting

on the floor of the gondola. Wearing a look of contentment, he held the jar nestled in his arms as if it were his own child. I thought his mood might make him talkative, and I asked him to tell me about the ocean's dream.

"A love story, you said?" I asked him.

"I was joking in a way when I said that, but what I meant was that my interpretation of what I have seen, the silver chronicle of what seems to be every single moment of one particular man's life, has a meaning that is greater than the sum of all its individual scenes. It is a total concept that lies just beyond my powers of description. This is why I call it a love story, because *Love* is a word I am familiar with, a word that haunts my own dreams, but for the life of me I can no longer grasp the concept of it. The significance of the story in the ocean and my inability to remember the meaning of this term leave me with an identical, unquenchable yearning. I feel they are one and the same thing."

"Are you any closer to them now from when you started?" I asked.

"I'm so close," he said, laughing. "So close now that everything is disintegrating. Perhaps if I had a long enough glass rod and jar with which I could dip into myself, I could bring out the answer."

I hadn't realized how badly I needed a cigarette until I found myself puffing on a lit Hundred-To-One that, without warning, materialized between my fingers. It tasted so good, I didn't bother to question its appearance.

"What about this man in the story?" I asked. "Who is he?"

"He's a man of great power and great weakness with the potential for both good and evil—a scientist and magician. The ocean has shown me this in detail. Once I saw him crack an egg and a cricket jumped forth, and once he built a crystal egg that held within it a world."

The wind rocked the basket in a circular motion. This and the Doctor's conversation made my mind spin. For the remainder of the ascent, I suffered from a sense of unreality as if I were the ghost of a ghost. All I had to anchor me was the insubstantial smoke of the cigarette. I pressed my hand against the pocket containing the green veil and remembered my own yearning.

13

WHEN WE FINALLY REACHED THE ISLAND, AND I STEPPED
out of the basket, Anotine was there to take my arm.
The moment my foot touched the ground, I realized
that our strange journey had wrought some change
in me. It was as if the mnemonic world had gained
a great measure of authority or validity, for everything appeared more vibrant, and I felt, for the first
time, comfortable with my existence there.

All of the doubt I had felt while ascending in
the basket was now gone, carried off by one of the
clouds we had passed through. The urgency of my
mission, which had been a constant nagging companion, had mysteriously vanished like the breakfast plates in Anotine's dining room. I concentrated
now on the touch of her hand, and that thrilled me
like nothing from my rapidly diminishing memories
of Wenau ever had.

We left the Doctor sitting on the base of the
giant winch, gazing into his sample of the ocean,
and headed through the wood, walking side by side
in silence. Anotine had let go of me by then, but I
wanted desperately to take her hand. The leaves fell
around us, and every so often a beam from that
immaculate sun would pierce the canopy overhead
and illuminate her face.

I was on the verge of touching her when I
looked up and saw something approaching. It flew

above the ground at shoulder height, threading a swift, treacherous path in and around the bases of the trees. My first
thought was that it was a large bird of some kind, but I quickly
came to realize it was the Fetch.

The sight of the flying head so shattered my state of mind
that I could do no more than grunt. For a second, I thought
the monstrosity was going to collide with us, and I froze in
place. Its face came hurtling directly at mine. I could clearly
see the milky whiteness of the eyes and an open mouth I
believed, in my fear, would swallow me. At the last second,
it lifted its left eyebrow slightly, and this subtle motion directed its course up and over us. It moved so swiftly that
when I turned to watch its departure all I saw were a few
tendrils of its black hair whipping around the trunk of a tree
some twenty yards off.

"The Doctor must be on to something," said Anotine with,
what I thought, an inappropriate complacency.

"You mean she is going to stare his discovery out of him?"
I asked.

"That's an interesting way of putting it," she said.

"Doesn't it bother you that your thoughts are not your
own?" I asked.

"My thoughts are my own," she said defensively, and I
could tell that I had touched a nerve that had to do with
something more than the processes of the Fetch.

I put my hand out and touched her forearm. "I'm sorry,"
I said. She lowered her gaze and sighed.

"Cley," she said, "you're not a specimen, are you?"

"That designation lies solely with you," I told her.

She looked up and stared as if trying to see through me.
I removed my hand from her arm. A minute passed; then
she turned, and said, "In that case, come with me. I have an
experiment I'd like to try." She set off ahead of me, walking
with determination.

Rather dejected, I followed her, seeking solace in the memory of the night I had shared her bed. We left the wood,
traversed the field, and took a short set of steps up into the
maze of the terraced village. It was late afternoon by then, and
the sun had begun its decline.

As we traveled the alleys and open-air corridors, I looked

up, studying the Panopticon. Noticing that the light was off in the dome, I tried to peer through the glass and detect movement, but it was far too distant for me to see anything. What I did see was the Fetch, returning from having feasted on the Doctor's thoughts. It flew around the tower a few times and then directly into one of the darkened open portals in its side.

I imagined the Doctor trapped in the green gaze of that horrible visage. I saw those twin beams scouring the halls and rooms of his mind, uncovering all of the knowledge he had risked his life to secure. It was with this thought that I realized that the Fetch probably possessed the very ability I needed. When it examined the researchers, it was probably seeing through their symbolic nature. Its bleached eyes were most likely Below's tool for decoding the reality of the memory world, restoring it into the valuable ideas he had hidden there. The Fetch's activity could, I thought, be proof that he was still conscious even though his body was cocooned in the diseased sleep. Following this thought, it became evident that some manifestation of him must reside in the tower.

I felt that I was close to some revelation, when Anotine stopped, and said, "Here we are."

I looked up as if waking from a dream and saw her standing next to a wall that had a small arched entrance like a large mouse hole, no more than three feet high.

"Follow me," she said, and with the mischievous look of a child, got down on her hands and knees and scurried through the hole.

I followed her, but not as quickly, for the fit for me was a tight one. When I came through on the other side, her hand was there, extended to help me up.

"This is my special place," she said.

I looked around and even before the beauty of it sank in, I smelled the perfume of the flowering plants that grew everywhere around the perimeter. The enclosure, which was open at the top, showing a view of the sky, was circular, about forty feet across. At the center of it was a large fountain in the shape of a scallop shell and rising from the middle of the fountain was a statue of a monkey, standing on one foot as if frozen in the middle of a dance. A steady trickle of water issued from the creature's penis and fell to slightly disturb the tranquillity of the pool beneath. Though the statue was rendered in bronze and covered with patches of a creeping oxidized green, I knew immediately that it was Silencio, the ingenious and good-natured monkey warder from my prison days on the island of Doralice.

"I am not a monkey," I said, a phrase that blew back to me on a memory breeze strong enough to cross two worlds. I laughed at the sight of him.

"The others have no idea this place exists," said Anotine. "Nunnly and Brisden would certainly think crawling through holes beneath them, and Doctor Hellman, who might do it, most likely has never seen it because he is always staring up into the clouds or down into the ocean."

"It's beautiful," I said.

"But this is my favorite part," she said, and took me by the shoulder to turn me away from the fountain. Behind me, at ten paces, I saw a tall shade tree, around the base of which was a circular stone bench like a marble ring on a wooden finger.

"Look there," she said, and pointed.

The branches were heavy with the white fruit of paradise. The sight of this tree, laden with potential miracles, made me want to speak so badly, but I held myself in check for the same reason I had in the gondola. My truth would be, to Anotine, like a poisonous serpent in this perfect place.

"Come sit down, Cley," she said.

We sat on the bench beneath the tree, and the fragrance of the fruit thickened the air with a sweet perfume that instantly put me at ease. It took no time at all before I felt a pleasant drowsiness descending over me. I looked to Anotine and her eyelids were partially closed, her lips turned up at the corners in a vague smile.

"I sit here and watch my monkey," she said. "If you sit long enough and stare, he begins to move." She giggled at herself.

"And what was the experiment you wanted to perform?" I asked in an intoxicated drawl.

"Experiment?" she said, and then after a moment of thought, "Oh, yes. Lie back on the bench," she said.

"As you wish," I said, and I could feel a sudden heat in my neck and ears.

"Roll up your sleeve," she said.

I did as I was told. When I was finished, she reached over and pushed it way up near my shoulder. Then she stood and moved over to sit next to me, resting my bare arm on her lap, palm up.

"I want you to keep your eyes fixed on the monkey over there," she said. "We are going to take a gentler course in order to find the moment this time." She pushed her fingernail into the exact center of the inner crook of my elbow. "Here is the spot that will stand for the present. I will start here, at the tip of your middle finger and brush my nails along the palm of your hand, across your wrist, and then up your inner forearm, moving in a circular motion that will make slow progress toward it. I will backtrack and continue and backtrack again, and you must wait until I reach the exact spot I indicated. At the instant I reach that spot, I want you to focus on the experience. Try to remember it clearly, so that I can question you about it."

The description of this experiment suddenly made me a staunch supporter of Science. I lay there submissively and stared at the bronze effigy of Silencio, remembering Below's enthusiasm for the creature. It was no wonder that he be immortalized, so to speak, in the Master's memory palace. My memory went back to Doralice and the nights I had spent there on the porch of Harrow's Inn, drinking Rose Ear Sweet and listening to the primate play his miniature piano. Another strange island in another place and time. I was considering the fact that islands seemed to be an important symbol in the story of my own life when Anotine began to skate the tip of her nail down across my palm in a circular motion. The sensation both tickled and satisfied me, an exquisite torture far more agreeable than the metallic chair.

"Something is changing me, Cley. I can feel it inside," she whispered. "I'm not sure if it is the death of the island or your arrival here, but it is as if I am rousing from some long waking sleep."

"I felt it today, myself," I said, "when I returned from my journey to the surface of the ocean."

"Perhaps Below has sent you to distract me in my final days," she said. "It's as if you have infected me with some disease."

"Never," I said.

"Yes," she murmured. "It is bringing the present within reach. I know it. Your appearance is no mistake."

I tried to speak, but she cut me off. "Shhh," she said as her nail doubled back across my wrist. "Concentrate."

The stone bench was as comfortable as a couch, and the scent of the white fruit, the splash of the fountain, the hum of bees among the flowers made me drowsy. It was growing late, and the dark was filtering into daylight. Her nails moved inexorably toward the present but never arrived and somewhere, perhaps minutes or hours after the experiment was begun, my eyelids barely open, I saw Silencio move. Then I realized that I was dreaming.

The monkey leaped down with a graceful somersault from his spot in the center of the fountain. He danced around the walled garden and climbed up into the tree. Sitting on a branch directly above, he picked one of the white, fleshy fruits and bit into it. When he had finished, he stood and, holding his member in one hand, directed a stream of piss down upon us.

I woke suddenly to find Anotine, lying asleep across my chest. Her finger pointed to the middle of my forearm a good two inches from the point she had been working toward. It was dark, but I could see well enough to tell that the monkey was back on his perch in the fountain. Still, I was getting wet. At that moment, a streak of lightning walked the sky, quickly followed by an explosion of thunder, and the rain came even harder.

"Anotine," I said, and shook her awake.

She sat up, surprised. "My goodness, it's raining," she said. "It hardly ever rains."

We were getting drenched. She got up and ran for the opening in the wall. I followed her, and she waited for me on the other side. We ran through the downpour, pursuing a meandering course across the terraced village. Her dress was soaked, and I could see her body beneath the transparent membrane. She sped on ahead of me, sure of every turn and step, and I tried to keep up. Although I knew I was now awake, the sight of her beauty ever receding before me, the flashes of lightning, and the cool rain made this seem more of a dream than the bronze Silencio dancing in the garden.

We arrived back at her darkened rooms just as the rain had begun to abate. Anotine lit the lamps and then lowered them. She stripped off her wet dress and flung it down the hall. I stood in the middle of the room and watched forlornly as she lay down on her bed. She curled up on her side and closed her eyes. When I believed she was asleep, I huddled myself down upon the brown rug.

A few minutes passed, and I listened to the water dripping off the eaves and down the innumerable steps of the village. Without opening her eyes, she said in a weary voice. "Take off those wet things and lie down here, Cley. I want to dream again tonight."

I did as I was told, and by the time I rested my head on half of the pillow, she was lightly snoring. As I lay there on my side, watching her again, I thought about my vision of Silencio eating the white fruit and remembered that I had actually eaten a piece myself before my journey into Below's memory. At first, I wondered why it hadn't as yet worked any magic for either good or ill on me, but as I stared at the complex weave of Anotine's wet braid, it came to me that perhaps she was my miracle. No matter how many ways I tried to return in my thoughts to Misrix and Below and Wenau, all of these paths wound back upon themselves like the strands in the braid, leading me always to her. I reached out and placed my open palm upon her back.

That night I had no dreams, and when I woke in the morning to bright sunlight, I found a lit Hundred-To-One waiting for me in the ashtray on the table across the room.

14

THE NEXT DAY PASSED WITH A SMOOTH PERFECTION THAT only memories edited by time can achieve. I was free of doubt and fear, and Anotine and I spent every moment together from breakfast on. There was no talk of work. She procured a bottle of Rose Ear Sweet from the dark closet in the hall, and we set out for the edge of the island.

There, sitting on a small rise that gave a clear view of both sea and sky, we played at finding faces, animals, cities, in the clouds while passing the bottle back and forth. My cigarettes appeared and she asked me for one. I told her those stories from Wenau that had nothing to do with Below. She was particularly interested in my role as a midwife and treated the idea of birth as some exotic concept, begging for me to recount in detail the looks and personalities of all of the children I had delivered.

"I'd like to go there with you," she said.

"That would be grand," I told her. "I have a house in the woods."

"Can I witness one of these births?" she asked.

"You could be my assistant," I promised.

She regaled me with stories of her associates, like the time Brisden, whose specialty was extemporaneous philosophy—a search for meaning through verbiage—had talked for two days straight and wound up his discourse at the exact place he had started. Or the time Nunnly and the Doctor had gone fly-fishing off the edge of the island for a type of brightly colored bird whose migration path passed directly overhead once a year.

"They have been good companions," she said. "I can't think of what I would have done without them here. But they are so enmeshed in their work most days that at times it gets lonely."

"I'll be with you now," I told her.

Then the Sweet made her conversation expansive, and she told me her theories of existence, the past and present and future, a mixture of mathematical and philosophical concepts that whirled time and god in a circular design outward from the center of the moment. Intellectually, I was confused, but the sound of her voice added to my intoxication, and I saw it all with great clarity, a multicolored, perfectly symmetrical blossom, that spun like a pinwheel in the wind.

We shared a long silence before she spoke again. "I dreamt last night," she said.

"Can you tell me?" I asked.

"Not now," she said.

By the time the sun reached its apex, the bottle of Sweet was empty. We both slurred our speech slightly, and, if we weren't drunk, we were no more than a drink or two from it. I lay back on the grass and she lay next to me. The alcohol gave me the courage to turn and kiss her on the lips. She was surprised but did not resist. She returned my kiss and put her arms around me. I rolled onto my back and she moved above me. Her hair, which was not braided that day, hung down all around my face.

She stopped, pulled her head back, and stared into my eyes. "I think I feel the moment coming on, Cley. The present is near," she said excitedly. She dipped down to put her lips on mine again, but the connection never came. A high-pitched animal squeal sounded, and we froze. Anotine sat up, resting back onto my hips, and as her hair came away from my face, I saw the Fetch, hovering above us.

The green beams shot from her eyes and into Anotine's, but this optic union lasted only seconds before the head disengaged. From where I lay, I saw the Fetch weave in the air and then suddenly lose altitude, nearly smashing into the ground. At the last instant, it regained its weightlessness and flew off, uttering a horrific cry.

"What was it after?" I asked.

"Our touching of lips," said Anotine. "It was hungry to know it."

"Did we scare it?" I asked.

"No, the alcohol sickened it and made it lose control. I could sense, when we shared sight, that it was confused." She leaned back and laughed triumphantly. Then she was off of me and running into the wood. "See if you can find me, Cley," she called back. I heard her laughter trail off as she moved in among the trees.

As I walked the trails, peering down the rows of trunks and listening for the scuffling of leaves, I thought about Anotine's reaction to my kiss. She hadn't even known the term for it. It seemed that love and sex were much like cigarettes and food on the floating island—something that had not been woven into the basic design of the mnemonic world. I was responsible for infecting this dying island with my desires. There was much more to ponder along these lines, but just then I caught sight of the hem of her green dress flapping behind a far-off tree, and I began to run as silently as possible.

That night, back in her rooms, after having spent the evening lounging and kissing in the hidden garden beneath the tree of white fruit, we lay naked on the bed together. Our touching had increased to a fever pitch. I moved between Anotine's legs and made ready to enter her. She was whispering the word *Now*, again and again, for it was clear that she equated her arousal with the discovery of the present. I was on the verge of penetration, when I heard another voice, much lower than hers, say from behind me, "Cley, what are you doing?"

The sound of this intruder so startled me that, in one fluid movement, I leaped off the bed and spun around. There was Misrix, wings parted, barbed tail dancing behind him. His yellow eyes glared from behind those ridiculous spectacles as he leaned back and brought his left hand up with all his might. It was too unexpected and swift for me to defend against. The blow struck me on the side of the face and sent me tumbling to the floor. I heard Anotine scream, and, from where I lay, saw her, through a blurry haze, crawl frantically from the bed and run out into the night.

The next thing I knew, the demon was helping me to my feet.

"I'm sorry, Cley," he said, "but I needed to prevent you from burrowing any deeper into this illusion."

"Interesting choice of words," I said, as I rubbed the side of my face. "You almost took my head off."

"You're wasting time, Cley. I've been watching your progress, and I think you've lost sight of what you are here for."

With his words, the thoughts of my neighbors at Wenau, which I had been successfully keeping at bay, flooded back to the forefront of my mind, and I knew instantly I was guilty as charged.

"These are not people, here," he said. "You must remember that none of this really exists. You are risking the lives of so many for so much air."

"You're right," I told him. "I will redouble my efforts to find the antidote."

"Look," said Misrix, "even if you do feel something for this memory woman, she is going to perish along with the island if my father should succumb to the disease. Think of that."

It was a fact I hadn't wanted to consider. I had been acting like a truant schoolboy, living, so to speak, for the moment. "You can trust me," I said.

"There is another problem now," he told me, shaking his head. "It was very difficult for me to get through here to you now. With the physical state my father is in, it creates a kind of interference in the process of connection between you and him and me. The worse he gets, the harder it will be to bring you out. If you stay, and we cannot find the antidote or if you take too long to find it, I may not be able to retrieve you. I believe you will perish with him."

"I can't leave now," I said.

From outside we could hear the shouts of Anotine and the others. She had roused them and brought the party to my rescue.

"They will attack me," said the demon. "I've got to be

off." He moved closer to me and put his hands on either side of my head, resting them there for only a second. "Good luck, Cley," he said. He bounded to the back of the room and perched up on the window opening.

As Nunnly and Doctor Hellman burst through the entrance, Misrix leaped into flight. Anotine came in then, followed by Brisden, who carried an empty liquor bottle by the neck. She put her arms around me, and I saw the Doctor run past us with the wide-barreled gun he had used from the basket the day before to signal our desire to return to the island. Leaning his arm on the ledge of the window opening, he took aim.

"Don't shoot," I said.

"Why the hell not?" asked Nunnly.

The Doctor fired and a pop sounded. The smoke flew back in the window and filled the room. I ran through the mist to look over the Doctor's shoulder just as a bright red puddle spread across the night sky. To my relief, I caught sight of Misrix's distant silhouette against the flare. He was climbing toward the moon with powerful wing thrusts.

"Did you hit the filthy dog?" asked Brisden, still breathing heavily.

"I doubt it," said Hellman. "I'm just glad I didn't shoot myself. I'm not exactly a man of action, if you haven't noticed."

Nunnly and Brisden laughed.

I thanked them for coming to my rescue. Brisden inspected the welt on the side of my face and whistled. The Doctor offered to leave the gun for me, and I accepted in order to seem as worried as the rest of them were.

"There are only two shells left for it," he said. "I reloaded it for you, and I have the other one back at my place."

"So, here we have it," said Nunnly. "The monster has returned."

"It was terrifying," said Anotine. "Cley, you're lucky he didn't kill you."

That is when I looked around and noticed that we were all standing there naked. The gentlemen finally left after offering assurances that we need only yell and they would come running. Anotine and I went back to bed, but she was no longer in the mood for experimenting. She fell asleep in my arms, and I was left to lie awake and consider how I was going to save everyone.

The following afternoon, we all stood, this time fully clothed, at the edge of the island a few feet behind the winch.

"It's some bad business," said Nunnly, pointing to where the ground had disappeared beneath half of the giant mechanism.

"Through the night, things have gotten worse," said Brisden. "The rate at which the island is disappearing seems to have increased radically. What would you say, Anotine?" he asked.

She nodded. "No question about it."

"I wonder if the monster's visit has anything to do with this?" said the Doctor.

"At this rate," said Anotine, "we don't have much longer. There is every indication that this process will continue to accelerate."

I could see that what they were saying was true. The winch now literally teetered on the rim, the process of disintegration readily visible.

"Do you think Below will leave us here to die?" asked Brisden.

"I'm not counting on him," said Nunnly. "He left us here with you, didn't he?"

Brisden tried to smile, but the intensity of his stare fixed on the precarious circumstances of the mechanism showed his concern.

"We need a plan," said the Doctor, "and I'm sorry to say, one that might run contrary to our host's prescribed protocol. Are you all in agreement?"

"You mean revolt?" asked Nunnly.

The Doctor nodded.

"Count me in," said the engineer.

"Anotine?" Hellman asked.

"On one condition," she said. "That Cley becomes a full partner and is no longer viewed as a specimen."

"What the hell," said Brisden. "Now that I think of it, this place bores me to tears. As for Cley, I have no objections."

The Doctor and Nunnly agreed that I was now part of the group. I thanked them for their vote of confidence.

"You can reserve your thanks," said Hellman, "until we tell you what happens when you go against the wishes of the island."

"What do you mean?" I asked.

"You mean Claudio?" asked Brisden.

The Doctor nodded.

"We shouldn't discuss this any more right now," said Anotine. "The minute our minds light up with these thoughts, the Fetch will be swooping down on us."

"True," said Nunnly.

"We discovered the other day that it can't pry into your thoughts if you are drunk," I told them.

"It wobbles like a one-winged bird," said Anotine.

"Well," said the Doctor, "I suggest we begin drinking as soon as possible."

"My place?" asked Nunnly.

"Sounds good," said Brisden, who separated from the group and walked over to the winch. "Say good-bye to your favorite toy, Doctor," he said as he reached his hand out and gave the heavy wooden base a slight shove.

That was all the force that was needed to send the huge thing sliding, slowly at first, and then with all its weight over the edge. The rest of the group joined Brisden at the rim to watch it fall. Plummeting with great speed, it punched through clouds and appeared to diminish in size as it went.

Nunnly clapped. "Your greatest accomplishment since arriving, Bris," he said.

"I feel now as if I had always wanted to do that," said Brisden.

"I'm wondering if it will disturb the dream of the ocean," said the Doctor as it splashed into the liquid mercury, raising a geyser of silver liquid that must have been an eighth of a mile high.

"Could the disturbance awaken its sleep?" asked Anotine.

The Doctor raised his eyebrows in contemplation of her question. "Perhaps," he said. "Or perhaps it might cause a nightmare."

As far as I was concerned, a nightmare was more to the

point. Events were now moving at an alarming rate, and a solution was nowhere in sight. I had forgotten for so long about the antidote that it was hard for me to again get my mind around the method of how I had even arrived on the island, not to speak of the absurdity of what I had meant to do there. I never thought that I would be thankful for being struck by a demon, but without Misrix's visit I surely would have drowned in the unreal reality of the place. The worst complication of all was that I had fallen in love with Anotine, and there was no amount of reasoning that would change that. Women I could never truly have, like the theme of islands, seemed to be a recurrent motif in my life.

The winch had surfaced after its fall—an insignificant dot in the infinity of the ocean below. I could commiserate with its situation. We all watched as, slowly, it sank again beneath the silver waves for the last time.

"Who's next?" asked Nunnly.

15

A STIFF NORTH WIND HAD BEGUN TO BLOW BY THE TIME we left the edge of the island and headed back toward the village. As we passed through the wood, the leaves now fell in torrents, swirling around us and moving along the ground in green waves. It was as if the trees had determined that they should be completely barren by evening.

"It looks like rain," said Brisden.

I gazed up through a hole in the now tattered canopy of branches and could see dark clouds passing in front of the sun. The day had taken on an autumnal feel, and that glorious light was slowly losing strength as the sky tinged toward a dull violet.

"Twice in the same week," said the Doctor. "I don't recall that ever having happened before."

"I remember entire years when it didn't rain once," said Nunnly.

Anotine moved in close to me, and I put my arm around her. I could feel her shivering slightly, and I knew it was not from the drop in temperature. She slowed her pace, and when the others had moved on ahead of us a short distance, she whispered, "You are here to help us aren't you, Cley? You've come to save us."

I stopped walking, surprised by her comment. She looked up at me.

105

I nodded. "How did you know?" I asked.

"The dream I had two nights ago. In it you revealed to me the secret for restoring the island. I tried so hard to remember what you said, so that I could take it back from sleep with me into daylight. But the second I opened my eyes the words that formed the plan dissolved like the boundary of the island, crackling into nothing."

"If I tell you now, the Fetch will come," I said. "Wait until later, and I will tell everyone. When I do, you must support me, for the others will never believe what I will say."

"I promise," she said, and reached up to kiss me.

As we began again our journey toward the village, a light drizzle started to fall. We walked without speaking, but I wanted to remind Anotine that a plan was not a guarantee of success. While crossing the field to the steps that would take us to Nunnly's rooms, we passed the Fetch, its green stare trained on a bird that lay dead on the withering grass. Not wanting it to notice us, we slipped quietly past, and once we were in the corridors of the terraced village, sprinted the rest of the way to the engineer's.

By the time we arrived, the drizzle had turned to a true rain. We came through the entrance to find cigarettes burning and quarts of Schrimley's and Rose Ear Sweet opened on the table. Nunnly and Doctor Hellman drank from glasses while Brisden directly engaged a pint bottle of the notoriously bitter distillation known as Tears In The River. Two seats and two glasses awaited Anotine and myself. We took our places and Nunnly poured. When we had our drinks in our hands, Brisden lifted his bottle toward us, and said, "Here's to chaos."

"Get the noise machine, why don't you," said Hellman.

Nunnly got up from the table, and as I followed his movement to the back of the room, I noticed for the first time that the walls were covered with diagrams of machines. The drawings of gears and hobs and axles rendered in a clear, clean black ink upon pure white paper were startling in their complexity and beauty. Arrows curled around the designs and indicated directions of rotation and thrust. They covered every inch of the back wall and much of the sidewalls as well.

Off in the left corner was a drawing table, its surface tilted at a forty-five-degree angle. Next to it on one side sat a stand, holding jars and cans full of brushes, quills, knives, half-melted candles, and bottles of ink. On the other side was a mattress that lay directly on the floor with no box spring or headboard. I pictured Nunnly late at night, overcome by exhaustion from working away at the depiction of one of his mechanical masterpieces: the brush drops from his hand as he falls from his chair onto the waiting mattress.

From under a stack of used paper, Nunnly retrieved a wooden box with a crank handle on the side and carried it to the table at which we were sitting. He placed it down carefully, and then, with his right hand, turned the squealing crank in a counterclockwise direction no less than fifty times. When he finally let go, the box began, very gently, to hum. He walked over and took his seat.

Anotine turned to me, her eyes closed, and said, "Shhh, just listen."

A faint noise of very fine glass slowly fracturing issued from the mechanism. Before long, though, it increased slightly in volume and arranged itself into a tinkling music that sounded like icicles being struck by minute tin hammers. The song was slow and sweet, eliciting a sense of nostalgia. I looked around at the company and saw that they all had their eyes closed and were following every note with emotional intensity.

I thought of them for the first time as a group, their different personalities and the focus of their individual studies, mixing together in a cocktail of inspiration. They were not merely symbolic objects containing secrets waiting to be remembered. If that were the case, there would have been no need for them to carry on lives and interact. I realized that Below was, through them, using the mnemonic system as a type of laboratory for creativity. Not only was he storing ideas here on the floating island, he was blending them to create new hybrids of thought. The researchers and their interactions, their conversations, constituted an imagination engine whose output was gathered and brought to consciousness by the Fetch. In short, Below was thinking without having to think about it.

When the box ran down and the last plinking note had sounded, Doctor Hellman turned to me, and said, "When I hear that, I can't help but believe that things are going to work out for the best."

"Very pretty," I said, and they all smiled at my approval.

"Let's have another drink," said Nunnly, "and then the Doctor can explain what happened to Claudio."

We each assiduously worked at our poison until our glasses were emptied and then refilled. Brisden polished off the bottle before him and reached down next to his chair to lift another pint he had at the ready. As he twisted off the top, he said, "I can hardly remember what Claudio looked like."

"I remember his thin black mustache," said Anotine.

"Hair that curled upon his head in a rather remarkable wave," said Nunnly.

"An altogether serious-minded fellow," added Doctor Hellman. "Claudio was a number man. He worked mathematics like an artist. The tune you just heard was composed by him. It is a theorem of his transposed into notes. For him, numbers had personalities, equations were like plays or stories, great comedies and tragedies that could make him laugh or cry. An interesting fellow, but ill suited for life on the island as it is prescribed by our absent employer.

"His vanity got the better of him, and he eventually came to the decision that he would no longer share his discoveries with the Fetch. We all cautioned him that to meddle with its work might be a tragic mistake. We did not know the extent to which we would be proven correct. One day when the head swooped down to extract his recent findings, he managed to duck beneath it, come up from behind and grab its long locks with both hands. It attempted to free itself, and the wailing it sent up brought us all scurrying to see what the commotion was. When we arrived he was swinging it by the hair, slamming the head into one of the walls in the courtyard outside his rooms. He gave it four or five bone-crunching whacks before it turned on him and bit his hands, finally liberating itself. It sped back to the tower emitting the sounds of a child weeping."

"He was very proud of what he had done," said Brisden.

"To say the least," continued the Doctor. "The next day, we were all sitting at the club, that room where you, Cley, initially materialized. We were drinking and playing cards, when suddenly there appeared a figure in the doorway. He was a tall, exceedingly thin man with a bulbous forehead and a chin that came nearly to a point. I remember his plain brown suit and how snugly it fit his emaciated body. His fingers were long and graceful, and they wriggled like unjointed worms when he spoke. 'Good evening, ladies and gentlemen,' he said."

"Wait," said Anotine. "Do you remember his head was shorn but for two long braids in the back?"

The others nodded.

"The look he wore on his face was what I imagine my expression will be when I go to the closet and find there is no more Tears In The River," said Brisden.

"Or mine when you next open your mouth to speak," said Nunnly.

Brisden grinned around his cigarette.

"A nightmare," said Doctor Hellman. "Then he said, 'I am looking for Professor Claudio,' in a high, whistling voice. We were all too amazed at the sight of another person on the island to respond. Claudio finally came to his senses, and said, 'I am Claudio.' The stranger excused himself to the rest of us and walked over to the mathematician. In an awkward manner, he leaned down. I thought he was going to whisper something to the professor, but at the last second, he put his lips over Claudio's ear, covering the entire thing. Then began the most horrifying process I have ever witnessed. I don't know how else to say it, but that he sucked the life right out of him."

"More than the life," said Nunnly. "Claudio's eyes imploded, his chest caved in, bones popped and broke, and his skull deflated like an overripe melon. The entire procedure took three agonizing minutes. The professor's screams exceeded any relationship to pain. I'll never forget it."

"Claudio was nothing but a limp husk when the stranger released him," said Anotine.

"A flesh puddle," said Brisden.

"The rest of you may not recall this," said the Doctor, "but when the thing, for I knew then it wasn't human, was finished, it belched, and through its open mouth, I could hear Claudio, as if at a great distance, crying unmercifully for help."

"I wish you hadn't mentioned that part," said Anotine, bringing her hand up to cover her eyes.

"Then, he wiped his mouth with the sleeve of his brown suit, turned to us, and said, 'Please excuse the interruption.' With that, he walked out of the room," said the Doctor.

"We did nothing to help," said Brisden, staring at the tabletop. "We sat by, paralyzed with fear, and watched our colleague get devoured. Since then, I often think of things I might have done."

There was a thick silence for some time before the Doctor went on. "Nunnly and I followed a short distance behind the creature to see where he went. He walked swiftly, taking the most direct route to the doors at the base of the Panopticon. As far as we knew that entrance had never opened in all the time we had been here. But he presented himself to the eye that is carved into the center of the emblem that adorns it. A green light shot out, much like the light that issues from the Fetch, engaging his eyes, and the doors slid open to allow his entrance. He stepped through, and they slammed shut behind him. And that," said the Doctor, "is what you can expect from interfering with the protocol of the island."

"What was it?" I asked.

"We call him the Delicate," said Anotine. "It was Brisden's name for him."

"I thought it captured the irony between his demeanor and his table manners," said Brisden.

"I hope you'll forgive us for not having mentioned it sooner," said Nunnly, "but we can barely stand the thought of it."

There was nothing I could say. Either we would perish by way of the disintegration of the island or at the gaping mouth of the Delicate, who I surmised was some kind of agent for the eradication of errant or dangerous thoughts from the mnemonic system. I merely shook my head. The glasses were filled again, cigarettes were lit, and Nunnly went over and wound the box up. This time the same tune seemed more lurid than nostalgic. While we listened, the Fetch flew by the window outside, then returned to stare in. The Doctor silently motioned for us all to laugh. We did, a false chorus of merriment that iced the eerie moment and convinced Below's spy to move on.

While I waited for the box to wind down, I weighed the words I would use in order to bring the others into my plan.

I knew that without them, it would be impossible to circumvent what the Doctor called the protocol of the island and get inside the Panopticon. Even with them, it was going to be difficult. When the last notes of the music had disintegrated and a contemplative silence still held sway, I lit a Hundred-To-One for courage and spoke.

"I have a confession to make," I said. The others looked up from their thoughts and focused on me. "I am not here to fulfill the position of specimen, but instead I am on a mission to save both yourselves and your employer, Drachton Below."

"Fancy that," said Brisden with a laugh. "Perhaps you should switch over to ice water now, Cley."

"No, hear him out," said Anotine. "I feel he is telling the truth."

"Go on, Cley," said the Doctor.

Nunnly leaned back in his chair and smiled in amusement.

"The island is disintegrating because there is something wrong with the health of Below. There is a direct connection between them. He created this place and is linked to it by means I can't fully explain."

"Try," said Nunnly, blowing a smoke ring.

"We don't have time for explanations," I said. "Below is infected by a sleeping disease that has put him in a coma, and his body is wasting. As he debilitates so does the island. There is an antidote to this disease and it is here on this very island. The only problem is that it is hidden in an object which I believe is in the Panopticon. If I don't find it, Below is going to expire, and if he does, so are we all."

Brisden started to laugh. "Cley, I appreciate your humor."

"You're starting to sound like Brisden," said Nunnly, poking a smoke ring.

"Anotine," I said, looking to her for help.

"I do believe you, Cley, but I can't say why or how."

"We haven't got time," I yelled. "Look, you know something has to be done, yourselves. That is why we are here. I think you are all just afraid to act."

The Doctor sat forward and placed his drink on the table. "I believe you, Cley." Then, turning to the others, he said, "I've got something in the way of proof that might convince you to follow him."

"Please let it be more than one of your rambling dream interpretations," said Nunnly.

"Have you got a mirror back in your workshop?" asked the Doctor.

Nunnly nodded.

"If you don't mind," said Hellman, and the engineer got up and walked down the hallway.

"Now, now," said Brisden, "doubling your image won't make you twice as believable."

Anotine seemed more certain after the Doctor had spoken. She smiled and put her hand on my back. I was as puzzled as the others as to the evidence he might have, but I stayed silent and hoped for the best.

Nunnly returned with a square mirror that was two feet by two feet. He laid it on the table in front of the Doctor, and said, "The last one in is a Fetch's leg."

The Doctor reached inside his coat and brought forth a small vial. He held it out in front of him so that we could all see. It glowed there in the dimness of the room like a silver flame, its reflection bouncing off the mirror and throwing bright dancing patterns onto the walls. I knew instantly it was a part of the sample we had taken from the ocean, and when I looked more closely, I saw miniature images swirling and twisting through the thick liquid.

16

"STAND AND OBSERVE," SAID THE DOCTOR. HE UN-
screwed the small glass stopper from the top of the
vial and very carefully poured the shimmering liquid onto the surface of the mirror. It flowed out with
a lazy thickness and puddled in a mound before
spreading flat to cover a good portion of the glass.

"What is that?" asked Brisden, standing now
and leaning forward to get a better look. He weaved
slightly from the drink and blinked his eyes twice
in order to clear them.

Nunnly also began to show an interest when the
shallow pond of silver started to swirl within its
boundaries. "A dream?" he asked.

Doctor Hellman shrugged. "A piece of the
ocean," he whispered, as if speaking too loud might
cancel the effect he was looking for.

"It's beautiful," said Anotine.

"Watch now," said the Doctor, "and you will
see what I am talking about."

Images began to form in the liquid mercury.
First there came the vague outline of a person. Then
it was clear that the figure was holding something
round up to his eyes. As the details slithered into
place like crease-snakes in the silver, I thought for
a moment that it was going to be me on the floor
of Anotine's bedroom, inspecting the steel ball. In-

stead the detail coalesced and began to move, revealing Below, biting into the fruit of Paradise.

"I see a man," said Nunnly. "He's eating something."

"Quite right," said the Doctor.

"Now it is changing into the same man, holding a kind of dog creature on a leash," said Anotine.

"Look carefully at the next scene," said Hellman.

Then I was there, sitting across from Below in his office at the Ministry of Benevolent Power back in the old days of the Well-Built City.

"Why, that's Cley," said Brisden.

"I see him," said Nunnly.

My head slowly spun into the fruit of Paradise from the first scene. Below lifted me and took a bite, and the series of tableaux began to play from the beginning again with perfect accuracy at the speed of dripping honey.

"The man you see in all of these scenes . . . Well, the ocean beneath us contains the entirety of this man's life, every movement from every instant of his existence. He is ever-present on the surface of the silver waves. This is the merest portion of that sea, and it happens to hold three distinct incidents. I believe the man whose life is being detailed is Drachton Below, our employer. Cley, as you saw, shares one scene with him, but it is proof that he must know him."

"Couldn't it all be a dream?" asked Nunnly.

"I used to think they were dreams," said the Doctor, "but now I think they might be memories. If this is so, then we have been trapped all of this time in a world that has as its essence the soul of Below. If you want to survive, I suggest we follow Cley's advice."

"I don't want just to survive," said Anotine. "I want to escape."

"If I can save him, I think I can convince him to return you all to the lives you left when coming to the island," I said, unable to look into Anotine's eyes as I made the false promise. I prayed that the Doctor would not have been self-effacing enough to realize that he and the rest of them were no more than the insubstantial stuff of thoughts. I let my proposition sink in for a moment before lifting my head, and asking, "Who is with me?"

Nunnly nodded in silence.

Brisden gave a grunt that was obviously meant as an affirmation.

Anotine said, "I'll do anything to leave here."

When I looked at the Doctor, he smiled and nodded, but in his expression I saw a hint of sadness. "There's no choice but to follow you," he said.

I was a little taken aback by his gaze, but I could not stop. I had them where I needed them. As long as I could attain the antidote without ever having to tell Anotine the entire truth, I would be able to continue.

"Very well," I said. "Tomorrow, when the sun is directly overhead at noon, I want you all to meet me at Anotine's. From that moment on, you will have to do whatever I ask of you, no matter how strange or dangerous it might seem. I will explain as much as I can as we proceed. But if I were to tell you the plan now, the Fetch would surely be upon one of us as soon as the alcohol wore off. You've got to trust me that your safety is my greatest concern, although there will be moments of doubt. From now until tomorrow, return to your work and work diligently. When you cannot work, sleep. Try not to consider, even for a moment, the possibility of what might happen."

When I finished speaking the others looked at me strangely for they had never heard me address them with so much self-confidence. For a moment I had fallen back into the autocratic speech patterns of a Physiognomist, First Class. I was somewhat startled myself, but managed to counter its effect with a smile.

By the time we left Nunnly's, it had stopped raining, and the sun shone in its final hours. The temperature had also nearly returned to its usual warmth. Anotine and I, ignoring my advice to the others of work and sleep, shuffled through the wet green leaves that littered the wood and marveled at the starkness of the naked branches silhouetted against a pink twilight. We said nothing but held tightly to each other. I wondered what she was thinking, but did not ask for fear that she would ask the same of me.

When we reached the edge of the island, it became obvious that the disintegration process had accelerated past the rate it had been earlier that afternoon. The clearing where we had all met and watched Brisden push the winch over the rim was now, itself, gone. Trees fell before us to the growing nothing, and the crackling sound of their disappearance, which at one point had been so faint, was now readily audible, like the feasting of an invisible swarm of insects.

On the way back to Anotine's rooms, we discovered that most of the blossoms that had filled the planters of the terraced village had shriveled and turned brown. She stopped to pluck one of the dead vines and crumble it between her fingers. At first, her look was that of the researcher, studying how the crumbs of stem came apart and floated away toward the stone of the terrace floor. Then her lips curled back and her eyes winced in a show of disgust. For the remainder of our walk back to her rooms, she kept wiping her hands together even after all trace of the dead plant was gone.

Later, we lay in bed and Anotine kissed me. She requested that we work toward discovering the moment again as we had tried the previous night before the monster's interruption.

"The time is not quite right," I said, gently pushing her back onto the pillow. Had she understood the signs, she would have seen that my body was yearning for a "discovery of the moment." In order to calm her and myself, I proposed that I would tell her a story.

"What about?" she asked.

"Wait and see," I said.

She seemed more interested in making love, but I coerced her with more lies, telling her that it would enable the discovery of the present at a much sooner time than if she refused to listen.

"Very well," she said, moving in close to me and resting her head on my arm.

I thought for a moment, staring at the face of the moon out the back window opening. She moved her nails in wide circles along my chest with the same graceful motion as in her experiment beneath the tree in the private garden. If I couldn't think of something to tell quickly, I would not have been able to hold myself in check, although my entire plan depended upon it. Then, like a ghost, a wispy cloud moved slowly in front of the moon, and I had what I was desperately searching for.

"This is the story of The Woman and the Green Veil," I began. "Once there was a very vain man with a position of great power . . ." I employed voluminous detail and slowly told the tale of my betrayal of Arla Beaton in the third person, as though the foolish hero were someone I had never met. Anotine's hand stopped moving, and I could tell she was listening intently. I spoke in as soothing a voice as possible.

More than an hour passed in the telling, and by the time I reached the part where the Physiognomist butchers the young woman's face in a foolish attempt to make her more virtuous, Anotine was, to my relief, fast asleep. I went on telling the rest of it, aloud, to myself, as if it were a confession of sorts.

The images came out of my memory in single file—Arla's face covered by the veil because I had made it so ugly that to gaze upon it meant sudden death, my imprisonment on the island of Doralice, my return to the Well-Built City. I saw the false paradise, an enormous crystal egg, that Below had built underground to house Arla and Ea, the Traveler from the wilderness of the Beyond. Then the Master bit into the white fruit, the city was destroyed through explosions, and we managed to escape. Again, I witnessed the birth of Cyn, Arla's daughter, whom I was forced to deliver one stormy night. Somehow, that birth had caused Arla's face to heal to its original beauty. She left the veil with me when she and Ea and their children had gone off to the Beyond. This last detail, my uncertainty as to whether her leaving it was to remind me of my guilt or a sign of forgiveness, was where I ended the story. The experience of giving voice to every memory left me feeling perfectly calm.

I had never felt so exquisitely comfortable in all my life as while lying there, but I had to fight my inclination to doze off. With great care, I rolled Anotine back onto her side of the bed and then slowly swung my feet around to sit up. After waiting some time to see if she was deeply asleep, I stood and went over to the brown rug. There, I sat down cross-legged as I had somewhere read the pagan holy men of the territory do to meditate. I concentrated and conjured a lit Hundred-To-

One; then I turned my attention to materializing something else that the mnemonic world could not as yet provide.

In my mind's eye, I pictured a Lady Claw scalpel, the kind the old Physiognomists, like Kurst Scheffler and Muldabar Reiling had once used. These instruments were supposedly more difficult to handle than the modern, double-headed type, but it had been said that they could cut bone as if it were pudding. The instrument glinted in the light of my thoughts, and I saw it from every angle. Even the fine, three-finger inscription on the handle did not escape me.

My self-induced trance lasted for as long as my story had, and when I finally opened my eyes, I stood and walked down the hallway to that mysterious dark closet. It had come to me in my meditation that the instrument would be in there on one of the shelves.

Once inside, I discovered that it was perfectly black. I felt along the inner wall of the room, letting touch be my guide. Before too long I found where the shelves began and started tentatively feeling around. These shelves reminded me of Misrix's Museum of the Ruins, and I thought of the pride with which he had shown me his display. My fingers came in contact with fur, ceramic, linen, and glass, and then with lumps of a soft unformed gel, which I guessed might be the element of things waiting to become.

I was beginning to think that my theory about the closet and the materialization of objects might have been all wrong, when I slid my hand across the dusty surface of a shelf and felt a sting on the tip of my index finger. Even a retired Physiognomist knows the feel of a scalpel, though it be the slightest caress. I knew the nick had drawn blood, and I smiled as I closed my fist around the handle. As I lifted it, I was startled by the sound of heavy breathing behind me.

"Cley," said a voice that I was sure was not Anotine's.

"Misrix?" I asked, rapidly placing the speaker.

"Yes," he said with a hiss.

"How long have you been in here?" I asked, careful to keep my voice to a whisper.

"I'm not here," said the demon. "I'm only speaking to you. I could not enter the mnemonic world again. It was hard enough to get my voice to travel over."

"How long have we been connected in reality?" I asked.

"Almost an hour."

"An hour . . ." " I found the discrepancy in time impossible.

"You've got to hurry," he told me. "The chances of retrieving you grow slimmer by the minute."

"My plan is mad," I told him.

"I can see what you are thinking."

"Absurdity seems to be the order of the day, though," I said, hoping he might try to talk me out of it.

A minute passed, and I thought he was gone. I prepared to leave.

"Cley," he said, frightening me again, "you are going to use the woman, aren't you?"

"For her own good," I said.

A wheezing laughter broke out around me everywhere, echoing in the small room. As it diminished, I could hear him very faintly call, "I'll be watching."

I brought the Lady Claw out into the bedroom and laid it on the table alongside the signal gun that the Doctor had left with me. Seeing the gun, I thought it might be better to have a weapon more truly suited for self-defense. Until very early in the morning, I meditated upon the derringer I had at one time carried, but no matter how precisely I saw it or desired it, it never appeared in the closet. I realized in dejection that there were probably limits to the complexity of the objects that could be materialized. As the dawn began to show itself out beyond the field and wood, I crept back to bed.

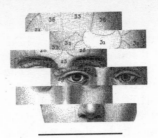

17

AFTER A LATE BREAKFAST THE NEXT MORNING, AS THE sun climbed a final step toward noon, we returned, at my insistence, to the bed. With Anotine sighing, "Now," and myself wrapped in ecstatic concentration, like a child in a final round of split the muggen, together we discovered the present, a gift from the future and the past.

This event was meant to be the initiation of my plan, but when I rolled onto my back and was breathing heavily in unison with her, I forgot all about disturbing Below's mnemonic world. If anything, I wanted it to remain as it was forever. What I had found in her was not the fulfillment of lust, but the origin of love. All of those questions of reality and illusion had disintegrated more completely than the edge of the island.

"Did you feel the moment?" I asked her.

"Yes," she said, "it exploded inside me. I was transported to another place." She reached out and put her hand around my wilting member. "Cley, you're a genius. Who would have thought."

Her comment about having gone to another place reminded me of Bataldo's revelation that sexual union was a temporary fusion of memories. I pondered this notion, and found that it coincided with the feeling that I had finally, after all my errant wandering in thought and deed, come home to myself. There was nothing left but to tell her I loved her, and that is precisely when the Fetch arrived.

It slowly drifted backward in through the window opening above us, its hair alive, its expression a startling mask of ecstatic rage. Anotine sat up to take its gaze as the green light streamed toward her eyes.

I rolled out of the bed in a fit of jealousy and made my way to the table across the room. There, I lifted the signal gun and turned to aim, determined not to share our intimacy with the creature. As I was about to pull the trigger, I realized that I might hit Anotine. Lowering the gun, I walked cautiously up behind the Fetch, steeled myself as if on the verge of thrusting my hand into a fire, and reached out to grab a shock of serpentine hair.

The instant I closed my grip, it began to scream. The unnatural sound of its cry roused me to action, and I pivoted on my heels, swinging the disembodied head facefirst into the wall. There was a sickening crunch, and I thought I had broken its nose. Behind me I heard Anotine cry, "Cley, what are you doing?" as I let go of my victim. The Fetch wavered in midair, then dipped toward the ground but managed to stay aloft. As it turned to lunge at me, its shrieking mouth wide with pointed cat teeth, I lifted the gun, aimed, and pulled the trigger.

It all seemed to happen at once—a pop, a cloud of smoke, and a sizzling explosion of red light. The force of the blast slammed the Fetch into the wall as I was thrown back a few steps in the opposite direction. I saw it hang there for a moment, like some strange decoration, before it slid to the floor and onto its face. With great care, I approached it, waiting to see if it was feigning death. The limpness of the singed hair convinced me it was safe to touch. Using the end of the gun, I flipped it over to reveal a blackened, tattered visage of melted green flesh.

I turned to look at Anotine and found her sitting straight up, her face pale, her mouth open wide. "Quickly," I said, "get dressed. The plan has begun." Only then did I remember that I had intended to kill the Fetch all along.

By the time the others had arrived, we were both clothed and had dragged the lifeless head into Anotine's laboratory.

They entered by way of the bedroom, and I heard the Doctor call to us.

"In here," I yelled.

They came down the hallway with Nunnly in the lead and Brisden bringing up the rear.

As they entered the lab, Nunnly said to me, "Brisden and I have been thinking this over, Cley, and we believe . . ." He never finished his statement, though, because at that moment I stepped away from the table I stood in front of, allowing them to get a look at what I was working on. Nunnly took a step back. The Doctor immediately brought his hand to his beard, and Brisden said, "Fa," closed his eyes, and turned his face away.

"There's no going back," said Anotine, casting a sick glance at the mutilated remains on the table.

"I should say not," said Nunnly, now stepping closer to study it.

"You know what this means, Cley," said the Doctor.

I nodded.

"The Delicate," said Brisden.

"It's the only way we can get inside the tower," I said.

"Do you think we'll be invited after this?" asked Nunnly.

"That's the part I'm unclear about," I said. "All I know is that the doors have to open for us to get inside."

The Doctor stepped closer and peered down at the head. "How did you stop it?" he asked.

"The signal gun you left the other night was a better weapon than I imagined," I said.

"What is that in your hand?" asked Nunnly, pointing to the Lady Claw.

"An instrument for cutting through flesh and bone. It's called a scalpel."

"Do you think it's necessary to dice the little beast up?" asked Brisden, grimacing at the sight of it as he moved alongside the others.

"I want to get inside the head," I told them. "I need to determine what it is that allowed the Fetch to see into each of your minds."

"Cley thinks there might be something there that will help him to discover the antidote," said Anotine.

"Stand back a little," I said. With this, I lifted the scalpel and began to cut away at the long strands of hair. My facility with the tool came back to me all at once, and I found a kind of pleasure in wielding it again. The Physiognomy also tried to pry its way back into my consciousness along with my appreciation of the grace of the instrument. It was all I could do to suppress the tenets of that crackpot philosophy, which slithered in mind-speech and flashing images through my thoughts.

I had shaved nearly the entire head when I stopped for a moment and looked up to see the others staring with expressions of astonishment at my work.

Brisden broke from his trance, and said, "Things have certainly grown more complex in the past few minutes."

"They're going to get absolutely intricate," I said, and went back to playing the barber.

I made the cut along the middle of the bald cranium with confidence, and the tight skin parted to release a viscous yellow fluid. It seeped out of the opening, pooled on the table, and dripped to the floor in minute wet explosions as steady as the ticking of a clock. Laying the scalpel down, I worked the fingers of both hands into the crease I had made and pulled back the flaps of flesh on either side to reveal the skull.

"There's nothing shy about Cley," Nunnly said.

"Doctor, how long would you estimate we have before the Delicate comes seeking revenge?" I asked.

"All we can go by is what happened to Professor Claudio. With this in mind, I believe we have a day." He turned to Anotine, and asked, "Was it the next day that it came after him?"

She nodded, and added, "But that is the only instance; a poor estimate based on one piece of evidence."

"I suppose we will have to trust to it," I said. "Now let's see what the Fetch is made of."

I tapped the scalpel against the yellow cap that lay exposed and was surprised to find that it was not hard like bone. There was a certain pliancy to it as if it were crafted from a kind of sturdy rubber. The Lady Claw dug into the substance with little resistance, and when I pulled the instrument in a circular motion to create a portal, it sailed smoothly along as though

I were cutting nothing tougher than the callused flesh of a sailor's hand.

When this was finished, I used the thin edge of the scalpel as a lever and pried open the plug, which encompassed an area a little larger than the size of my fist. As soon as this piece was removed an acrid stench rose out of the cavity and filled the lab.

I was nearly overcome by the aroma, which smelled sharply of chemicals and shit. It was necessary to take a step back and let it dissipate before continuing. The others, having never experienced the scent of the latter, groaned audibly. Anotine's nostrils flared, she gagged, and I could see a ripple of fear run through her. Nunnly reached for his handkerchief. Brisden and the Doctor stepped briskly over to the open window and took in draughts of fresh air.

When the odor had lessened, I asked Anotine to light one of the candles and bring it over so that I could look into the dark hole I had opened. As she prepared this, the others returned and gathered around me. She brought the candle, and I leaned down, holding it as close to my face as possible so that its glow would illuminate the cavity.

At first glance there appeared to be nothing but space and the inner walls of the skull. "Harrow's hindquarters," I thought, "the damn thing is empty." I looked again, and then I saw a small shiny protuberance glint in the light from the flame. Giving Brisden the candle, I reached with my opposite hand inside the head. Up near the front, just behind where the eyes were positioned in the face, I felt a small sac filled with fluid. Further tactile investigation told me it was connected by two stalks to an area of smooth flesh. I grabbed these cartilaginous tubes tightly with my fingers and yanked on them. They came free with an audible snap, and I drew the entire assemblage of tissue out into the daylight.

Holding the organ in the palm of my hand, I looked down at it, amazed that this little bag of green liquid could have animated the Fetch.

"Not much of a prize for all that work," said Brisden.

"Is there nothing else?" asked the Doctor.

"Just this," I said.

"I don't understand how the thing worked," said Nunnly.

"Surely that can't be enough of an organic engine to power a flying head."

"Unless that gas that was released was the source of its energy," said the Doctor.

"And what would that be?" asked Nunnly.

"Dreams, perhaps," said the Doctor.

"Noxious ones at that," said Brisden.

"Another delivery," said Anotine, referring to what I had told her about my midwifing duties. She smiled at me as though proud of my accomplishment.

"For that, I'm going to have my essence sucked out through my ear?" asked Brisden, pointing with his pinky finger.

"It may be more valuable than you think," I said. Now that the initial puzzlement had worn off, I realized that it might just be what I had been looking for. The fact that it had been attached to the back of the eyes led me to believe that it had something to do with the Fetch's ability to probe the inhabitants and objects of the mnemonic world. Of course, it was all so much dangerous conjecture, but I wondered if perhaps it was the key to releasing Below's secret knowledge from those symbolic forms in which it was hidden.

"Anotine, do you have a beaker, something I can pour the contents of this into?" I asked.

She turned away and began searching the other tables.

Nunnly laughed. "Time for cocktails?" he asked.

"Precisely," I said.

The others remained silent as I cut the small bag of green with the scalpel and drained it into the bottom of the flask Anotine had found. When the organ was empty, I threw the whithered sac back into the open skull. Lifting the container, I swirled it around, the inch of liquid at the bottom circling in a miniature wave.

Now came the moment of reckoning. If I were to ingest it, I considered that there were at least three possibilities of what might happen. The first was that it would do nothing, perhaps make me ill. The second was that it would poison me, and I would die both in Below's mind and also back in my reality, where Misrix waited for me. The last was that I would be privy to the knowledge Below had stored on the island.

As cold as it is to say, I thought nothing of the predicament of my neighbors in Wenau, but only of Anotine. I could not lose her. The only prospect for her survival would be to find the antidote. It was this alone that convinced me to gamble.

"You're not really going to drink that muck, are you?" asked Brisden.

I walked past the others and took a seat in the metallic chair, which now frightened me less than the thought of what I was about to do.

"I can't allow this," said the Doctor. "Cley, this is senseless. There is no evidence that this will do any more than sicken you."

"I'm with the Doctor," said Nunnly. "We are going to need you when the Delicate comes. You're the only one who knows this foolish plan of yours."

"I'm only going to take a little of it," I said.

"Absurd," said the Doctor.

"We'll have to prevent that," said Brisden.

"Wait," said Anotine. "He knows what he is doing. You said you would trust him. Now is the time for trust. Stand away from him."

I watched as the gentlemen all bowed their heads and reluctantly moved a step back. It confirmed what I was beginning to suspect, that Anotine was really the leader of the group. Although Hellman had always spoken with the most conviction, it was evident that she had an unvoiced authority over the rest of them.

"I'm grateful to you all for your concern," I told them. "If this wasn't necessary, believe me, I'd rather a Rose Ear Sweet any time."

"What if you perish?" asked Nunnly. "What are we to do with the Delicate?"

"Kill him," I said, "and take his head to the gate. Align his eyes with the eye on the emblem. Hopefully it will open for you. The Panopticon might save you from the dissolution of the rest of the island."

"And if it doesn't?" asked the Doctor.

I had no ready answer for him, for I had barely thought

that far ahead myself. To my surprise, I found a lit Hundred-To-One in my right hand. When I looked up, Brisden, Nunnly, the Doctor, and Anotine were all smoking. After a few puffs, I swirled the liquid one more time and put the flask to my lips.

"Cheers," said Brisden.

The green fluid trickled across my tongue and then down my throat, leaving an almost unbearably bitter taste. I did not take all of it in case it proved useful and more would be needed later. Handing the flask to Anotine, I sat back and waited.

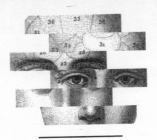

18

Twenty minutes passed and the only noticeable effect was that my stomach had begun to ache. The others pulled up chairs and sat quietly, watching my every breath.

Doctor Hellman had been right in that there was no scientific basis to my belief that to ingest the brain liquor of the Fetch might afford me its special power of vision. All I could have said in my defense was that in light of the Fetch's remarkable abilities, the near emptiness of its skull was enough to prove that science had little to do with the natural laws that governed the island. To do so, though, would imply that all of the work the researchers had done in their long confinement had been nothing but an elaborate game of make-believe.

Every now and then, Anotine would ask me how I felt, and I would give her the same report as to my status. During her fourth inquiry, Nunnly interrupted, and said, "I think it is fairly evident he has a stomach ache. While we are waiting for Cley's head to take flight, could we at least discuss what we are going to do with the Delicate when he comes in search of us."

"Agreed," I said, and they all seemed relieved that I felt well enough to carry on a conversation.

"One thing we must take into consideration," said the Doctor, crossing his legs and then uncrossing them, "is that we do not know what our menacing friend is capable of."

"The signal gun seemed fairly effective against the Fetch," said Brisden.

"There is only one remaining shell for it, though," said the Doctor.

"With anything else, we are going to have to get danger-ously close to that mouth of his to kill him," said Anotine.

"Could you create some weapons?" I asked Nunnly.

"It's not my specialty," he said, "but I guess I can put together just about anything in my workshop."

I thought of the crossbow that the people of Wenau had supplied me with, but I had no idea as to how to describe the operation of the firing mechanism. "What about a couple of long poles with sharp blades attached to the ends?" I asked.

"What about a big rock I can hit him on the head with?" said Brisden.

"We could just have him spend some time with Brisden," said Nunnly. "With that strategy, he might be persuaded to cut his own head off."

"What about a trap?" said Anotine. "I think we should trap him first."

"Do we have a net somewhere?" asked the Doctor.

"Slingshots for everyone," said Brisden.

I was about to suggest that we shock the Delicate into unconsciousness with the same technology utilized by the me-tallic chair in which I sat when the whole room suddenly tilted to the left. Gripping the armrests, I tried to steady myself as everything tipped back in the opposite direction. This seesaw effect rapidly increased in speed, giving way to a brutal spin-ning that made me feel as if I were descending into the funnel of a whirlpool.

"Something is happening," I yelled to my friends as they spun past. I was forced to close my eyes against the dizzying motion of the world around me, which elicited a sudden attack of intense nausea. The disorientation also disturbed my hear-ing, because though I knew the others were only a few feet from me, their voices seemed very distant. I could only catch snatches of what they were saying. Somewhere in my motion-addled mind, I began to believe that it was the chair I sat in that was rotating. The phenomenon soon reached an unbearable speed that took my breath away. With my last shred of consciousness, I flung myself out of the metal seat.

For quite some time it felt as if I were turning somersaults in midair. Although I kept anticipating a sudden crash, it didn't happen. "Perhaps I have gained the power of flight," I thought. I finally opened my eyes, expecting a view from somewhere near the ceiling only to find the floor in my face. A moment later, the impact of the fall registered, as if my entire body suddenly remembered the collision. I grunted with the delayed pain, but the spinning had stopped, and the nausea began to dissipate.

Hands grabbed at my arms just beneath the shoulders, and I was being hoisted to my feet. At the same time, the others' voices became clear, and I heard Brisden behind me say, "Cley is quite a duffel bag full."

"The weight is all in his head," said Nunnly.

As soon as my field of view became more than the stone floor, I realized a change had occurred in my vision. The room appeared submerged in a clear, lime green light, and all of the objects that filled the tables gave off a mild incandescence that seemed associated with a vague jumble of whispering in my mind. The transformation was unsettling to say the least. I closed my eyes, and the indistinct voices fell silent.

"Are you all right?" asked the Doctor.

I nodded to him. "I'll be fine," I said, and my speech sounded low and throaty, almost unrecognizable to me.

"Cley, it's me, Anotine," she said, and I felt her hand upon my face. "Wake up if you can."

I wanted to tell her I was not asleep or faint, but I did not want to hear that foreign tone in my voice again. Nunnly and Brisden still held firmly to me, and I felt another hand reach down along my wrist—I assumed it was the Doctor's—in order to find my pulse.

"Come back to me, Cley," I heard Anotine say. Then she lightly slapped me.

I smiled to let her know I was fine, and when I opened my eyes her face was before me, an absolutely radiant green. Her lips moved, and I knew she was speaking to me, but her words were blocked by the whispering inside my head, which had begun again the moment my eyes focused on her.

In addition to the alien voices, I also saw pictures that did not obscure my view of her, but played over it in a strange palimpsest. Numbers and chemical formulae were scribbled across her forehead. They wavered and swam in circles along with a school of words that spoke the meaning of it all to me. When I saw an image of Drachton Below superimposed upon her right cheek, holding up a beaker of violet liquid that became the center of her iris, I turned away. Shrugging off the supporting hands, I ran out of the lab, down the hallway, and out into the village.

Frantically, I fled from this new attribute whose power seemed to increase with every second. The architecture, the dying flowers in their planters, the steps in the myriad stairways I climbed and descended, all revealed themselves to me in a dizzying barrage of information. I had found the key that unlocked the symbols of Below's mnemonic design, and the secrets came at me from every direction, clamoring to have me know them, accosting me with their detail, leaping upon my back like so many malicious demons and riding through the alleys.

I flew rapidly through states of knowing—the formulae for deadly explosives, equations that equaled fear, philosophies of chaos and order and the insubstantial border between them. I saw phantoms, some I recognized from the Well-Built City, step forth from sculptures to expound upon their lives, and cornices and arches oozed music and poetry. When I was finally exhausted, I fell to my knees in front of the fountain of the pelican whose breast spurted an arched stream of water. The stone bird told a tragic tale concerning the death of Below's sister. There was no running away from the Master's brilliance. All I could do to stop it was close my eyes.

The relief that darkness brought calmed me, and I was able to regain my rationale. I crawled forward and reached up over the edge of the fountain to cup some water in my palms. Splashing this over my face, I breathed deeply.

"They are only ideas," I said aloud to myself. "They can't hurt you. Only notions." My eyes remained closed as I leaned back against the base of the fountain and began to cry. These tears had nothing to do with fear. The reason I had run, the reason I felt then an overwhelming sense of desolation, had to do with what I had seen in Anotine's face. Like the purported power of the false science of Physiognomy, the Fetch's borrowed vision had read the cues of her outer form and revealed to me her essence.

That flask of violet liquid that the image of Below had held up to her eye was nothing less than sheer beauty. In the Master's memory palace, she was the symbolic manifestation of the formula for the vicious drug I had so long been a slave to. My desire for her was clear to me. It was the recultivation of an addiction that had at one time nearly cost me my soul.

"He's over here, by the fountain of the pelican," I heard Nunnly call.

His message was followed by the sound of footfalls on the pavement. I felt them all around me, and my recent revelation made them seem like ghosts who had materialized to torment me. Doctor Hellman could very well have contained at his core the process for turning men and women into werewolves. Brisden or Nunnly might have been the receptacle of Below's recipe for the sleeping virus. In my mind, I cried out for Misrix to bring me back. I wanted nothing but to awaken from the nightmare. Again I felt Anotine's hands on my face, and I flinched at her touch.

"Please, Cley, open your eyes," she said, and, with that, everything changed.

The pleading in her voice, the touch of her fingers on my forehead, an image of our making love, came suddenly together, like some magic spell, to completely obscure the horrible knowledge I had of her. I was like a traveler at a crossroad. One path would, if all went well, deliver me back to my placid existence at Wenau. The other most likely led toward death, but for the duration of the journey I would be with Anotine. My decision to embrace the illusion was almost instantaneous. Until then, I had been solely focused on the ramifications of memory. It was time to succumb to the mechanism of forgetting.

I opened my eyes to find that the green affliction had passed. The day was bright, and Anotine's face was more beautiful than ever. She leaned forward and kissed me.

"There's an odd custom I don't think I will adopt," said Brisden as he helped me to my feet.

"Can you stand on your own, Cley?" asked the Doctor.

"I'm quite all right," I said.

"What did you see?" asked Nunnly. "What frightened you?"

"It was just the weirdness of it all," I said. "A rush of information. The place is brimming with knowledge."

"Will you be able to take the stuff again when we get inside the Panopticon?" he asked.

"I'll be able to do it. I know what to expect," I said.

"What did you learn about us?" asked the Doctor.

"Nothing. I didn't have a chance to really focus on any of you," I said. When it was evident from the quizzical look he gave me that my answer was hardly sufficient, I spoke quickly before he could question me further. "The weapons," I said. "We have to prepare for the Delicate. Nunnly, do you understand what I'm looking for?"

The engineer nodded. "I think so."

"Brisden," I said, "I want you to go to the edge of the island and check the rate of disintegration."

He bowed as low as his stomach would allow and set off, surprisingly, without a word.

"I'll get the remaining shell for the signal gun," said the Doctor.

"Meet at Anotine's as soon as possible," I called.

Brisden waved without looking back, and the other gentleman turned away to their tasks. I was left alone then with Anotine.

"I thought I was going to lose you," she said.

"Nonsense," I told her. "I'm not leaving here without you. No matter what happens, I will find a way for us to be together."

She smiled and put her arms around me. I pulled her close and could feel every inch of her body against mine. Putting my lips to her ear, I meant to whisper, "I love you," but instead the words came as, "I believe in you."

19

Back in Anotine's bedroom, I had only to tell her my idea of using the technology of the metallic chair as some sort of weapon, and she immediately came up with a way it might be put to use.

"The seat and back are the only pieces that carry the charge," she told me. "We remove the arms and legs, and then lay the effective parts in the entrance, so that when the Delicate tries to come in we can use the black box from a distance to disable him. Once he is weakened, we can finish the job with one of the cruder weapons that Nunnly comes up with."

"Perhaps we should then fire the signal gun at him," I said.

She shook her head. "From what you said before, the signal gun should be held for emergencies. If you destroy his face with it like you did the Fetch's, we may not be able to use him to gain access to the Panopticon."

"You're right," I said, impressed with the speed and clarity of her thought. I could see now that she had shrugged off her fear and was attacking the situation as if it were a research problem.

I followed her down the hall to the laboratory, and stood back as she moved quickly from table to table collecting an armful of implements. The way she launched into the project of cannibalizing the

chair showed me why my conjecture as to her being the leader
of the group was correct. Although Nunnly was the engineer,
Anotine herself was a wizard with tools. She was altogether
focused and graceful in her work, and when she needed my
assistance, gave orders with an authoritative voice that told
me I had better pay attention.

As we set the makeshift trap up in the entrance to her
bedroom, I asked her how the black box was able to affect the
chair parts from a distance.

"I haven't the slightest idea," she said, kneeling to check
our placement of the device. "The apparatus was here when
I arrived long ago. I can tell you, my discovery of how it
worked was rather interesting. I had always thought that the
chair, being made of a metallic alloy, must have some impor-
tance beyond being another piece of furniture, but I just
couldn't find the key to its significance. One day, after long
hours of research on trying to study the instant between a
candlewick's being lit and my extinguishing of it, I sat down
in the chair. Back in those days, I believed my stay on the
island would have a limit, and I wanted to make the most of
it. Instead of simply resting, I thought it would be a good time
to take another look at a certain black box with buttons I had
also found here in the lab."

I laughed. "Happy accident," I said.

"A shocking discovery," she said. "I think it proves something that Brisden always says: with enough time and the right
degree of curiosity, all secrets will be revealed."

"Maybe," I said, thinking of my own problems in locating
the antidote.

"The time has come for another discovery, Cley," she said,
standing up from where she had been adjusting the sections
of the chair. From the manner in which she dipped her head
and arched her eyebrows, I realized she wasn't speaking
hypothetically.

"What would that be?" I asked.

She paused for a moment before speaking. "It came to me
before by the fountain of the pelican. You said you believed
in me. Why would you have to say that? None of this is real,
is it? Nunnly, Brisden, the Doctor, myself, we're all merely the
afterthoughts of some other greater place, aren't we?"

I walked over and took her hand. "Listen," I said. "I'm from another place, and there is no one there who doesn't wonder the same thing. We may have the curiosity, but there will never be enough time to answer that question. Live your life, Anotine. Be real for me, and I'll be real for you."

Her look softened, and then she smiled. "Agreed," she said, and shook my hand.

I was going to put my arms around her, but Brisden came in then, overheated and babbling at an alarming rate. He walked directly between the two of us, pushing apart our hands, and took up a seat at the table near the back of the room. I had never witnessed the weighty philosopher practice his verbal profluence. The words came in torrents, strung together by a frayed ribbon of exotic grammar.

". . . and the ineluctable presence of the not-there is evident in a materially vanquished nuance of equal parts matter without regard to structure and spiritual gravity in the falling off of the centeredness beyond the point of diminishing . . ."

"Brisden," Anotine said.

He continued to spew.

She stepped over to him and smacked him across his meaty face. His head turned with the blow, and perspiration flew off. He went silent, and his lips turned down at the corners. It seemed as if he suddenly came awake, looking up at us with a dazed expression.

"What is it?" I asked.

"Tell us so we can understand," said Anotine.

"Pass out the wings," he said.

"The disintegration has increased yet more?" she asked.

"I almost went over the side," he said, smiling. "I was standing about midway through the wood, and the edge was now there. It moved so rapidly, I was amazed and could not help but gape. Before I knew it, I looked down and saw the ground beneath my feet disappearing. I just managed to dig my heels in and throw myself back onto my rear end at the last possible second. Nunnly would have been beside himself had he seen me scrabbling to my feet and running—I actually ran."

"Well?" said Anotine.

"It's going to keep increasing in speed. I'd say we have two days at the most, taking everything into consideration."

"Hardly enough time for me to perfect my swan dive," said a voice from behind us.

I turned around to find the engineer standing at the entrance upon the back of the broken-down chair, holding three five-foot-long pointed shafts made of polished steel.

"How about these, Cley?" he asked, and came forward to hand me one.

"Not bad," I said.

"They're partially hollow inside, making them light enough to handle, but I ground down the ends to a wicked sharpness."

"I'll take one," said Anotine, and he handed one over.

"Bris?" asked Nunnly.

Brisden waved his hand, begging off. "Maybe later," he said.

"You should practice jabbing with them," said Nunnly. "It would be a good idea to get used to the feel of them. They might also be thrown a short distance."

"Your technological prowess astounds me," said Brisden. "I think it's called a spear."

"There's no substitute for simple elegance," said the engineer.

It was an absurd scene, the three of us moving around Anotine's bedroom, jabbing at the air with the silver javelins. Nunnly stood in front of Brisden and poked his an inch away from his friend's vital areas. At one point, Anotine's slipped out of her hand and sailed across the room to skewer the pillow to her bed.

"I wasn't aware the plan had changed to group suicide," said Brisden.

"Wait a second," said Anotine, as she retrieved the spear. "Where is the Doctor? He was only going to get the last shell for the signal gun."

"Did you see him?" I asked Nunnly.

"I walked him as far as his rooms and then went back to my place to get to work."

*   *   *

We took the spears and the empty signal gun and set out in search of the Doctor.

"He's probably poring over his notes, still looking for the ultimate interpretation of everything," said Nunnly, but his words did little to ease the obvious tension.

Outside, along the passageways and across the terraces of the village, the pervasive sound of the disintegration of the island could be heard, like an infinite number of bootheels treading upon an endless supply of hard-shelled beetles. I pictured the mile-long fall and could almost taste a burning mouthful of liquid mercury. That fear I had experienced on the fields of Harakun during my approach to the ruins of the City was now back with a vengeance, weakening my legs and leaving my mouth dry as dust. At one point I had to stop and take a drink from one of the fountains.

"To hell with the water," said Brisden, as they waited for me to compose myself. "I hope no one minds if after we return to Anotine's, I stay at least moderately drunk for the rest of this fiasco." He lifted the empty signal gun as if it were a bottle and pantomimed a healthy draught.

"Come on, Cley," said Anotine, "be real for me."

I looked back at her, and she appeared focused and determined.

"I'm with you," I said, and, after a few deep breaths, managed to carry on.

Nunnly led the way, the spear in his right hand and suddenly materializing Hundred-To-Ones in the left. He chain smoked through alleys and corridors, and at one point had to lean against a wall for a second to catch his breath. "Right now, I'm thinking about what fear would be like if it were a machine," he said.

Brisden stepped up and put his arm around him, helping him back on course.

When we reached the Doctor's rooms at the bottom of a long flight of steps, Anotine called out his name. There was no reply.

"How are we going to do this?" asked Nunnly, but Anotine had already taken the initiative and passed through the entrance, holding the spear out in front of her with both hands.

The rest of us followed reluctantly, not wanting to be left alone on the terrace. Inside, the candles had not been lit and the room we entered was cast in the subtle shadows of late afternoon. Whereas Nunnly's place had been lined with the schematics of his imaginary machines, the Doctor's walls were taken up by bookshelves crammed with hundreds of volumes. There were also stacks of books at different heights sitting here and there like a mountain range of pages and words. The passes that led between them were sometimes too narrow to fit through, and we would have to backtrack in order to find a way through the maze. Down the hallway, which ran off to the left, we found another of the dark closets like Anotine had at her place, and beyond that a larger area he obviously used as his living quarters.

We stood there in the middle of the bedroom, looking at each other. In one corner was a four-poster bed, and at the other end of the place, beneath a large window opening, sat a desk, facing into the middle of the room. On the desk, I could see what remained of his sample of ocean, glowing in its lidded glass jar, and an open notebook lying next to it.

"Perhaps he took another route to Anotine's while we were coming to get him," said Brisden.

"The Doctor has a tendency to let his mind wander," said Nunnly, "and while it does his body does the same. I just hope he hasn't walked off the edge of the island, daydreaming."

"Let's get back, before we miss him again," said Anotine.

"Perhaps we should check his notebook and see what he was working on before he left. It might give us an idea as to where he has gone if he wasn't heading for your rooms," I said.

"Allow me," said Brisden, and he stepped over behind the desk to read the open pages.

"I can see we're going to have to keep Doctor Hellman on a leash until this is all over," said Nunnly.

"Oh my," Brisden said in a weak voice. "I think I've located him."

We turned to him, and Anotine asked what was in the notebook.

"Not the notebook, the chair," he gagged out, doubling over with his hands grasping at his chest.

As Brisden moved away to sit on the bed, we took his position behind the desk. Lying on the seat of the chair, like some discarded heap of pink leather, was a wrinkled pile of flesh, resting upon the Doctor's empty clothes. There were two dark eye sockets and an opening where his mouth had been. Perhaps the most gruesome detail of all was the indistinguishable area that still held his beard.

Anotine and Nunnly stepped away, both of them in shock. I meant to follow, but as I turned, I noticed something was scrawled on one page of the notebook. The writing was nearly illegible and moved in a downward slant across the page. I leaned over and made out the message. "*Shell in pocket*" it said.

It was necessary to step away for a few minutes before I could work up enough courage to disturb the pitiful remains. Brisden was lying back on the bed, whispering to himself at lightning speed. Anotine and Nunnly both had found places against the wall, where they had leaned back and sunk down to cover their faces with their hands. Their crying and Brisden's babble was enough to make me insane. In addition, I played out in my mind the scenario of the Doctor's last minute. As his insides were drawn out of him, bones splintering and brain becoming oatmeal, he had the courage to lift his pen and try to help us.

I shook my head, then returned to the chair to retrieve the shell. When I pulled on a trouser leg to expose the pocket from beneath the heap of flesh, the mess came with it and spilled onto the floor. The sound of it hitting made me dizzy. I wasted no time in fishing in the pocket and bringing out the canister. Once I had it in my hand, I backed away from the desk and shouted to the others in a voice cracking with fear. "Now, let's go!"

I went around the room and, using my foot, nudged everyone sharply and ordered them to move. Anotine was the first to come around, and she helped me rouse Brisden and Nunnly. Before we could leave, Brisden insisted that he take the glass jar of ocean as something to stand in as a symbolic presence we would now find difficult continuing without. Once he had it in his hands, we dashed down the hallway and out into the village. Anotine led us through the passageways, and I was last, using my spear to prod Brisden in the rear end when he tried to slow down. Our flight was a nightmare, and at every turn I expected to see the gaping maw of the Delicate. Though I had only been told about it, it was now more real to me than anything I could remember.

20

Brisden kept to his own plan and was well into a pint of Tears In The River. He sat at the small table in the back of the room, the signal gun resting in his lap, staring into the glowing ocean sample he had retrieved from the Doctor's. Nunnly was in the chair opposite, following the trail of smoke that rose from his cigarette. I stood by the entrance, looking down the steps and across the moonlit terrace below for any signs of movement while Anotine sat cross-legged on the brown rug, her spear lying next to her and the black box in her hand. No one had bothered to light the spire lamps when twilight gave itself up to darkness. No one had spoken since our return. The loss of the Doctor had left us weak, our mourning compounded with the other impossible elements of our predicament.

As I stood guard, I thought about Hellman and how incredibly I missed him. He had been more vibrant than many of the people I had known on a daily basis back in Wenau. It came to me in the midst of my vigil that he had to be, no more, no less, than some manifestation of Below's personality. I had a hard time reconciling this. In fact, all of my companions on the island were first-rate human beings. Was there an aspect of the Master I had missed? I supposed that everyone, even the most heinous of criminals, could think himself, in some way, righteous and good. This type of delusion could have been the impetus for the creation of the four moral souls I had met, or perhaps Below did harbor a positive side.

It was all too confusing to consider, especially in light of the fact that our time was quickly running out. The sound of the island disappearing had grown stronger since our foray to the Doctor's. What was quickly becoming evident through our siege was that the Delicate was too smart to enter a room full of armed enemies. His plan became clear to me—draw us out into the night, separate us, and devour us one at a time. I had a sense from the little I knew that he was patient and methodical, perfect attributes for a beast of prey.

I hated to have to implicate the others in my decision, but without taking action at this point we had absolutely no chance of survival. It was obvious that we would have to do exactly what the Delicate wanted. As I turned back into the room, I found Nunnly standing behind me, spear in hand.

"Let's go," he said, and one look into his eyes told me we had reached the same conclusion in our thinking.

Anotine got up and came over to join us.

"Stay here with Brisden. Nunnly and I are going to try to lead the Delicate back to the room. As the Doctor said, we don't know what he is capable of. I think we have a better chance of taking him here with all of us working together," I told her.

"I want to go," she said.

"I want you to, but someone has to be ready to charge the trap when we lead him through the door. You're the only one who knows how to work the box."

She reluctantly nodded.

Nunnly leaned over to her and whispered. "Get the signal gun away from Bris. He's more of a danger with that thing to himself and us than to the Delicate."

"Forget about what we discussed earlier," I said. "If the creature comes through the entrance and the trap doesn't work, shoot it. We'll have to risk damaging its face."

"I know what to do," she said. She kissed me, then went back to sit on the rug.

"Someday you will have to explain that lip maneuver to me," said Nunnly as we stepped out into the night.

In addition to the spears we carried, I also had the Lady Claw secreted away in my boot with a piece of sponge protecting the blade. I almost relished the idea of getting in close to our nemesis and practicing some of my old technique. Even considering the dexterity I had lost since my renouncing the mantle of Physiognomist, I was confident I could surgically fillet the bastard with a few passes.

A strong breeze now blew in toward the center of the island, a phenomenon caused, no doubt, by the disintegration at the edges. The noise from out there where the wood was rapidly falling into nothing was a constant distraction. We moved along cautiously, keeping close to the walls of the rooms where the shadows were thickest, communicating only with hand signals and the merest whispers. At one point Nunnly proposed that we not move too far away from Anotine's room, but that we should think of it as the center of a circle, and our wandering should not exceed a modest circumference. With this tactic, we would always be the same distance from it. I agreed, seeing that we were only trying to attract the Delicate. Neither of us thought it feasible that we could actually hunt him down.

After following this strategy for over an hour, having made at least ten orbits around our point of departure, we had ceased whispering and now spoke in normal tones. The anxiety that had accompanied us at the start had all but diffused, and Nunnly made the suggestion that we might have been too stealthy.

"I think we need to be more obvious, Cley," he said.

"Should we split up?" I asked.

"Not completely, but we should make it appear as if we have," he said. "You know the course we've been following. Stay on it, but I will follow twenty yards behind you. This way if he shows up, we'll still be close enough to come to each other's rescue."

"If that should happen, try not to engage him, but instead lead him back to the room," I said.

"I understand," he said, and brought his hand to his mouth with a lit cigarette now in it.

As I started off, he said, "You know, Cley, while we were walking just now, I had a memory of my other life. Perhaps it is the fact that everything is falling apart that allows me to see into my past."

I stopped to listen.

"It wasn't much," he said. "I definitely recall having had a black dog, though. A rambunctious animal, courageous and trustworthy, but verging on the insane. I can just about see him, running in circles. That's all."

"Interesting," I said, knowing full well that what he told me was impossible. "No doubt you'll remember more and more as we proceed."

He took a drag of his cigarette and smiled, smoke leaking from the corners of his lips.

I moved on ahead, happy for Nunnly, even if he had somehow absorbed my memory and taken it for his own. It was just this kind of absurdity that made everything seem so dangerous.

We circled and circled. I passed forty times the mousehole opening to Anotine's secret place, and thought about my dream of the monkey dancing. It was the first time since I had arrived that I began to get a sense of how the village was laid out. I finally knew that if you were to take the alley to the right of the pelican fountain and go up a flight of stairs, you would pass the corridor that led to Nunnly's. Other landmarks became familiar and I began to plot, from certain points, the best course to get back to Anotine's should I hear a scream or the firing of the gun. At the end of every circle, I would wait up for Nunnly by the fountain, and we would have a word in order to make sure each of us was still safe.

It must have been only two hours or so till morning, and I was treading wearily along the path we had defined, having nearly forgotten what I was doing, when I heard a distinct sound rise above the background din of the disintegration. Like a single note struck on an out-of-tune piano, it brought me up short, and my fatigued mind worked to place it. I saw a picture in my mind before I realized what it was—the sound of Nunnly's steel spear, hitting the stone floor of the corridor I had just turned out of.

I began to run, backtracking down the alley and turning the corner onto the corridor beside the pool that was lined with columns. At the opposite end, by the steps leading down from a terrace, I could see two figures that appeared joined in a dance. They moved in and out of the shadows, and my approach made it clear that a large-headed man in a dark suit had his arms wrapped tightly around Nunnly, his lips covering the engineer's.

The Delicate didn't notice me, so engaged was he in his business. I gave no shout of warning, but used the momentum I had built up with my charge to drive the steel spear into the middle of his back. The brown suit jacket split, and the creature arched his spine, releasing a high, throaty whistle. Nunnly dropped to the ground, still writhing, his body only partially deflated.

"My, that smarts," said the Delicate in a voice both masculine and feminine.

I stepped back, waiting for him to fall to the ground. Instead, he whipped around to face me, and the steel shaft was flung out of his back with the violence of the motion. It hit the stone and rang out. He winced with the sound of it, and, for the first time, I got a look at him. The bald head was enormous, suggesting either brilliance or idiocy, I wasn't sure which, but in the face's long descent toward the chin it grew exceedingly thin, coming almost to a point. The twin braids, which Anotine had spoken of, were draped forward over the shoulders and tied together in front. His body seemed too thin to support the weight of that head, which appeared to ride atop it like a pumpkin on a flexible broom handle.

"Good evening," he said to me, adjusting his shirt cuffs inside the sleeve ends of his jacket.

I stepped back even farther and reached down into my boot for the Lady Claw. As I straightened and pulled the protective sponge off the end of the instrument, Nunnly caught his breath and let out a most pitiful scream that scrambled my senses. Weak with fear, I held the scalpel up in front of me and made ready to defend myself.

"What have you there?" asked the Delicate as he took a step closer to me.

I sliced at the air to let him know I meant business, but now I was not half as sure of my abilities as I had been when we set out.

"This is all a misunderstanding," he said in a placid voice.

He reached out toward me with those long rubbery fingers, and I sliced the Claw down across them.

He flinched and drew his hand back. "Excuse me for hitting your weapon with my hand," he said, giving me a sincere smile. "Perhaps we should get to know each other."

I lunged again with the scalpel, this time for his throat, but he was deceptively fast. His neck seemed to move separately from the rest of his body, pulling itself in, as his hand came up and caught me. Those fingers grew and circled my wrist, applying a pressure so intense I had to drop the Claw. In reaction to this, I threw a punch with my free hand, and with no effort at all, he intercepted it and held it fast. Then that circle of braided hair rose of its own volition off his chest, wriggling like the body of a snake, and passed over my head to rest around the back of my neck. I wanted to struggle, to kick and break free, but his vacant eyes, which were now only inches from mine, told me not to.

"Someday you will have to explain that lip maneuver to me," he said in Nunnly's voice. His mouth opened wide and a blast of warm breath, reeking of spoiled meat, stole my last shred of will. In my mind, at a place hidden from consciousness, I was wild with fear, though my body was completely limp. From deep within the Delicate's bowels, mixed with the digestive gurgle, I thought I could hear the Doctor crying for help. His lips moved over mine, and I felt an incredible pressure begin to build in my chest. There was a muffled explosion that turned the night red, and I thought I had died.

Then I was falling to the pavement, gasping for air. I landed on my back, and could see the Delicate step over me and begin walking quickly away. His back was ablaze with a red light, and there were small flames and smoke issuing from the brown suit.

"Sorry to have to leave unexpectedly," I heard him say as if holding back a groan. He lurched forward down to the alley I had come from and disappeared around the corner.

Anotine was there in a moment with the signal gun in one hand and her spear in the other. She helped me to my feet and asked if I was all right. I nodded as I caught my breath, and then we turned back to see what had become of Nunnly.

Brisden, the sample bottle of ocean cradled in his arm,

knelt above the engineer, whose body was jerking and rolling
back and forth. Weak cries of pain, like dry whispers, were
issuing from his open, disfigured mouth. One side of him was
deflated, leaving the flesh loose and puddled as had been the
case with the Doctor. It was obvious that his ribs were broken
on the bad side and that his leg and arm contained no trace
of skeletal structure. I finally managed to get my voice back,
but the combination of Nunnly's suffering and the ordeal I
had just been through prevented me from speaking for a time.

"We heard a scream and came running," said Anotine. "I
can't believe I actually managed to hit the Delicate in the back
with a shot from the top of the stairs there." She paused for
a moment, and her eyes filled with tears. "Cley, what are we
going to do?"

I had to struggle against despair. Things had gone from
impossible to hopeless. Although the Delicate could be hurt, I
couldn't imagine what it would take to kill him. The island
was growing ever smaller. The Doctor was dead. Nunnly was
soon to follow, and Brisden had lost his mind in the face of
tragedy and had given himself up to ceaseless babbling.

Anotine leaned over and picked the scalpel up off the
ground. She came over to where I was standing, and whispered to me. "You've got to kill him, Cley. There is nothing
that we can do but end his suffering." She handed me the
instrument, and I accepted it.

The thought of taking Nunnly's life made me physically
ill, but what Anotine had said was true. Still, my mind worked
feverishly for another solution. I thought about Wenau, where
I was a healer, and wondered what I would do there. There
were no herbs or roots of the forest that could reverse the
effects of the Delicate's attack.

"Give it back to me, Cley. I'll do it," said Anotine. "I can't
watch this anymore."

As she reached for the Lady Claw, I stopped her hand.
From out of the storm of confusion in my mind, a single white
image presented itself. I thought of Anotine's secret place and
the tree that grew there. I had seen the fruit that hung from
its branches work miracles in my own reality. Its effects could
be short-term or long, for better or for worse, depending somehow upon the morality of the person ingesting it. I knew it

had saved Arla Beaton's life after I had butchered her, trying to rework her physiognomy. I also believed it was the long-acting effects of it that had years later erased the hideous scars from her face and allowed her to remove the green veil. It was the catalyst that had destroyed the Well-Built City after Below had partaken of it. I hoped now that in this world it could save Nunnly's life.

21

THERE WAS NO TIME FOR ME TO EXPLAIN TO ANOTINE THE history of the white fruit or what I hoped it would accomplish. Searching the ground for the sponge I had removed from the scalpel, I quickly found it and secured the instrument, putting it back in my boot. Then I walked over to where Nunnly lay and gently helped Brisden to his feet.

"Take the spears," I said to Anotine as I bent over to gather up the wriggling, loose parcel that was now the engineer. As I hoisted him into my arms, he groaned unmercifully. He was surprisingly light, but hard to get ahold of because of the state the Delicate had left his body in.

"Where are we going?" she asked.

"To your special place with the fountain of the monkey," I said.

We merely exchanged a look, and I believe she knew I had something in mind. As I trudged down the corridor with Nunnly draped across my arms, I thought of myself in the arms of Misrix, flying through his memory above the forests of the Beyond. Anotine gathered up the spears and prodded Brisden along in our direction. We were particularly vulnerable to an attack just then, but luckily the Delicate seemed to be somewhere else, no doubt tending to his wounds. I knew, from having passed the low opening in the wall so many times that night, exactly where I was going.

We traversed two alleys and a terrace. After that there was only one flight of stairs to climb, in the middle of which I almost dropped poor Nunnly. By the time we made it to the top, my arms were cramped with pain and my heart was pounding. The engineer's breathing had grown erratic, and his supplications had withered to near-inaudible whimpers. Anotine moved ahead of me as we got closer to our destination, making sure that Brisden kept pace with her. As I staggered across the last courtyard toward the wall with the opening, I saw her kneel and toss the spears into the secret place. She then crawled through herself and helped Brisden to enter.

I carefully placed Nunnly down at the opening, and she reached out and took him by the shoulders. She pulled, and I pushed, and we managed to get him through the portal. Once I had entered, myself, I lay back on the stones and rested. My body was aching from the exertion, and my breathing was nearly as erratic as that of the engineer's.

"Cley," said Anotine, "why are we here?"

"Help me up," I pleaded, and she leaned over and grabbed my hand.

The place was as serene as ever, the fountain water quietly splashing, the monkey frozen in his dance. Then I turned, and to my delight, the tree bearing the white fruit had, unlike the rest of the plant life on the island, not succumbed to the disease of disintegration. As I had hoped, it stood strong with all its leaves, the pale globes of fruit hanging ripe and heavy. Brisden sat, with the glowing sample jar beside him, on the bench that encircled its trunk, and the peaceful nature of that scene made me momentarily forget the danger we were in.

I walked toward the tree with Anotine beside me, and only then did I begin quickly to describe the properties of the fruit as I knew them. Continuing with my explanation, I stepped up onto the bench next to where Brisden sat and reached into the low-hanging branches to pick a large specimen that in its bleached complexion seemed to emit its own light. Holding it in my hand, I could again smell that sweet aroma I associated with my daydreams of paradise. It brought me back to Misrix's Museum of the Ruins, where I had, myself, tasted the flesh of the delicacy. My discourse trailed off as I wondered for a moment how and when the fruit would change me, or if the fact that I had survived as long as I had in the mnemonic world was already a sign of its miraculous influence.

"It seems you are expecting quite a lot from it," said Anotine, bringing me back from my thoughts.

"Perhaps," I said, stepping down off the bench.

Brisden, who had been unusually silent for some time, let loose another stampede of words that I think had to do with the nature of miracles.

Anotine and I returned to Nunnly and knelt down on either side of him. I retrieved the scalpel from my boot and removed the protective sponge, flicking it off with my thumb. With the other hand, I brought the fruit up in front of us and made ready to cut it. The idea was to get as thin a slice of the pulp inside as I could so that it would melt in our patient's mouth. I trimmed away the skin from the outside of one half of it and then cut three hair's-width slices. When I had collected them in my palm, I handed Anotine the scalpel. Leaning low over Nunnly, I forced the wafers into his mouth.

"We'll wait for a few minutes and see if there is any effect," I said, resting back on my knees.

"If there isn't?" asked Anotine.

"I'll end his life," I said.

Anotine looked up, away from me, and took a deep breath. "Look, Cley," she said, "the sky is lightening. Day is coming."

From her expression, I couldn't tell if she was pleased with this or if it frightened her more than the night. I tilted my head and saw the stars fading into a sky of black and blue. Nunnly gave a sudden grunt, and I quickly turned my attention back to him.

"No," I said, as I watched the flesh of the engineer's face begin to pucker into wrinkles. I had no idea what was about to happen, but I had a sudden feeling in my stomach that it wasn't going to be good.

"He's turning black," cried Anotine, pointing to some spots that were forming on the skin around his mouth. These blemishes spread like spilled ink, dyeing every inch of his skin, the texture of which was also undergoing some rapid metamorphosis.

Before our eyes, in no more than a few seconds, Nunnly's body was transformed into a shriveled, dark mass, like a fallen plum that has rotted and dried in the sun. Anotine leaped to her feet and backed away from it.

"What kind of miracle is this?" she asked as if accusing me of some evil.

I shook my head but could not speak, and watched helplessly as she walked away to where Brisden was sitting. At the worst, I never expected an outcome so horrific, but I should have. This fruit of the memory world was not the fruit of paradise, but in its dripping pulp, its core, its very seeds, it was a beautiful symbolic mask for one of Below's million nightmares.

I sat there, trying to remember Nunnly, but I couldn't. What remained of him bore absolutely no resemblance to anything human, save for the fact that it was clothed in a shirt and trousers. All that came back to me was the image of a wisp of cigarette smoke. I left the mess where it lay and went over to the bench at the base of the tree, where the others sat. Brisden, eyes wide and perspiring like mad, was jawing away at a remarkable rate as if coming to some crescendo, and Anotine sat with her face covered by her left hand.

"If I had wanted to do him in, I never would have risked my life against the Delicate to save him," I explained to Anotine.

"I know, Cley. I'm sorry," she said, and waved away my comment.

"Have you got any ideas?" I asked.

She shook her head and stared past me at the fountain. "The disintegration will reach the village soon if it hasn't already, and then it won't be long."

"Are you giving up?" I asked.

"Aren't you?" she said.

"I could go out in search of the Delicate, but I doubt I could overcome him on my own."

"I doubt the two of us could overcome him," she said.

Just then, Brisden ceased his rant. He wiped his brow and looked up at us as if we had suddenly appeared before him.

"You've returned," I said, smiling.

"I was never gone, Cley. While you were turning my good

friend, Nunnly, into a prune, I was arguing myself into a solution."

If it were anyone else speaking, I might have been offended, but I had grown accustomed to Brisden's unique sense of humor. "Who won the argument?" I asked.

"Who else?" said Brisden. "Now you two are going to do as I say."

"We're listening," said Anotine, who seemed to be taking him with perfect seriousness.

"Nunnly was a part of me, and I can hardly stand to continue living, myself, without him. I wish I had the time to sit and reflect on the loss of my companion, but now it is time for revenge. I want the Delicate, and I know how to destroy him."

"What should we do?" I asked.

"You two have already done enough. I want you to take your ridiculous spears and go hide behind the fountain over there. Whatever happens, and I mean whatever, don't come out of hiding. If you do, all will be ruined," he said.

"You can't defeat the Delicate by yourself," I told him.

"I won't be alone," he said. "I'll have the Doctor to keep me company." He placed his hand atop the lid of the glass sample jar and patted it. "Now go, quickly and keep quiet."

"What are you going to do?" asked Anotine.

"Be off," he said.

I was very apprehensive since, for most of the night, Brisden hadn't seemed to be in his right mind. Anotine took my arm, though, and pulled me away in the direction of the fountain. We stopped and lifted the spears where they lay near the entrance.

"There's a chance that he knows what he is talking about," she whispered to me as we took up our positions behind the fountain.

"There's a chance we might find a flying carpet and escape the island too," I said.

"Brisden has often amazed me with his insights," she told me. "His revelations are either uncanny in their brilliance or so bizarre they have no bearing upon reality."

"I think I know which this one is," I said, and my statement was confirmed when I heard the philosopher begin whistling, as loud as he could, the tune from the wooden box at Nunnly's.

"Give him a chance," she said.

We could watch him from where we knelt on the cold stones in the shadows. He was whistling with great vigor and swaying back and forth. After a few minutes, he stopped abruptly and sat in silence. I was about to tell Anotine that Brisden was out of his mind, when I heard the sound of footsteps echoing from the other side of the wall near the opening.

"He's here," she whispered, and I tightened my grip on the spear.

At first, I didn't think his enormous head could squeeze through the portal, but it did, like an infant's appearing from the birth canal. The Delicate was born into the secret place, pointed chin, twin braids, singed brown suit, and all. Once he was through, he stood and leaned over to brush the knees of his trousers.

"Hello, there," said Brisden, waving to him as though he were seeing an old friend.

"Greetings," said the Delicate, and waved back.

"Come sit down," said Brisden.

"One moment," he said, and stopped on his way to kneel over the remains of what had been the engineer. The huge head moved up and down the length of the shriveled carcass, sniffing and licking it here and there. When he had finished his investigation, he stood and continued on to the bench.

Anotine must have known what I was about to do, because she put her hand on my arm to restrain me from charging. "Let's see what he has in mind," she said.

"Thanks for stopping by," I heard Brisden say, and refocused my attention on the bench beneath the tree.

"Quite a night of excitement," said the Delicate.

"Well," said the philosopher, "the island is disintegrating, you know."

"Oh, I don't trouble myself with those things," said the creature. "I'm only out for some air."

"Mine, by any chance?"

"You are Brisden, aren't you?"

"I am."

"Mouth or ear?" asked the Delicate.

"I prefer the ear, because that will give me a few more moments to speak."

"Are we ready then?"

"Just a second, I'd like a last drink," said Brisden, and lifted the sample jar. He unscrewed the lid and dropped it on the stones at his feet.

"Oh, my," said the Delicate.

"Proceed," said the philosopher as he put the jar to his lips and tilted it, swallowing the liquid mercury in four gulps.

At this moment, the Delicate's braid came up and encircled Brisden's neck. He was pulled sideways toward the creature, his ear fitting into its open mouth. As the process began, the sample jar dropped to the floor and smashed into splinters. I held on to Anotine and she to me as our friend's screams filled the secret place. We closed our eyes to the sight of his dissolution. We should have run to his rescue, but there was little point. Anotine had stopped me by whispering, "Cley, don't. He wants to die." I knew she was right.

There were all manner of terrible noises, sucking and gagging, the breaking of bones, the slosh of blood, and when I opened my eyes to look, Brisden had been reduced to a formless bag of flesh lying on the bench. The creature belched and wiped his mouth with the sleeve of his suit.

I nudged Anotine in order to get her attention. I wanted her to run for the portal while I made a foolish attempt to subdue Below's walking death. When she did not move or turn to look at me, I realized that she was in shock.

"Anotine," I whispered, and tapped her cheek lightly.

She didn't move, but continued staring in the direction of the bench. Looking again at the Delicate, I now saw him looking directly back at us. I tried to crouch as low as I could, and I put my arm around Anotine as if this would serve to hide her.

The creature's broad mouth broke into a smile. "Hello, there," he said, and rose from the bench. "I've been looking everywhere for you two. I have a secret to tell you both."

22

As the delicate moved toward us, I broke from the shadows behind the fountain in an attempt to draw him away from Anotine.

He had only taken two steps before I came at him, walking quickly, spear in hand.

"Have you tried the fruit?" I asked.

"I couldn't possibly," he said. "I've just eaten."

I lifted the spear in both hands and lunged at him, thinking I could keep him at a distance. He smiled at me and continued to advance.

"Stay back," I yelled, and lunged again.

"An impressive maneuver no doubt," he said. "I think we are going to get along famously."

In another step, he would have been close enough to wrap those rubbery fingers around my throat. I aimed for his head and threw all of my weight behind the weapon. That jab should have put the steel tip directly through his left eye, but his head simply flopped to the side, like a dead fish, at the last possible second, and I missed him completely. At the same time, his hand came up and grabbed the shaft of the spear.

"Let me hold that for you," he said, and nonchalantly ripped the weapon from my hand.

I backed away from him as his head returned to an upright position. He dropped the spear, and it clanged against the pavement.

"Anotine," I yelled, and looked over my shoulder to see if she had heard me. She remained crouched in the shadows. When I turned back to the Delicate, somehow he was there, right in front of me, though I had never heard him move.

"Rest now," he said, his eyes like stones, his stinking breath all over me.

I didn't have the chance to react. His arm moved like a whip, and his fist caught me right beneath the jaw. My head snapped back with the impact, and I fell to the ground, landing on my side. I felt no great pain, but I was stunned, unable to move my arms or legs. Consciousness was a tenuous thing, but I managed to hold on to it. Struggling to move my head, I looked over to see the Delicate standing above Anotine. He reached his hand down to her as if she were a child.

"It's time to go now," he said in a soothing voice, coaxing her to stand.

I opened my mouth and tried to yell her name, but it came as a rasping whisper. His strategically placed blow had momentarily paralyzed me, and now that some feeling was beginning to return to my limbs all of my muscles were twitching like mad. It took the greatest effort to roll onto my stomach and lift myself to my knees.

"Come now," he said to her, and reached for her hand.

I judged from the slowness of my movements that I would never revive in time to help her. A great anger surged through me but did little to hasten my recovery.

Then Anotine suddenly burst from her crouch with a terrific grunt, swinging the butt end of the spear around and catching the Delicate on his pointed chin. The creature was knocked back two steps. As he worked to regain his balance, she flipped the spear around and jabbed him in the right shoulder, retrieved it, and jabbed again in the same spot.

"That will put a damper on my day," he said, his smile never fading.

Before she could attack him again, he had his hand around her back and had grabbed a handful of hair. His thin arm twisted unnaturally like a wet towel being wrung out and with this spiral motion brought her ear up to his mouth. With his free hand he relieved her of her weapon as easily as he had taken mine.

No matter how hard I worked to stand, I could not. The best I could accomplish was to crawl forward and watch as he attached himself to the side of her head, covering her ear. Anotine struggled wildly, but she could not break free. She called to me, and her eyes looked down into mine. I did not want to watch, but I couldn't look away.

"Don't," I yelled, my full voice returning, echoing through the enclosure. To my astonishment, the Delicate released her hair and stepped away from her.

"Oh my," he said, and the wriggling fingers of both hands clasped above his stomach. His enormous head again flopped to the side and his mouth opened, releasing a belch that was laced with Brisden's babble. A trickle of silver fluid seeped out from between his fingers. We watched as liquid mercury ate its way like acid through his stomach and shirt. It came from a hundred tiny openings that quickly grew together into a huge wound and spilled onto the pavement. Swirling designs full of life puddled at his feet.

"My apologies," he said, no longer smiling. He staggered toward us a step, then fell forward, that enormous head losing its battle against gravity.

Anotine ran to me and helped me to my feet. I was still somewhat weak, but I managed to stand on my own.

"Brisden knew what he was doing," she said as she put her arms around me.

I drew her close and held her tightly, closing my eyes. "I wish I did," I said.

"Cley, listen," she said.

Now that the threat of the Delicate had been canceled there was room for a new fear, and I was able to concentrate on the sound of the disintegration. It had increased from an annoying background hum to an obvious roar. I looked up and noticed that the stars had vanished and the sun would soon be up.

"The wood must be completely gone," she said, "perhaps the field too."

"We've got to move quickly," I said. "Where is the scalpel, the Lady Claw?"

"I dropped it behind the fountain," she said as she let go of me and went in search of it.

I walked over to the Delicate and, using my foot, flipped

him onto his back. Two steps behind him I noticed the puddle of liquid mercury, which was eating its way down into the stone of the pavement. Just before it seeped out of sight, I was able to distinguish a remarkable scene coalescing from its animated lines. The images I saw were of a young man standing beside a tall transparent block of what might have been ice. Embedded within that block was the figure of a woman. I quickly bent low to get a better look, and right before the silver tableau sank out of sight, it came to me that the woman was Anotine.

"Are we to take his head?" she asked, holding the scalpel out to me.

It was difficult, but I recovered without letting on how bewildered I was by what I had just seen. "Yes," I said, "the head."

I took great pleasure in separating the Delicate's head from his body. The precision of my cut, the clean circularity of it, proved this. I only wished I had been able to do it while he was still alive.

"No blood," said Anotine, looking over my shoulder as I worked.

"Where do you think everything went when he ingested Nunnly and Brisden?"

"Away," I said, not wanting to divulge my theory that the Delicate had contained somewhere within him the same phenomenon of disintegration that was dissolving the island. "Where do ideas go when we discard them?" I wondered to myself, and discarded the idea as it became clear to me that its spine did not grow up into the neck.

"Look here," I said. This explains how he could drop his head so quickly to either side."

"Beautiful," she said, "but don't we have to return to my rooms before we go to the tower?"

"Why?" I asked.

"The green liquid from the Fetch," she said. "How else will we find the antidote?"

I had forgotten all about that part of the plan. "Harrow's hindquarters," I said. "As if things aren't complicated enough."

Even free of the body that head must have weighed more than forty pounds. When I first attempted to lift it, I nearly

pulled my arm out of its socket. Using two hands, and grabbing it just beneath the chin, I managed to lift it off the ground.
I leaned it awkwardly against my stomach as if toting a small
boulder, and took short, halting steps toward the portal in
the wall.

After squeezing the oversize cranium through the opening
and out of the garden, Anotine suggested I use the creature's
braids to strap it to my back, making it easier to carry. She
helped me make that adjustment, and then we were off, moving as quickly as possible toward her place. When I looked
over at her, it appeared she was yelling words of encouragement to me, but it was impossible to tell, so deafening was
the noise of the island's demise.

Backtracking past the fountain of the pelican and around
the corner to the spot where Nunnly was attacked, we were
brought up short by the obvious absence of half the staircase
from which Anotine had fired the last shell from the signal
gun. Although she had been in the lead, she now stepped back
next to me and put her arm on my shoulder. Leaning in
toward my ear, she shouted, "It's here," and pointed.

It suddenly became clear to me, the rushing loss of pavement and architecture as it eddied away into twisters of dust
and then into nothing. Beyond the quickly diminishing steps
of the stairs, there was only blue sky. Her rooms were unques-
tionably gone, and it was clear that the green liquid from the
Fetch should instantly be dropped from the plan. The island
was a rapidly diminishing circle, and the advance of the nothing moved inexorably toward the Panopticon like a noose
tightening around a neck.

Anotine led the way to the doors at the base of the tower.
The weight of the Delicate's head in addition to the outlandish
exertions I had already suffered through the night combined
to reduce my running speed to an uninspired pace. I had run
like this before in nightmares—filled with fear, giving my all,
only to make a snail's progress. As I staggered up stairs, across
terraces, through alleyways, the nothing howled in pursuit,
less than a hundred yards behind.

At one point, after reaching the top of what was to be the
final set of stairs, I tripped and fell under the weight of the
head. It was lucky that Anotine chose to look back at that

moment, because if I had had to rely on calling her to my rescue, she never would have heard me. I struggled to get to my feet, but even with the threat of annihilation, I could no longer lift the weight. She understood my predicament, and without speaking pulled the head off my back and slung it across her own. With the drag of the hideous cargo gone I was able to continue. Whatever time we lost to my mishap we made up by the speed with which we now proceeded. I could run, and she stayed a few steps ahead of me, advancing with incredible stamina. I remembered the Doctor telling me, "It would be a mistake to underestimate Anotine's strength."

The journey to the gate seemed so inordinately long with so many twists and turns, I thought more than once that Anotine had forgotten the route and we were lost. Although the Panopticon was readily visible from every point of our approach, it never appeared to get any closer. Just as I was considering catching up to her to get her attention, we rounded the corner of a building and our destination was in front of us. At the end of the long corridor we had entered stood the two massive doors that gave entrance to the tower that loomed immense and unsympathetic to our frantic efforts.

When we finally stood in front of the doors, it came to me that I really had no reason to believe that merely holding the Delicate's head up would cause the mechanism in the emblem to allow us to gain entrance. Though I searched my memory, I couldn't for the life of me remember why I thought something so simplistic would work in such a complicated world. At this point, though, there was no alternative. I helped Anotine remove the head from her back. Setting it down for a moment, we each took a side. Then, on the soundless count of three, just my reading her lips, we hoisted the thing high and held it up to the emblematic eyeball, one-half of which had been rendered on each of the separate doors.

We waited for something to happen, and in that stretch of time it was all I could do to prevent myself from considering how we would save ourselves even if the doors were to spring open and we were immediately to discover the antidote. There was an extremely slight possibility that Misrix might appear and swoop me away to our reality, but either way, Anotine would soon cease to exist.

After it was clear nothing was going to happen with the current position in which we had situated the head, we began lifting it and lowering it to different heights in order to find the exact place where the Delicate's eyes might have been had I kept the body intact. The process we went through, though frustrating, was clear proof of the connection Anotine and I shared, because without the power to speak, and at that point not even bothering with speech, we remained always in synch with our movements, as if sharing one mind.

Eventually my strength gave out, and we were forced to rest. As we placed the head on the pavement, I turned and noticed that the disintegration had just entered the corridor that led to the doors. We now had mere minutes to find a way inside the tower. Along with the onrushing nothing came an incredible wind caused by the violence of all that memory matter being forgotten. The fear was instantly upon me, and I could not take my eyes off the wave of disaster and the calm blue sky behind it.

That was when Anotine struck me on the shoulder in order to get my attention. When I looked over to her, she had, still supporting the head, stepped around to the front of him, and with her thumb and middle finger lifted the closed lids of the creature's eyes. The nothing was twenty yards away when we hoisted the Delicate's head again to a place just a few inches above my own. Instantly, a green light similar to that which had emanated from the Fetch shot out of the emblem on the door. The gradually widening beam struck the open eyes of our trophy, and the doors slowly began to part.

Once it was possible to gain access, we lowered the head and, with a coordinated heave, tossed it behind us. So close were we to the dissolution that the last remnant of the Delicate did not land on pavement but went over the ever-diminishing edge of the island in a mile-long fall toward liquid mercury. We did not stop to watch its descent, but ran forward into the dark opening of the Panopticon.

23

"IT'S AS EMPTY AS THE FETCH'S HEAD," I CRIED, AS MY eyes adjusted to the shadowed interior. The light that streamed in through the portals set intermittently along the vertical length of the tower was enough to show me that there were no objects waiting to be deciphered. The inner base of the Panopticon was merely a round floor, in the exact middle of which began a spiral staircase that wound its way toward the dome a hundred feet above.

"What now?" asked Anotine, breathing heavily.

As soon as the words had left her, the circular wall around us began to dissolve. Tiny holes were forming and light shot through them in a confusion of bright beams. It was clear that soon these holes would join together to form the absence of a wall.

"Up," I shouted, and we made for the stairs. As my foot touched the bottom step, the doors we had worked so hard to breach disappeared, and the nothing began to creep across the floor toward us.

The fatigue that had earlier slowed me in our retreat to the tower was now thoroughly forgotten. If we were to rest for a moment, the world would slip away beneath us, and the glorious dive into the silver ocean that I had once imagined would become a reality.

We scrabbled ever upward around the twirling metal beanstalk that was the stairs while beneath us we could see the nothing climbing just as quickly, negating the steps we had trod only seconds before and vanishing the walls of the tower as it followed us toward the dome. Beneath all this was an unobstructed, breathtaking view of the glimmering ocean a mile away. The wind was so fierce at times that if there hadn't been a banister along the outer edge of the steps, I might have been blown off like a handkerchief.

The climb seemed both endless and pointless, and I could hardly catch my breath as we turned the tight circles in our ascent. Anotine was a few steps ahead of me, and I had the feeling she could have gone faster, but was regulating her speed to make sure I was safe.

As we approached the halfway point, I looked above and could see that there was a small landing illuminated by light from one of the portals. We came up through a hole in the floor of the landing, and Anotine didn't stop. I had no intention to, myself, but as my eyes came level with it, I noticed that on a circular shelf, which defined the edge of the landing, were positioned a series of hourglasses, each separated by only a few inches. Without thinking, I leaped off the stairs, bounded over to the closest one, and grabbed it. The entire procedure took less than five seconds. I turned and headed back for the stairs, and then with a sick feeling realized that the nothing was upon me. The landing was coming apart. I lunged for the steps, trying to grab the banister in order to pull myself back on course, but I missed. Instead, I felt a hand clutch tightly to my wrist. I don't know how she managed it, but with one powerful tug and a fluid swinging motion, Anotine placed me back on the next step just as the twenty or more hourglasses fell away toward the ocean.

I didn't need any extra incentive at that point to move faster. With the hourglass cradled in my arm, I bounded two steps at a time. When I thought my heart was about to explode, I looked up and saw an aperture in the floor of the dome, like an open trapdoor.

Anotine reached it and jumped through, and I was no more than a second behind her. As I hit the floor inside the dome, I rolled over and kicked the trapdoor shut. I let the hourglass tumble out of my hand as I found Anotine, and we entwined each other in a viselike embrace, our bodies heaving, in syncopation. I could feel her heart pounding against mine as I closed my eyes and waited to fall.

We waited and we waited, and my obvious expectation that the floor would dissolve beneath us did not seem soon to be fulfilled. The howling wind of disintegration suddenly died, and there was complete silence. I opened my eyes and saw Anotine open hers.

"Well?" she said.

I shook my head.

Then we dropped, not through the floor, but with the dome intact around us. The fall seemed to have been slowed by some force, for we did not plummet the way the Doctor's winch had, but instead dropped with the lightness of a feather. Still, we held tightly to each other for a long time until there came a modest collision with the surface of the ocean, the impact of which bounced us a few inches off the floor. The dome settled on the surface like a boat, and the hellish roar of the wind was replaced by the thick liquid sound of rolling mercury. The motion of the waves rocked us gently and, dismissing my fears that we would soon sink or the dome would be melted, I reveled in this moment that did not call for physical exertion.

"We should get up and see what predicament we have gotten into now," said Anotine.

"Why?" I asked.

She smiled and closed her eyes. I did the same and found myself falling yet again, this time into the deep sleep of utter exhaustion.

I was delighted eventually to awaken in that it was a good sign we had not been consumed by the ocean, but at the same time, my entire body ached so thoroughly from all of the punishing work I had required of it that existence was now barely preferable to the alternative. My knees cracked as I straightened them, and even the simplest movements elicited a groan. It soon became clear to me that Anotine was gone. As I rolled onto my stomach to find a position from which I could use my arms to push myself up, I heard her call my name.

"Cley," she said, "you've got to see this."

With a good deal of effort, I rose to my feet, staggering somewhat in the process. I stretched and rubbed my eyes be-

fore turning around and getting my first true look at the inside
of the dome. Of course, it was circular to match the cylindrical
form of the tower. The trapdoor, which I stood next to, seemed
to be the central point of a wide space. There was a short wall,
no more than four feet all around, and then the dome began,
some kind of crystal or glass that arched upward at its center
at least twenty feet. I fully expected to see some kind of beacon
or light source, remembering the way the structure had glowed
at night, but there was nothing. Instead, the substance that the
dome was made from generated its own luminescence. The
glow of it lit the interior more efficiently than even spire lamps
might have.

"Come here," said Anotine, waking me from awe at the
architecture of the marvelous place. When I turned to find her,
she was off to my left, standing next to a chair whose back
was to me. As I approached, I could see that it was no ordinary
chair, but more like a black, leather throne without legs. The
seat hovered two feet off the floor and appeared connected in
front to a low metal rail that, I just then noticed, ran the entire
circumference of the inner dome.

All of this was interesting, but the sight of Anotine standing there, still alive, diverted my attention and almost brought
tears to my eyes. Her clothes were torn and there were scuff
marks of grime on her cheeks and arms, but she was beautiful.
The fact that we were now prisoners in this structure, adrift
on a seemingly limitless expanse of silver ocean, did not faze
me as long as I was with her.

I moved close in order to touch her, but as I approached,
she put her hand on the back of the chair and pushed. It
remained stationary, attached to the device that connected it
to the rail, but it spun around so that the seat faced me. Sitting
in it was an old man with a white beard. He was bald on top,
and the same white hair grew at the sides of his head. His
eyes were closed and his lips were drawn into a subtle grin.
If I had any doubts that it was Below, the blue silken pajamas
he wore erased them. It was the exact outfit he had been wearing back in the other world.

"The sentinel," said Anotine, and laughed horribly. "The
judge of our lives on the island. I knew he must be sleeping.

It was all for nothing." She began to cry, then turned and slapped Below across the face, screaming for him to wake up.

She brought her hand back to strike him again, but I caught it and restrained her. "It won't do any good," I said, trying to put my arm around her. She shrugged it off and stepped away.

"This isn't even death, Cley. I should have given myself up to the Delicate. Where are we? What are we? This is forever."

"Easy, easy," I said to her. "We'll find a way out of this," but as I spoke, I could feel the crushing weight of loneliness that she was feeling. We had each other for the moment, but beyond us, there was nothing. I fought back my desire to tell her everything I knew.

"Look here," I said, noticing that the device that connected the chair to the rail also had another part, a console that, when the seat was turned toward the outside, could be controlled by the occupant. It was a black board with switches and dials and two long levers.

"This reminds me of your black box," I said. "Perhaps you could figure out what its purpose is."

She refused to take the bait I hoped would divert her attention from the deplorable state we were in. Turning her back, she moved away to the opposite side of the dome. I left her alone for the time being, knowing there was nothing I could say that might change our situation, and anything I could tell her would only serve to reveal greater depths of hopelessness.

The fact that Below, or some mnemonic representation of Below, was there in the dome did not surprise me all that much. From the beginning of my journey, I always expected that I would find the Master. And why not? It was his world. We were breathing his imagination. I only wished he had been in a condition that might have allowed me to reason with him. "If only I could awaken him," I thought, "I could simply ask him what the antidote is." At that point, though, I was uncertain if Misrix would be able to bring me out. It became clear to me as I stood there above the old man, staring down at him, that the demon had lost me.

I reached over to the console and slowly turned one of the knobs. As it spun, the light thrown off by the dome diminished in brightness. The more I moved the knob, the more the darkness of night outside became evident, and I realized then that my nap had lasted for an entire day. Wanting to see the extent of the device, I brought the glow to a bare minimum, then turned it out altogether.

"Cley," Anotine called.

"It's all right," I said. "I'm making it happen." Looking up through the clear crystal of the now extinguished dome, I could see a multitude of stars above. They shone with fierce clarity, and I wondered what they were in relation to Below's mnemonics. The absence of the light made the inner dome seem more still and quiet than before. Straight ahead, out through the transparent membrane, I saw the ocean rolling—shadowy hills on the move, glistening here and there in the wash of light from a half-moon that hung low, off to our left.

"It's pretty," said Anotine, who had found her way back to my side.

"Yes," I said.

"I suppose this is Below," she said, nodding toward the chair.

"I'm afraid so," I said.

"I have only one question, Cley. What is the point of all of this?"

I don't think she could have faulted me had I admitted that I had no idea, but I thought hard for an answer. After a long time of watching the waves moving in the night, I said, "It has something to do with Below's fear of uncertainty."

"I can taste that fear right now," she said.

"Rather bitter," I agreed, "but, believe me, I know from experience, not half as bad as the taste of its opposite."

She took my hand, and, leaving the light of the dome extinguished, we moved to the middle of the floor. I understand how impulsive it sounds given the circumstances, but there we undressed and lay down on the floor. We worked at finding the moment with all our might, as if trying to assert our reality. In the midst of making love, there was at least the illusion of freedom.

When we were finished, Anotine rolled over next to me,

and whispered sleepily in my ear. "Do you still believe in me, Cley?"

I told her I did, and soon after that, I could tell from the easy measure of her breathing that she was asleep. That is when a familiar sensation began to move through my body. I sat up and turned my head as if listening, but in actuality I was trying to place in my memory the feeling of a flower blossoming in my solar plexus. I remembered, like an old friend, the circumstance of tiny bubbles bursting in my head. The transformation that was taking place in me was strange, but not unpleasant. I chanced a look back down at Anotine, and it became clear to me.

What my body was experiencing was the identical reaction that had been brought on, years earlier, by my injecting myself with the drug, sheer beauty. The tentacles of the hallucinogen began to wrap around my mind, and it all made perfect sense. I knew that Anotine's hidden essence was the formula for the beauty, and now it did not hide itself from me. It felt wonderfully warm and invigorating. Thoughts rushed through my mind like a bright stream, and one that leaped out was the question of how I had gone so long without an injection.

The ever-present sound of the waves organized themselves into music, and the stars above flew in erratic courses like fire flies. I began to laugh and couldn't stop. Everything became clear to me. The disintegration of the floating island was merely the first piece of Below's memory to go as the effects of the sleeping disease wasted him. The reason for this was because it was the most highly organized, what with its symbolic system. Anotine and I had escaped into another part of the memory, perhaps that part we acquire by merely going through our days with our eyes open.

As was the case with the drug when I had taken it by injection, an apparition began to appear before me. It solidified out of thin air, first appearing as a shimmering phantom, and then a mirage of flesh and bone. Four feet in front of me sat the black dog, Wood. There were scars on his flanks, and one of his ears was missing.

"Come, boy," I said, and held out my hands.

He walked over to sit right in front of me. I petted him

and put my arms around him. His coat was smooth to my touch, and the place where his ear was missing was still wet with blood. It gave me the greatest comfort simply to pet him.

"You're alive, " I said.

He barked, and I opened my eyes to sunlight.

24

I woke groggy and confused into the harsh sunlight streaming through the dome. My first inclination was to look for the dog, hoping against reason
that he might have been able to stay with me. What
I found was that not only was he gone, but Anotine
was also nowhere to be found. I got nervously to
my feet and spun around, calling her name. Five
times I revolved in a circle, until dizziness set in,
and I staggered forward, nearly falling on my face.
The sudden fear of being alone, stranded on a memory ship upon a memory ocean was overwhelming.
In my mind, I had an image of myself as a character
on a page ripped from a storybook and thrown to
the wind. I was frantic with the sense of having
been buried alive. Running over to the unconscious
Below, I begged him to return her.

I had my hands on his shoulders and was shaking him when I heard a distinct knocking sound.
Looking up, I saw Anotine, standing outside the
dome, waving to me. The sight of her there plunged
me further into confusion. For the longest time, I
simply stared at her. She knocked on the dome
again in order to break my trance, then pointed her
finger. I thought she was pointing at me. I put my
hand to my chest and nodded. Her lips moved, and
I was able to read their message. "Turn around,"
she was saying. I did, and behind me on the other

side of the dome, I saw what I had missed in my panic. A doorway stood open in the low wall that defined the circumference.

I went over to it and, getting down on my knees, was able to see that there was a walkway with a railing outside that encircled the platform. It was a feature I had never taken notice of back on the island from my vantage point at ground level. The opening reminded me of the entrance to Anotine's secret place, where we had defeated the Delicate. I crawled over the rail and out onto the walkway. Once outside I could more clearly hear the movement of the ocean. The sharp breeze and direct sunlight were instantly refreshing, driving off the last shreds of the previous night's intoxication.

Since the passage was rather narrow, the railing low, and the pitch of the dome more pronounced outside, I stayed on my hands and knees and started around the path toward the other side. Eventually my head bumped into Anotine's knees, and I looked up to see her laughing at me. I should have been embarrassed, but I didn't care as long as she was still with me. I grabbed the railing with one hand, and she took the other to help me to my feet.

"I thought you were gone," I said to her, and put my arm around her for support.

"I'm sorry," she said. "I should have told you. I was playing around with the switches on the black board of Below's chair, and I discovered that one of them opened that small door. Isn't the view here magnificent?"

I mustered what courage was left in me and turned to look out over the silver ocean. The waves swelled and died beneath us, and now that I could see them, their rhythm and regularity seemed somehow reassuring.

"I can see now the Doctor's fascination with the ocean," she said. "The scenes, the little illustrated plays, are endlessly entertaining. I believe I saw you in one not too long ago."

"Was I crawling?" I asked.

She laughed. "No, I think you were making Below drink something from a cup."

"What else have you seen?" I asked.

"So much, but there is almost too much rushing by to make sense out of it. It's forever curling and changing and becoming something other than what it once was. If I were still a researcher of the moment, I would say there were interesting implications here."

"Interesting implications," I said, and smiled.

I don't know how long we stood there, but it was a considerable time. The undulation of the liquid mercury was hypnotic, and the constant flow of scenes, disjointed in time, but each obviously an integral part of some complete story, made me think that always the next one would tie it together and the entire saga would make sense.

While I watched them, feeling content with Anotine at my side, my mind wandered. It came to me that I hadn't eaten in quite some time, but I felt no hunger or use for food. I would have liked a Hundred-To-One just then, but found that my ability to conjure cigarettes had dissolved with the island. "How long would this last? Should we make an attempt to awaken Below? Now that I knew that Anotine was still with me, did I want it to change?" These were some of the questions I pondered as I witnessed the Master's life flowing by beneath me. With what we had just been through on the island, and now this, I had the impression that I was awake inside the bubble of a dream.

The sun rose to its apex and began to descend before I managed to turn away from the ocean's performance. My last subject of contemplation was that the sun, which shone brightly, was an indication that Below, back in my old reality, must not yet be too close to death. As soon as that thought had passed, I began to get an uncomfortable sensation in my head as if my brain were itching. Severe chills accompanied this symptom, and though I was feeling strange, I had an unquenchable desire to make love to Anotine.

The unstoppable urge made me bolder than I might normally have been. "Shall we find the moment?" I asked.

She smiled and pointed for me to make my way back inside. By the time we found our place on the floor, I was overwrought with desire, almost physically ill with necessity. This painful craving only began to be alleviated when I moved atop her and was working away in rhythm with the rocking of the waves. In the middle of this dalliance, I happened to look up and see Below, sitting there as if in judgment upon our love. It was then, as we teetered on the edge of the moment, that I realized the discomfort had been born of withdrawal and the desire of addiction.

When we finished, I again experienced the narcotic effects of the beauty while Anotine slept. This time, I looked out through the top of the dome to where the Fetch materialized, flying high above us. Her speed left a rapidly fading green line in its wake, and her aerial acrobatics spelled out a message against the blue. "Truth lies at the end of a circle," she wrote, and its meaning for me was profound. Everything made sense filtered through this aphorism, but the minute the hallucination ended, I lost the thread of my discoveries, which unraveled into a dullness of mind that forced me into sleep.

Two more days and a night passed in this same manner, and I combine them in the telling because, for the most part, they were indistinguishable—a hazy stew of sex, hallucination, ponderous thought, and splinters of drama, riding the backs of waves. Anotine was very much both the essence of sheer beauty and a real woman in this time. As often as my physical contact with her would send me off into flights of fancy, the conversations we shared would ground me by way of her intelligence and depth of feeling. She was both metaphor and matter, a hybrid I could never quite get my mind around.

One early evening out on the walkway we sat in the twilight with our backs to the dome. The sky was growing dark, but the last rays of sunlight streaked the silver, setting it on fire. She held my hand in her lap, and the serenity of that moment made me feel as if she had always been with me.

"I want to talk to you about the future, Cley," she said.

"I thought you specialized in the present," I said.

"I want you to know that it is all right if you must leave me."

"Nonsense," I said. "Where am I going?"

"Back to the place where you have a past."

"I've forgotten it," I said, and realized that those words might be truer than I ever could have imagined.

"What about the antidote we were trying to find?"

"We did our best. Now I am going to concentrate on being with you. That is my antidote," I said.

"Won't people die without it?"

"People will die anyway."

"What if we never find a way off this ocean?"

"We'll make this our home," I said.

"How am I your antidote?"

"You help me to forget the past, and the future is so perfectly uncertain. My guilt falls away behind me, and there is
no responsibility to tomorrow. With you I am in the present.
The present is a kind of paradise."

She leaned her head on my shoulder. "I long for the past,"
she said.

"The island?" I asked. "You miss your friends?"

"I miss them terribly, but what I meant was, I don't think
I was ever a child. I can't see my mother's face or even remember a favorite toy."

"We can create a past for you," I told her. "Even people
who remember their mother, father, toys, the house they were
born in, create the past for themselves. Memories can be a
record of how things were, but they can also be a record of
your desire for the way things should have been."

She was quiet for some time, and I could tell she was
thinking about what I had said. When darkness fell, we went
back inside the dome in order to find the moment, our third
heated search that day.

When I wasn't conjuring phantoms from the past at the
behest of the beauty or reflecting on the enigma of Anotine's
dual nature, I watched the ocean. Hours upon hours were
spent staring down into the billowing spectacle of Below's life.
Although the plot eluded me, there were more than a few
revelations I managed to glean from my time on the walkway.

I witnessed the death of his sister. She had been a child
with bangs and plump cheeks, and then, through various fractured scenes, I saw her grow frail and painfully thin. I will
never forget the tableau of Below as a boy of thirteen, kneeling
on the floor before a fireplace, crying into his hands.

I did not tell Anotine, but I also spotted Hellman, Nunnly,
and Brisden playing their small parts in the silver theater.
Apparently, they had all been actual figures in Below's real
life. Hellman was the doctor who tried to heal the young girl.
I saw him sitting at her bedside, dozing off in a rocking chair,
his hand moving through his beard. Nunnly appeared to have

been a schoolmaster, and I caught sight of Brisden, sitting at a table, drinking and talking, having done in Below's life exactly the same thing he was to do later in the mnemonic world. As the vanishing depiction of the philosopher passed beneath the dome, I thought I saw him wave to me. Why the Master had, after so many years, chosen these people to symbolize certain ideas remained a mystery.

In addition to the three gentlemen of the floating island, I came across myself quite a few times—scenes from my days of the Physiognomy. These made me cringe. I also spotted Silencio, the monkey, lying on a table with his chest open and wires attached to inner organs. Below stood beside him, dressed in an operating gown, laughing uproariously. There was Corporal Matters of the day watch from the island of Doralice, Calloo as a mechanized gladiator, Ea and Arla, Greta Sykes, Winsome Graves, Pierce Deemer, and so many more I was both familiar with and ignorant of. By the end of that second day, the dizzying cavalcade of persons and places made me tear myself away from the edge of the walkway for fear that I would literally vomit with gorging myself on the past. I went in search of Anotine, hoping again to reach that special state of amnesia.

On the second night of those lost days, after making love to her, I sat in the dark at the center of the dome and again stared up at the stars. The beauty swam through my bloodstream, making me wonderfully weary and light. To my great joy, I heard Wood bark behind me, and I turned to stare into the shadows. Anotine was fast asleep, so I called to the dog.

"Come, boy," I whispered, but his silhouette stood its ground. I got up and walked over to where I thought I had seen his figure. He was nowhere to be found, but instead I discovered the hourglass I had rescued in our dash to the top of the Panopticon. I had forgotten all about it in the face of my intense involvement with Anotine. It lay on its side, a one-foot wooden frame securing the glass figure eight. Inside, gathered into one of the clear compartments, was an hour's worth of bleached sand. I sat down next to it and stood the object upright with the sand at the bottom. Out of the fog of the past came a memory of the scrap of paper I had found in the Master's laboratory bearing its likeness, showing it as equivalent to an eye. "Harrow's hindquarters," I thought, "another buzzing dung heap of mystical pretension." The comedy of it all was exaggerated by the influence of the beauty, and I laughed till I cried.

"Let me mark this hour," I said. I lifted the timepiece and flipped it over. The grains began to fall, bleached atoms dribbling three or four at a time into an empty, other world. It was the first instance of my registering the passage of time since we had entered the dome of the Panopticon. There was something alluring about the phenomenon, and I could understand how Misrix must have felt when, being born into humanity, the light of the Beyond went out in his head and he initially became aware of himself.

I heard someone speak, and thinking it was Anotine, I looked away from the hourglass. From where I sat, I could see that she was still sleeping. I turned in the other direction, and there I saw someone coming toward me out of the shadows. As he moved across the floor, he dragged behind him an unfolding light. Inside this light I saw a room with wallpaper and furniture, and it blossomed outward, quickly replacing the shadows of the dome and obliterating my view of the stars above. It happened so quickly, I could do nothing but stare.

I realized that the young man approaching me was unaware of my presence.

"Watch out," I said, but he ignored my warning and continued on his course, passing through me as if I wasn't there at all.

He stopped and turned around, and I saw his face. No more than twenty, and strikingly handsome with his dark hair and piercing eyes, I immediately knew it was Below in his youth.

"Please, Anotine," he said, as if addressing someone behind me. I looked around, first noticing that I was no longer in the dome but rather in some room in a house, and then I saw her, sitting on a pink chair, dressed in the very yellow dress she had worn when I first met her on the island. Her long hair was in ringlets, and she wore an ironic smile.

25

THE HOURGLASS PROVED TO BE THE REPOSITORY OF JUM-
bled scraps of memories I was able to splice together
into a love story of sorts involving the Master and
my Anotine. A series of scenes melted one into the
next around me, out of order but each completely
convincing in its reality. I remained an invisible
presence through the course of their unfolding,
and though I could no more affect the outcome as
stir with my phantom breath the flame of a candle
within the tale, I found I had a clear omniscience
about everything that transpired. This ability that
came with the hallucination allowed me to auto-
matically rearrange the events into a chronology.
The beauty released me from its embrace at precisely the end of the hour, and I found myself
sitting on the floor of the darkened dome, the
moon and stars overhead. I woke Anotine and told
her everything.

In the summer of his thirteenth year, after the death
of his younger sister, Below left home never to return.
Being an exceedingly sensitive child, the girl's passing
so frightened and confused him that he fled from the very
thought of it. He traveled as far as he could on the small
amount of money he had been able to put away. It took
him as far as the seacoast to a town called Merithae. The
winter was coming on and he found himself in dire
straits. Without so much as a scrap of bread, he was

*forced to hire himself out as a servant to an old man by the name
of Scarfinati.*

*Although Below had never heard of him, Scarfinati was famous
throughout much of the realm for possessing a limitless imagination
and the ability to bring his dreams to life. His specialty was a kind
of technomancy, and he dabbled in those regions where science and
magic mingled. Through his wealth, acquired from work for various
patrons, political, military, artistic, religious, he had been able to
amass an impressive fortune. With this money, he had a palatial
house built out at the tip of a spit of land that jutted into the ocean
a mile south of Merithae. It was to this place he called Reparata
(named for Scarfinati's own sister), he brought the young Drachton Below.*

*There were many rooms in the house, and Scarfinati hated dust.
Below worked from early in the morning to late at night continually
dusting books, furniture, scientific gadgetry, glass, primitive sculpture. When he finished every room, he was instructed to begin again.
Scarfinati, though old, was large in stature and stern in his demeanor. During the first month of Below's employment, his existence
was barely recognized. He was fed well, paid a modest sum, and had
a comfortable bed to sleep in. There was one day off a week, and he
had access to the books in the libraries granted he returned them to
their precise locations. When the snows came, he decided he had
better stay until the spring.*

*At the end of his first week at Reparata, Below saw a girl his
age cooking at the kitchen stove. He tried to speak to her, but she
completely ignored him. When he realized she wasn't going to speak,
he sat down and watched her work. He would have stayed there all
afternoon if Scarfinati hadn't come through and warned him to get
back to his dusting. As the days passed, he learned the girl's name
was Anotine. He also began to see that she was not just a cook, but
also a kind of student. Occasionally, Below would enter to dust a
room already being shared by the old man and the girl. He would
eavesdrop on their conversations. For the most part, she listened and
he spoke, instructing her in processes that Below had no understanding of. He often found them in the basement laboratory, working
together over a small fire with glass beakers and golden tongs.*

*Through the long winter, the mysterious nature of his employer
and the huge house were enough to keep away memories of his sister
and the tragedy of her death. When spring arrived, young Below*

decided he would again take up his traveling now that he had saved
some more money. This time he found himself fleeing not death but
love. He had become completely enamored of Anotine, even though
she had not said one word to him or cast a single glance in his
direction. The situation, as it was, had become sheer torture, as he
planned out entire days to try to get as little as a mere glimpse of her.

One day, when the snow had all but melted, Scarfinati entered
one of the libraries where Below was dusting. The young man cleared
his voice and explained to his employer that he would soon be moving
on. Scarfinati said he was very sorry to hear that, because he had
had it in his mind all along to request that Below become one of his
students. Below most likely would have declined the invitation had
it not been for Anotine, but he saw the old man's offer as a way to
get closer to her. He agreed to become an apprentice—of what, he
wasn't exactly sure.

A week later, he retired his feather duster and rags and joined
Scarfinati and Anotine in the basement laboratory for his first lesson,
the production of a chemical ice that could not melt. In the beginning
his ignorance was always evident, and his inability to grasp the
concepts the other two discussed fluently made him physically
clumsy. He broke equipment, burned himself, and dribbled a highly
corrosive acid onto the toe of Scarfinati's boot. The old man had a
great deal of tolerance for his ineptitude, but the girl was impatient,
rolling her eyes and calling him a fool.

On a rainy afternoon in late spring, as they all sat quietly
having tea in the library on the third floor, Scarfinati, by mumbling
and tossing a pinch of blue powder onto the carpet, conjured for
Below the spirit of his sister. The little girl walked out of thin air
and up to her brother. His immediate reaction was to bolt from the
room, but the old man commanded that he return and stay seated.
With this, he found he couldn't move. "Is there something you
wanted to say to your brother?" asked Anotine of the spirit. The
little girl nodded. "Drachton, your mind is in a fist with the thought
of my death. If you love me, you will relax it, so that I may travel
over into the next world. Release me and open yourself to possibility." The girl vanished then, and Below broke down in tears.

From that time on, his ability to learn seemed to grow exponen-
tially. The lessons that had seemed so obscure to him just a week
earlier, mathematics and the properties of chemicals, all began to fall
into place in his mind. He began to notice that with every procedure

he was able to accomplish in the lab without spilling the contents of the beaker, every complex problem he was able to solve without benefit of pencil and paper, Anotine began to grow more interested in him. This extra incentive charged his newly discovered intelligence.

As the years progressed, he learned at an alarming rate all of the secrets that had made Scarfinati rich and powerful. The old man had become like a father to him, but Below saw the girl as anything but a sister. Things began between them with a conversation one day in which she instructed him in some terms that would help him to discuss that area of study where magic and science merged. From that purely innocent conversation grew a friendship, which led, after months of talk, to a kiss, and then quickly to secret rendezvous in the middle of the night while the old man slept.

Things continued in that fashion for quite a few years, until the time both Anotine and Below turned twenty. It was then that Scarfinati announced that they would no longer take their lessons from him together. He told them that Below would continue on his course of alchemy, philosophy, and mathematics, whereas Anotine would be taught the memory book. A flare of jealousy leaped to life within Below, for he knew that the memory book was the last step, the most important element in one's progress toward becoming an adept.

Both Below and Anotine had been lectured in how to understand and utilize mnemonic systems. Each had built in his own mind a kind of crude memory palace, and used it in order to store information. Scarfinati had always stressed, though, that this was only the first step, and that the ultimate achievement of the mnemonics was to turn the memory into an engine of creativity. In order to do this, he said, "You must introduce life into it. The elements of it must continue to interact, commune, intermingle, even when your attention is elsewhere. This way new ideas are forever being born, and all you need do is harvest them."

The memory book contained lists of symbols and their values. Scarfinati had told them that those symbols, for some reason, could not be stored as a list, within the memory palace itself. Whenever he tried to hide them in the mnemonic structure, they would disappear, so the physical existence of the book would always be necessary. He also revealed that in order to introduce life into a mnemonic system, one had to learn how to manipulate the symbols from the book in one's mind. The correct juxtaposition of symbols would create an environment that was conducive to mnemonic life, and where this was achieved, imagination would surely grow. It was also a certainty that if you tried to use the symbols and did not know how, it could result in serious damage to the memory and the mind in general.

Knowing all of this, Below felt slighted that he had not been chosen to learn the book. From the time Scarfinati and Anotine began on their private lessons concerning the text, the young man tried to get her to talk about what she had learned. They would still meet at night and would discover the moment, but even in the throes of passion, or the dreamy time that followed, Anotine never uttered a word about the book. She told him flatly one day that if he were to keep interrogating her about it, she would have to stop seeing him. At her words the secret knowledge he was being left out of became in Below's mind almost like a secret lover whom Anotine was surreptitiously seeing.

Scarfinati noticed the young man's new sullenness and confronted him about it. Below asked why he was not also chosen to learn the book. The great adept told him he was not ready. "You have made great strides in the acquisition of knowledge, but that is only the beginning. I am leaving you an incredible legacy in what I am teaching you, and I don't want it squandered by impatience and immaturity." "But I'm ready," he told Scarfinati. "The very fact that you say that means you are not," said the old man.

Below tried to ignore the issue of the book and dedicate himself to his studies. He neither asked Anotine nor Scarfinati about it, but went through his lessons with a false smile and an exaggerated show of determination. Still, the book always worked its way back into his thoughts, and it began to drive him insane. It was his belief that when Anotine had finished with the special course of study, she would be so superior that she would no longer notice him. Then it struck him that Scarfinati had been planning all along to make her his wife. Such machinations led Below to one overriding desire—he must see the book.

He sneaked into Scarfinati's private study one night when the others were asleep and found it lying on the table, where it had been left from the day's lesson. The cover was fashioned from stiff leather boards with only three straps of leather serving as the spine. Upon opening it, Below saw that the pages were not sewn together as with a bound book, but were merely placed between the covers. There were no numbers in the corners or on the bottoms of the pages, and he wondered how Scarfinati kept track of their arrangement. The text was handwritten in black ink, rows of symbols (stars, circles, squares, florettes, depictions of animal paw prints, a water droplet, the sun, etc.) followed by equal signs and either other symbols or numbers. He carefully perused each page, bringing all his vast knowledge to bear on the system, but in the end found it meant nothing to him.

He was not content to leave things as they were, though, and so he decided to steal one of the pages. Searching through Scarfinati's study, he located the old man's paper and ink. With great care, he produced a facsimile page, using symbolic designs that were much like the others in the book, but of his own invention. The forgery of his mentor's drawing style was exquisite, driven to excellence by the idea that he now had insinuated himself into Anotine and Scarfinati's secret. When he finished, he folded the original page and placed it in his pocket. After returning the book and the writing implements to their appropriate places, he sneaked quietly back to his room. The mask of affability he wore for Anotine after this theft was his first true work of genius.

In his private moments away from the others, he would pore over the original sheet from the memory book. Days passed and he tried to implant some of the symbols that he found on the page into his already-existent memory palace, hoping they might imbue it with creative energy. He felt as if he was really beginning to understand the strange system when one day, while reaching into his mind to retrieve a basic mathematical formula, he discovered that his mnemonic world was slowly disintegrating. The steady forgetting confused him and made him physically dizzy.

He grew concerned when it became evident that he would not be able to halt the dissolution of all the knowledge he had worked so hard to acquire over the years. The idea of confessing what he had done to the old man in hopes that there was some way to reverse its effects was quickly becoming his only option. During this time, Anotine could sense there was something wrong with him. She promised that if he could be patient for a few more days, she would beg Scarfinati to let them go on a vacation. During one of their midnight meetings, she wondered if it wasn't time they should be married.

The feelings of jealousy began to disintegrate along with his memory, but they were replaced by a sense of guilt. Anotine's concern for him, her desire to be with him, showed that his paranoia had *been unfounded. During a particularly troubling night, he decided to confess the following morning. He only hoped that even if Scarfinati could not forgive him, Anotine might find it in her heart to.*

The next day, before he could present himself to his mentor, he heard Scarfinati calling to him from the private study on the second floor. As he mounted the stairs, he wondered if his theft had been discovered. When he reached the closed door of the study, he knocked meekly on it. "Enter," Scarfinati said from the other side.

He opened the door and saw Anotine sitting at the study table in front of the open book. She looked straight ahead with a perfectly blank expression, her mouth slightly open. Next to the open book was the original page that Below had stolen. How it had gotten there, he could only surmise. Scarfinati must have been aware of the theft all along and taken it back through some act of magic. The mysterious old man was nowhere to be found.

Scarfinati never appeared again at Reparata. Below came to realize that the bogus symbols he had inserted into the book on the forged page had been studied by Anotine and put to use in her mind. Because of their ill effect, her thoughts had seized. She could neither think ahead nor remember, but sat perfectly still, staring into that moment when everything came to a halt. He now could no longer deny the truth of his selfishness, and this plunged him into a great depression.

Using a formula the old man had taught him, he entombed Anotine in a chemical ice that was impervious to heat. In that way he hoped to preserve her until he could conceive of a way to free her mind. With the last of his own fading knowledge, he set about learning the symbology of the memory book. This he finally mastered and, almost at the last second, was able to reverse the effects of his mnemonic disintegration. Even when his thought processes had returned to full efficiency, and he was using his mnemonic world as a creativity engine, he still could not discover a cure for Anotine, who lay completely immobilized in her clear sarcophagus.

Her presence tormented him so that he invented a drug that would, for the short time it took control of his body, make him forget the pain of his guilt. Sheer beauty, as he called it, became his refuge, but when even that lost its effectiveness against his anguish, he knew he had to escape. He finally sold Reparata, and with the fortune it brought, he hired a ship and a crew in Merithae. Anotine was loaded into the hold of the ship, and Below gave orders to the captain that he was to stay perpetually out on the ocean. Once a year they would be allowed to dock in order to take on supplies and change crews. It was an odd request, but he had the wealth to back it up. The thought of not knowing with any certainty where Anotine was at any given moment came as a great relief to him.

He spent the next few years searching for Scarfinati, but never found him. The lessons the old man had taught him proved exceedingly valuable, though, and he sold his services to the wealthy and powerful in order to survive. Each spring, he would make his way back to Merithae and wait for the ship to put into port. Then he would visit the hold where Anotine lay like a beautiful insect in amber. It was on his last visit to the coastal town, as he was watching her sail away again toward the horizon, that all at once his mind conceived of a magnificent city. This seed of a thought began to sprout behind his eyes right there on the dock as the outgoing ship diminished against the horizon to a speck of white sand and then fell through the neck of the hourglass.

26

WHEN I FINISHED TELLING ANOTINE ABOUT WHAT I HAD witnessed, she remained perfectly still, staring vacantly at the hourglass as if the symbols of the story had again caused her mind to seize. I feared that it had been a cruel thing for me to reveal the secret of her past, and I admonished myself for having been so foolish.

"I thought you would want me to be honest," I said to her.

She broke from her trance and looked up at me. "I'm not angry, Cley," she said. "I'm merely confused. I know the Anotine of your story is not me, only a kind of distant relative, and yet now that you have recounted the tale, I am having memory flashes of that time and that place, Reparata."

She stood up and walked over to where Below sat sleeping. I followed her and stood at a distance, wondering how she might feel toward this man who had both destroyed her and then given her life in his memory. I heard her whispering and saw her hands moving in an expressive manner. She walked back and forth in front of him, continuing to expound, while he sat slumped in the chair, his arms limp at his sides. This went on for some time, but I could not hear what she was saying. I chanced a look out through the dome and saw that the sun was beginning to rise.

She suddenly stopped talking and moved in close to the body to run her hand over his hair. Remaining in that pose for almost a minute, she studied his features, maybe trying to remember what he looked like in his youth. She then leaned over him, her breasts flattening against his chest, and brought her hands up to either side of his face. I pretended to turn away, but watched from the corner of my eye as she proceeded to kiss him on the lips. It lasted a moment, and when she was done, she leaped back and screamed in surprise.

I could hardly believe what I was seeing, but the sleep-weighted body of Below abruptly sat straight up in the chair. Rushing over to where Anotine had backed away, I put my arm around her. Together we watched as the old man, with eyes still closed, turned the chair around to face the console. His wrinkled hands came up slowly, like the hands of a marionette, to turn dials, flip switches, and adjust the two long levers in front of him. As he performed his tasks on the board, I could feel the floor of the dome begin to rumble.

"We're moving," said Anotine, and she was right. The dome had come to life at Below's insistence and was now cutting through the thick waves under its own power.

No sooner did we realize this than the Master fell forward, the effect of his miraculous animation leaving him as if the invisible strings had been severed all at once. His head and shoulders landed on the console, and in the process must have activated one of the controls, for the chair began moving along the low rail it was connected to, traveling smoothly around the inner circumference of the dome.

I tried to catch up to the orbiting throne and turn it off, but I couldn't get close enough without risk of being run down. Eventually I gave up, and Below continued to make his rounds like the hand of a clock made to indicate seconds. While he circled, Anotine and I dressed.

"What did you say to him?" I asked her.

"How often does one get to express herself directly to god?" she asked with a smile. "I told him how much I hated him, thanked him for bringing you to me, and then begged him to release us."

"Why the kiss?"

"I could feel his fear. I remembered very clearly the day

in the library at Reparata when Scarfinati materialized Below's sister's spirit. The kiss was for that part of him that is the confused child. That boy is trapped in here as much as we are."

"You remembered?" I asked, uncertain as to how this was possible.

"When you told the story, there were parts of it that I saw so clearly in my mind, it was as if they were my own memories."

It was a dangerous business getting out onto the walkway with Below on the move in his chair. We had to time our slipping over the rail and through the portal just right so that we wouldn't be run down. Once outside, we stood in the early-morning sun with our backs to the dome, and watched as it sliced through the lazy waves of the silver ocean. It was obvious we were heading somewhere, for the unconventional craft seemed to stay on a direct course.

After an hour of watching the scenes in the waves and wondering what force had taken charge of Below's body, I looked up and saw something looming on the horizon. At first, I thought it was a cloud bank moving in, and I mentioned it to Anotine. She shaded her eyes with her hand and peered outward.

"Cley," she said, "I think it's land."

Not only was it land, but it was huge, a coastline stretching in either direction as far as the eye could see. I was amazed with the discovery of this memory continent, and was beginning to understand that the mind had an almost limitless storage capacity. I also realized that the memory had duplicate processes for retaining information. There had been the island, the ocean, the hourglasses, and now this vast territory that grew more distinct with our approach. These were both deep insights, but they did me little good. In the end, all I could hope for was that I still had some time left with Anotine before the complicated world that was Below went out like a match in the rain.

About a mile or so from the coast, we passed a boundary after which the liquid mercury of the ocean became a clear, light blue water. Anotine had never seen anything like it before, and she marveled at its beauty. We had remained on the walkway throughout our approach, and now as we looked over the side, we could see the shadowy forms of large fish passing beneath the dome. Off in the distance, a flock of birds was headed for shore.

"Do we have a plan?" asked Anotine while shading her eyes to get a better look at our destination. Although we were still a few hundred yards offshore, it appeared that the course set by the comatose Below was going to land us on a smooth beach of white sand.

"Do we need one?" I asked. "We seem to have traveled beyond any influence of a purpose."

"Are we free?" she asked. "Or just lost?"

"For the time being, both, I suppose."

"I like that," she said.

Eventually the heavy vibration coming from the floor of the dome stopped, and the gentle action of the waves pushed us right up onto the beach. All there was to do was hop down over the railing of the walkway. I turned and took one more look inside through the clear barrier. There was Below, riding his chair in a continuous loop. The sight was so absurd that I had to laugh. Anotine came up next to me and also looked in.

"I tell you, *there's* a dream in need of interpretation," she said.

Then I turned and climbed down off of the walkway and onto solid ground. I was a bit shaky from having been at sea for so long, and it took me a moment to find my balance. When I felt more steady, I reached up and helped Anotine down. Once we started up the beach, we never looked back.

We walked for more than two hours through an intense heat before we saw our first signs of foliage. For miles there had been nothing but white sand and outcroppings of a rust red stone. I was beginning to fear that Below had delivered us to a barren wasteland when finally the sand turned to dirt and then grass began to appear. By late afternoon, we found the edge of a forest and stopped to rest beneath a thicket of tall trees.

The ground was soft with moss and fallen leaves, a welcome bed after the hard floor of the dome. I lay there with Anotine next to me, enjoying the breeze that rolled out of the forest, carrying with it the scent of pine and the distant sound of birds. I closed my eyes and the peaceful nature of the place brought back a memory of us lying in Anotine's bed on the island. "So many memories," I whispered, half-asleep, and as I began to drift off, I pictured myself inside a memory having a memory of a place created to store memories, lying next to a memory woman who stored within her the memory of the formula for a drug invented to ease the pain of memories. The mental exercise wearied me even more than the walking had, and finally the whole thing dissolved into a dream of the green veil.

Night had fallen by the time I awoke. I came to with a splitting headache and that certain crawling of the flesh and itching of the brain that signaled withdrawal. Groping in the dark, I found Anotine next to me and initiated a round of lovemaking, even though I knew she was not fully conscious. At that point it had been almost an entire day since I had my last infusion of the beauty, and I wasn't concerned about the ethics of the situation. She lay there with her eyes closed as I lifted her dress and moved her legs apart. I worked quickly to quell the urgency in my very blood.

At one point my ear was near her mouth, and I heard her say the name "Drachton" very faintly. Had I not been driven by addiction, I would certainly have stopped to ponder this, but as it was, nothing could have stopped me. When I finally backed off of her, I felt ashamed of what I had done, and wondered how I could explain it to her when she woke up. The beauty, a hundredfold stronger than my conscience, was turning me into an animal.

These self-recriminations lasted only as long as it took for the drug to produce its euphoria. Then my mind raced, spinning twisted philosophical theories that eventually smothered my guilt. I shelved my apprehensions by telling myself that Anotine would understand. As pleased as I was to have dispersed these troubling thoughts, I was now again aware of my surroundings. The fact that I could see no more than a few feet in front of me, and that we were in a strange forest in some country of the Master's mind brought with it a brand of paranoia worse than anything I had previously been feeling.

Twigs cracked and something moved through the fallen leaves. Who knew what nightmare creatures roamed this tract

of Below's addled mind? I considered waking Anotine for
company, but I didn't want to have to explain just yet. Instead,
I huddled up, my arms clasped around my knees, and listened.
The effects of the drug made everything more uncertain, and
I began to see misty white forms moving through the trees in
the distance. For the first time, I noticed that the temperature
had dropped considerably from late afternoon, and I started
to shiver.

Anotine mumbled a phrase in her sleep, and I looked over
at her to see if she was awake. Her eyes were closed, but it
was obvious she was having a bad dream, for her face went
through a series of grimaces and winces. When I turned back
to look out into the night, there was a man standing in front
of me. He was tall, and at first, my heart leaped because I
thought the Delicate had somehow returned to life and tracked
us. I tried to cry out, but I couldn't. The beauty had, as always,
left my throat incredibly dry. By the time I worked up some
saliva and could have given voice to my fear, the shadowy
figure had put his finger to his lips, motioning for me to be
quiet.

He sat down in front of me, folding one leg under the
other and wrapping himself in his cape. The fact that he
adopted this nonthreatening posture did much to relieve my
fear. When I saw his smile, I relaxed and asked his name.

"Scarfinati," he whispered.

"I know you," I said.

Though his body appeared to be in remarkable shape, his
face, a veritable web of wrinkles, showed his age. Still he
seemed very spry, and there was a certain light in his eyes
that couldn't have been a reflection.

"I know you," he said. "Cley. Am I right?"

I nodded, incredulous at the fact that he had my name.
"This is Anotine," I said, pointing to her.

"She is still beautiful," he said. "But don't wake her."

"Why are you here?" I asked.

"The same reason you are. To save you and Anotine, and
in the process even this son of a dog turd, Below."

"Do you know . . ."

"I know a few things. I have it within my ability to follow
the events of this world. This forest is my prison, so to speak.

I can go no farther than its boundaries, but I still see with the eyes of an adept. Many things are clouded but some things are clear. Unlike your friend there, I am aware that I'm a memory."

"This world is dying," I told him.

"Yes," he said. "That's why I am here. I can't stay long, but I've come to tell you how to reverse the ravages of the disease."

"Please," I said. "Do you know the antidote?"

"The antidote you speak of is more dangerous than the disease. I will tell you a better way to cure the illness. Enter the forest, and before long you will come across a path. Follow it. A half day's journey from here, due west, there is a large field, and in the very center of it lie the ruins of a City that Below was once the ruler of."

"The Well-Built City," I said.

"I would have used that title, but I can't say it without laughing uncontrollably." He reached out and put his hand on my shoulder. "Now listen. You must go to that place and find the memory book. I can tell you know what I am speaking of. Find in the book the page that begins with these three symbols: the eye, the hourglass, and the circle. When you have located it, burn it, but do not let the ashes fly away. Gather all of the ashes together and ingest them. I have calculated that once this strand of symbols has been obliterated from the mnemonic world, the disease that infects Below will be neutralized."

"But I thought the memory book could not be kept in the memory," I said.

"No, it can't be kept in the memory palace. It's too difficult to assign symbolic meaning to symbols that already carry a complex of assigned meanings. You are no longer in the specialized environment of the floating island, though. This is the country of things one cannot help remembering, the everyday memory, if you like. Here, it is not the meaning of the book that is preserved, only the book itself. Do you understand?"

I nodded in order not to offend, but I was never more unclear in my life. "Where will I find it in the city?" I asked.

"I don't know," he said. "I must be going."

"Wait," I said. "If the time should come when I leave here

and return to my reality, I want to find the ship that Anotine sails on."

Scarfinati laughed. "Did you really believe that fairy tale?"

"It was a memory," I said.

"If only every memory was truth," he said. "Very little of that story has anything to do with what actually happened. That is why I didn't want you to wake Anotine. I believe it will be less tormenting for her to believe the lie. Below wasn't powerful enough at the time to carry out those achievements. Anotine's mind never seized. He and she had a child together while they were studying at Reparata. I think he might have even loved the child, but it made him nervous because of his memory of his sister. He engineered some drug he would take in order for him to be calm enough in her presence to spend time with her. No, there was nothing miraculous about it. He simply stole the memory book and abandoned his family."

"And what became of you?" I asked.

Scarfinati grinned. "He knew he wouldn't be able to make off with the book while I was still alive. The night he left, he poisoned my dinner and slit my throat. With anyone else, I might have seen it coming, but I had begun to think of him as my son. I still want to save . . ."

The old man couldn't continue, and I immediately saw the reason. A dark line of blood began to appear like a necklace around his throat. He brought his hand up to it quickly and gurgled some curse. Then he slowly got to his feet and staggered away into the night.

27

Anotine slept fitfully through the remainder of the night, occasionally calling out and at times waving her arms. As for me, I found it impossible to rest after my meeting with Scarfinati. If what he had told me was true, I could possibly save Anotine. But he, himself, pointed out that all memories are not truth. Besides that, he might have been an hallucination generated by the beauty. What were the chances of my meeting him so soon after my experience with the hourglass, and why of all places would he be relegated in Below's memory to this forest? My thoughts revolved with no destination like the Master in his chair.

By the time the sun rose, I was thoroughly confused, but in the end decided that if during our journey I were to come upon the fields of Harakun, I would enter the ruins and locate the memory book. Since the island had been destroyed, there was little chance I would be able to discover the antidote that Misrix had mentioned. One thing that Scarfinati had said stayed with me, namely that it was better to let Anotine believe in the fairy tale that had been projected by the hourglass.

When she finally woke, I immediately confessed my having taken advantage of her through the night.

"I was so tired," she said. "What dreams I

had—Scarfinati and the weird goings-on at Reparata." She shook her head.

I told her I was sorry again, but she seemed perplexed by my apology. The fact that she did not see my taking advantage of her as an affront to her dignity troubled me. It only stood to remind me that she was a mnemonic creation when what I wanted was for her to be a woman. The phenomenon that linked the sheer beauty to sex became like a snake swallowing its tail, breaking down, through repetition, my perception of her. If I ignored this, she remained absolutely real to me, and I loved her, but the minute the urge was upon me, I could not help myself from again seeing through the illusion.

"Come, Cley," she said. "Let's see what's in this forest." She reached out to take my hand and we began walking.

It was peaceful beneath the pines and oaks, sunlight filtering down in spots onto the carpet of fallen needles and leaves. In order to circumvent my troubled thoughts, I began pointing out for Anotine the different types of plants and mushrooms I was familiar with. She was truly curious as to what each of them might be used for, and I described in detail the physical illnesses and mental afflictions they cured.

"See here," I said, bending low to snatch a rosy piece of flush fern from between the exposed roots of an oak. "This plant induces amnesia, a total forgetting. If you were to take it, you would remember nothing."

"Have you ever administered it?" she asked.

"Once, to a young fellow who had lost his entire family in a fire. He was so grief-stricken, he could not continue with his life, and thoughts of suicide were always upon him," I said.

"Did it work?" she asked.

"I was loath to give it to him, but he pleaded so pitifully that I finally prepared him a tea from it."

"And did he find happiness?"

"He spent the next three years trying to find out who he had been and what had become of him. He discovered the names of his wife and children, but he could never acquire what they had looked like or any of the moments he had spent with them."

Anotine asked no more questions after that, and realizing my mistake, I relented on my pharmacopic lecture. As we walked along, I saw her very subtly lift her hands, as if she were merely adjusting her hair behind her ears. When she did not think I was looking, I saw her wipe tears from her eyes.

We came across the path that Scarfinati had described to me. It wound through the forest with unnecessary turns and loops as if it had been forged by a drunkard. Nevertheless, I made a point of sticking to it. Anotine hummed the tune from Nunnly's music box as we walked, and I lost myself for some time in the beauty of her voice and the haunting nature of that melody.

Sometime after midday, we came upon a small lake that the path cut across the middle of in a narrow land bridge. Being hot and tired, I suggested that we take a swim. Anotine said she had been feeling somewhat faint and agreed that it was a good idea. Leaving our clothes on the bank, we eased into the cool water.

I let myself slip down beneath the surface and slackened my muscles so that I sank slowly like a dead man. In that dark and quiet place, I remembered sinking in a similar fashion toward the bottom of the river at Wenau on the day that Below's metal bird had exploded. This brought to my mind images of the settlement and my own humble home off in the woods. I saw behind my eyes all of my neighbors, and for the first time in what seemed years I thought about the situation I had left them in. Jensen and Roan, the women I had assisted in childbirth, all of the children I had always thought of in some part as my own, beckoned to me for help.

I carried these troubling images with me to the surface, but the minute I burst through into the atmosphere of Below's memory and took a deep breath, I wanted only to find Anotine. Turning to look for her, I was startled when she appeared from under the water right behind me. She neither smiled nor spoke, but swam to me and put her arms around my neck. Her breasts gently pushed into my chest and her legs came up around my waist. The ends of her hair swirled on the surface of the water in spiral patterns as I joined with her and moved toward the moment. Wavelets began to break against the bank, and in the midst of our passion, she told me one of her dreams.

"I was paralyzed in the present, trapped in a block of unmelting ice in the hold of a ship bound for nowhere. I could not breathe. I had no pulse or heartbeat, yet I could see through the clear substance that was my tomb. Time had no hold on me, and all that passed before me, I saw only in the present, so that I saw it all at once. The faces of the crew when they would come down into the hold to stare at me, Below when he would make his yearly visits, the monkey that was bought by the captain during one of the voyages, the destruction of the ship in a typhoon, volcanoes and krakens at the bottom of the sea, my rescue by a strange race of amphibious people, a great city of dripping mounds where my frozen image was worshiped, and you, Cley. You were there somewhere," she said, climaxing with a sigh that sounded like dying.

When we finished, she swam backwards away from me. "It was a love story bound within an instant," she said, and then dived underwater.

The beauty had me in its clutches before I even climbed out of the lake. We dressed without drying off so that we would stay cool well into the afternoon. I felt refreshed and calm as we again began our journey along the twisting path. The effects of the drug helped me to remember the loss of my neighbors I had felt while floating beneath the surface of the lake. It all came back to me with the same vitality that my visions of Wood and the Fetch and the scenes from the hourglass had when wrapped in the afterglow of Anotine's love. What I experienced this time was a single thought, but one so powerful that it caused me to stop in my tracks. What, I wondered, was to be our future? Were we destined to wander aimlessly through Below's memory until it dissolved?

I turned to look at Anotine and in that very second, she put her hand to her forehead and fell into me with a great sigh.

"What is it?" I asked.

"I feel weak, Cley," she said.

"Are you simply tired or are you ill?"

"I'm dizzy and I cannot feel my hands or feet." Her eyelids were half-open and fluttering madly.

I quickly moved my hands beneath her arms and carried

her off the path. Finding a moss-covered spot that looked soft, I laid her on the ground and knelt at her side.

"Just give me a moment," she said. "I need to rest." With this, her eyes closed and she either fell asleep or passed out.

I didn't know whether to wake her or to let her sleep. "Anotine," I called to her, brushing the hair away from her face. I was relieved somewhat to see that she was breathing steadily. Leaping to my feet, I began pacing around her. My instinct told me that there was something truly wrong. Although I kept telling myself that she was merely resting, I knew that what had happened carried deeper implications.

The beauty heightened my paranoia of being left alone, and I began to circle frantically. "Just sleeping, just sleeping," I repeated aloud to myself. I changed directions and walked across to the other side of the path. While I still had my back to her, I heard a voice, not hers, say, "She's not sleeping, Cley."

I spun around and saw a misty figure sitting on the ground next to her. It was a man, someone familiar to me. I squinted, and this brought, what appeared to be, the ghost of Doctor Hellman into focus.

"Doctor," I said, the hair on the back of my neck rising, my pulse quickening, "how are you here?"

"Nothing in the memory is ever really destroyed unless the mind that contains it is destroyed. I have suffered a mild erasure through a willful act of forgetting, but Below can't eradicate me completely. Traces of me will exist as long as he does."

The sight of him back from the dead brought tears to my eyes. I could barely continue in the face of this new assault on my reason. "I have been through too much," I said to him.

"Listen, Cley. She is losing energy now that she is away from the island. We were designed as complex memory markers. You will lose her unless you do something."

"What? I'll do anything," I said.

"Go to the ruins of the city and find the book," he said. "Destroy the page as Scarfinati instructed."

"How do you know about Scarfinati?" I asked.

"I now have all the knowledge of one who has died," he said.

"But where do I go?" I asked.

"You must hurry," he said. "I will wait with her, but I can't remain for too long. My being here requires great effort. You must go, now."

Anotine then opened her eyes. "Doctor," she said weakly. He smiled at her.

I walked over and knelt down. "I am going to leave you for a short time," I said. "Do you understand?"

"Don't go, Cley. Stay with me," she said, a look of panic in her eyes.

"I'll only be gone for a very brief time. I have to do something that will make you feel better."

"Promise you will come back," she said.

"I promise," I told her. I reached into my shirt pocket and pulled out the balled-up green veil. Reaching down, I put it into her hand. "Keep this for me until I return. This is my promise to you."

Her hand weakly grasped the veil, as I leaned over and kissed her. Before I could pull my head up, she put her arms around my neck and pulled me gently down again. I could feel her breath on my ear. "I believe in you," she whispered.

"You must leave," said the Doctor. "Hurry."

I stood and began running along the path. When I reached the first turn, I looked back at the scene of Anotine lying there with the shimmering form beside her. She seemed to once again be asleep and, just as he had appeared in the silver ocean's tableau, keeping vigil next to Below's failing sister, the Doctor's hand rested upon his beard.

The journey along the convoluted path to where the fields of Harakun came into view could have lasted minutes or hours. My panicked concern for Anotine, my astonishment at the sudden appearance of the Doctor, the overwhelming uncertainty and weirdness of everything, boiled madly in a stew liberally seasoned with sheer beauty. I couldn't think clearly as to what my purpose was. All I could remember is that I had to get to the ruins.

I left the path, passing over a fallen tree and through some underbrush which eventually gave way to the barren plain. My very first thought upon setting foot amidst the dry dirt and saw grass was, "What about the werewolves?" I had traveled an enormous circle only to return to where I had begun.

The whole exercise seemed futile at that point, but if I didn't continue, what else was I to do? "Damn the werewolves," I thought, and took off toward the ruins in the distance at a pace that was more a stumble than a run.

The sun was still high and the heat was intense out in the open. I perspired past the point of sweating and felt myself beginning to parch. The soles of my feet burned in my boots, and my tongue had turned to cotton. The breezes were both a blessing and a curse, for although they were my only respite from the heat, they also made the saw grass shift, and then I thought werewolves were on the move.

Needless to say, the running did not last long, having early on given way to simple stumbling. I kept my sight fixed on the shattered column that was the Top of the City and advanced as best I could. The whole city wavered in a liquid mirage, making it appear a lost kingdom sunk into the sea. I swam through the heat with the determination of a salmon moving upstream, and finally, after hours, I walked headlong into a portion of the fractured circular wall and bounced back onto my rear end.

Following the wall around, I found a place where there was a gaping hole and entered the ruins. I laughed out loud at my success as I moved into the shadows of the rubble to rest and cool off. The beauty had long been sweated out of me, as had all my fear and confusion. I knew now I had to find the book and find it quickly. There was no time to delay, since the afternoon would soon begin to turn to night. I had promised Anotine I would return, and that is what I intended to do.

When I felt that some of my strength had returned, I left my hiding place and started up a street that I knew would lead me to that part of the city where Below's lab had been located in the ruins of my reality. I hadn't even taken twenty steps before I heard behind me an odd sound, something lightly tapping on the coral pavement. Before I turned, the smell had already permeated the air. There was the sound of growling. Greta Sykes, I thought, and saw in my mind's eye the lean, savage figure of the wolf girl, silver fur, head studded with metal bolts and, burning in her eyes, the desire to tear my heart out.

28

GRETA ROSE UP ON HER BACK LEGS IN ORDER TO LEAD ME through the remains of the city as her prisoner. She walked behind me and a step to the left, slightly hunched, the tips of her long claws resting on the back of my neck. I could tell from the sounds she was making, beastly guttural rumblings, that it was a great effort for her not to kill me. I remained silent and followed the direction her claws dictated. At any other time I might have been unable to walk from fear, but in this instance there was something I feared far more than death. I had to get the memory book, and I knew she was leading me directly to it.

When we arrived at the laboratory, she shoved me through the entrance, and I tripped and fell to my knees. Looking up, I saw that the place was almost exactly as it had been when I visited it with Misrix to search for the antidote. The only difference now was that everything was intact, the glassware was unbroken, holding the various colored powders and liquids that, upon my previous visit in the other world, had been strewn across the floor and walls. The lighthouse contraption that projected intermittently the images of birds was there as was the operating table and metallic chair. Nests of wiring lined the ceiling, and, over the edge of one of the tables, I could see a stern female face framed by wild hair, staring down at me from where it floated within a huge glass jar.

Then a hand came into view, and I heard Below laughing. He helped me to my feet. "Wonder of wonders," he said. "If it isn't the Physiognomist."

"Master," I said out of habit, and nodded. Although he had lost much of his hair on top and had shrunk in stature somewhat from the days when the city was in one piece, he appeared quite vital, and his face, I dare say, might have looked younger than mine at the moment.

"I knew you would come back someday, Cley. I imagine life out there in shantytown must be a little tedious."

"Not at all," I said.

"As you can see," he said, "I've been keeping myself busy." He turned and swept his arm in a gesture that directed my attention around the lab.

"You always were a busy fellow," I said.

He looked sternly at me for a moment, then broke into laughter. "I'm a family man now, Cley," he said.

"You don't say."

"I thought you would be more surprised," he said, looking somewhat disappointed.

"I'm here for a reason," I said.

"Well, it's good to see you," he said. "I'm glad you came. Come, we'll go to my quarters, where we can talk."

I followed him out of the lab and around the corner of the building. Behind the structure, in a lot cleared of the ubiquitous rubble of the city, we passed a row of ten large cages, each containing a man. Upon seeing us, the occupants cried out to be released in the most pathetic voices. I noticed that the two at the end of the row were not men at all but had begun some process that was transforming them into werewolves.

"Silence, gentlemen," said Below to his prisoners. "Who needs a visit to the metal chair?"

His words made them cease their groaning as they cowered away from the doors of their cages.

"What is this atrocity?" I asked.

"Now, now, Cley," he said. "These men came to my city with the express purpose of robbing me. They are criminals. I'm helping them to become useful."

"What have you done to those two on the end?" I asked.

"Well, that's the way they are all headed. Greta needs some playmates. What better way to protect my city than a pack of werewolves? Consider the lesson they are all learning. They are being transformed from thieves into guardians."

"That's horrible," I said.

"Let's try not to judge each other while you are here, Cley. Ideological differences shouldn't come between old friends. I hope that we can agree to disagree."

It was hard for me to ignore the suffering I witnessed, but I told myself that there was nothing I could do about it. These men would become werewolves, and I, myself, would kill quite a few of them. I had to concentrate on getting the book. "Very well," I said.

"Very well, indeed," said Below, and patted me on the back.

We walked through the rubble, heading, for the Ministry of Information.

"I understand you have become a vegetable salesman," he said, smiling.

"I gather and trade herbs and other medicines of the forest."

"Primitive," he said. "But, you also deliver children. Now, being a father, I can appreciate this."

"Do you have a son or daughter?" I asked.

"A son," said Below, actually beaming with pride. "You might say he is much like me in many ways."

"I look forward to meeting him," I said. "And who is the mother?"

"She is wild and untamed . . . deep and mysterious, but paradise is in her heart."

"Who is she?" I asked.

"The Beyond," he said. "My son is the demon I brought back with me from the territory. I tell you, Cley, I am not lying to you in any way when I say that I truly love him."

"I beg your pardon, Master, but this creature . . ."

"I know what you are thinking. It is hard for you to imagine how I have helped him. He speaks human language. He no longer eats meat. He reads. He thinks. He is good, Cley.

You will approve of him, I'm telling you. Perhaps it was the last result of the white fruit. After it completely destroyed all of my possessions, it left me one gift. The ability to love. I would do anything for him."

"I am amazed," I said, and even though I knew the tale, to hear Below speak these words was a miracle I never thought I would witness. "What is his name?"

"Misrix. I named him after a certain adept who lived three centuries ago. A great man as I expect my boy to be someday." He stopped walking and put his hand on my arm. "You must try very hard not to react to his demon appearance. Please, treat him as if he were . . ."

"Normal?" I said.

The Master quietly nodded, and we continued. For the remainder of our journey, he questioned me quite specifically about the daily life at Wenau. He inquired about certain people he had known who might still be alive and also as to the whereabouts of Arla and Ea. When we reached the Ministry of Information, we did not enter through the remains of the public baths, but Below produced a key, and we went through a side door in a part of the massive structure that was still completely intact.

He led me down into the basement and to one of the rooms in the long hallway lined with doors, at the end of which was the very place that in my true reality of the future, he lay wasting away with the sleeping disease. It twisted my thinking for a moment when I considered that if I went down the hallway to that room and waited long enough, I would meet myself.

The room, with the exception of the fact that there were no windows, was an exact duplicate of the parlor in which I first met Anotine back on the floating island. I took a seat at the table. He very cordially served me a glass of Rose Ear Sweet and pushed a pack of Hundred-To-One's, a box of matches, and an ashtray toward me.

"Relax for a moment, Cley. I'll be right back," he said, leaving me alone in the room.

I tried to appear calm, knowing that my only chance of snatching the book was in waiting and watching for just the right opportunity, but every moment longer I spent exchanging small talk, Anotine withered toward a memory form I would no longer be able to touch. I sipped my drink and lit a cigarette out of nervousness.

The door opened, and Below entered. "Cley, I want you to meet my son, Misrix," he said.

I stood and put my hand out. The demon came forth with his head bowed and his hands folded in front of him. There would have been no hope for me if I had been seeing him for the first time. I probably would have run screaming from the room, but as it was, I think Below was impressed with my calm demeanor as I coaxed Misrix with a nod of my head to shake hands with me.

"I like your spectacles," I said to him. "You appear to be a very intelligent young man."

"Yes, the spectacles. A little much," said Below.

"No, I'm serious," I said.

"Thank you," said Misrix, his fangs showing in a bashful smile.

He sat down with the Master and myself at the table, and I asked him about the books he was reading. The demon took to me and was expounding on some of the more recent volumes he had gone through, when Below interrupted.

"He's quite a fan of the Physiognomy," he said.

"Your father is a genius," I said to Misrix, and from the corner of my eye, I could see Below smiling.

I offered the demon a cigarette from the pack lying in front of me, and though he immediately declined, I could see his nervousness when the subject was brought up in front of his father.

Finally, Below dismissed Misrix, telling him to go back to the lab and check on the prisoners. When the demon had left, Below turned to me, and asked, "All right, Cley, you handled yourself very well there. What is it you want?"

"I know you have been working on the production of a certain disease that induces sleep," I said.

"Very good, Cley," said the Master. "We have both been doing some spying I can see."

"I want the antidote," I said.

Below grinned and rubbed his chin. "You want the antidote," he said. "Well, I can give you that."

"You can?" I said.

"Why not. But first, for old time's sake, I want you to indulge in the beauty with me. I have perfected the drug to be a hundred times more powerful than it was. The tiniest droplet mixed with water will do the job that an entire syringe of the stuff uncut used to do. If you'll do this with me, I'll tell you anything you like."

I would be a fool if I wasn't suspicious of the deal he laid out for me, but there was no choice. Besides, the day had progressed to the point where I would soon be needing a fix to quell the urge of my addiction.

"Yes," I said. "Certainly, for old time's sake."

The Master seemed a little surprised at my willingness, but with a fluttering of his hands, he conjured two needles. "I haven't lost any of my magic," he said as he passed one of the needles across the table to me.

He immediately went for the vein in his neck as I had seen him do on many an occasion in the past. For me it was more difficult. I had not taken the needle in years, and I had to think for a moment through the process of self-injection. I rolled up my sleeve, bent my arm, and made a fist. The moment I lifted the hypodermic it all came flooding back to me. I got into the vein as easy as putting a key in a lock. In making love to Anotine the effects of the drug were somewhat delayed in comparison to the needle, which deposited the beauty directly into the bloodstream.

When the empty syringes lay on the table between us, and we stared into each other's bleary eyes, Below asked, "How did you know about the sleeping disease?"

"The same way I know about the metal, exploding birds," I said, and laughed at finally having the upper hand on the Master.

"You've been delving into magic?" asked Below.

"Just your mind," I said. "Now, you promised me the antidote."

"I've already given it to you," he said.

"I'm not that high," I said. "What is it?"

"I just gave it to you," he said.

"No . . ." " I began to protest, but then it came clear to me. "The beauty?" I asked. "Is it the beauty?"

He nodded. "It has many purposes. When you are awake, it makes you forget; but when you are asleep, it reminds you to wake up."

"No," I said.

"Cley, you somehow know about the bird and the disease, so let me tell you the rest. The antidote has to be the beauty, because once I infect the people of Wenau with the sleeping sickness, I can then show up on the scene and become a hero for curing them. They will learn to respect me because I will have saved their loved ones' lives. In addition to this, I will introduce the beauty into the culture of Wenau, and soon I will be a most necessary figure since I am the only one capable of making it."

"Your plan is to spread addiction?"

"Call it what you like," he said.

"But why?"

"I want your people to accept my son, and I know they won't unless I coerce them. I must persuade them to see him as part of your society. I won't live forever, and I need to be sure he will have a normal life ahead of him. If he stays here with me, he'll become as mad as I am, and when I die there will be nothing to stop him from reverting back to his savage ways."

"You mean, you are doing this out of love?" I said.

"He's my son. Not having had any children, I don't expect you to understand the depth of my feeling."

"But there is no need for this. He would be accepted anyway, on his own merits."

"Don't be a fool, Cley. They would drive him out of town, hunt him down, and kill him."

"You speak of love, but your methods are all about tyranny, slavery, murder."

"It's too late for me to change completely. I know now there is a better way, but I am too tired to go back to the beginning. Truth lies at the end of a circle, Cley. We both have learned that by now. It's also too late for you. I can't have you ruining this plan as well. I happened to have forgotten to water down the beauty that was in your syringe. When next you awaken, I will be making a wolf of you. So good to have seen you once more. After tomorrow, you, like the other thieves, will have become my guardian.''

He stood up a little unsteadily, walked to the door, opened it, and left. I jumped to my feet, took two steps, and then my head exploded.

29

WHEN NEXT I OPENED MY EYES, I WAS STRAPPED TO THE operating table in Below's lab. I could see through the entrance and places where the walls had broken down that it was morning, meaning I had spent the entire night under the influence of the new, more potent sheer beauty. There had been visions, hallucinations more intense than anything I had ever experienced. Of this, I was certain, but exactly what they were was unclear. I vaguely remembered conversing with Brisden about some philosophical point, and at another juncture I had danced with the monkey, Silencio. There were other scraps of images that also returned—a three-masted ship battling high seas, a bitten piece of the white fruit sporting half a green worm, an animated etching in liquid mercury of the Delicate pursuing us. The only part of it that I was sure of was that a radiant vision of Anotine had been with me through it all.

I was dazed and weak from the experience, but I longed to see her and worried about her condition. My promise had been that I would return quickly, and I felt each minute that had passed since I left her side to be another brick in a wall that would separate us forever. Looking to the left of me, I could see clearly the open entrance to the lab, my path to freedom, but try as I might I could not budge the straps that were tightened around my chest and legs. To the right were all Below's bizarre experiments, the tables holding clear jars of heads, jars of gilled fetuses, liquid rainbows, gears made of bone. Every now and then, at odd intervals, the diminutive lighthouse would begin to glow and the lab was filled with the darting figures of birds. These songs, in conjunction with the howling of the prisoners out back in their cages, combined to make a music that was driving me mad.

I tested my bonds again, this time crying out in order to add the force of my voice to my overall effort. When that didn't work, I simply began screaming, because I could think of nothing else to do. Thrashing my head back and forth wildly, I let loose with the sum total of my frustration.

I had nearly grown hoarse when Misrix appeared at the entrance. He stepped into the lab and passed by me, trying very hard not to make eye contact. I turned my head and followed his progress. Walking over to one of the tables, he lifted an object and started back. I couldn't help but smile when I saw that what he had retrieved was the memory book. This was my last chance.

"Misrix," I called to him. "Demon, I have a secret for you."

He averted his eyes from me as he made for the doorway.

"I can tell you the meaning of that white fruit you found in the ruins."

He stopped for a second, his back still facing me.

"I can tell you how it fits into the story of the city," I said. Of course, I had no idea what I was going to say, but I needed to get his attention.

He slowly came around to face me. "How do you know about the white fruit?" he asked.

"It's in your museum, is it not?"

He stepped closer, moving his wings, and their breeze washed over me.

"My father told you," he said.

I shook my head. "I simply know. That fruit is the key to the story you have been piecing together, and I know exactly where it fits in."

"Tell me," he said, using a claw of his free hand to push his spectacles back up the bridge of his thin nose.

"Loosen my straps, here. Let me get up and stretch my arms and legs, and I'll tell you," I said.

He laughed like a goat bleating. "My father would be very angry if I were to do that," he said. "He's waiting for me to bring him his book. I must go."

"No, you can't. He's going to turn me into one of those creatures," I said.

"He said you need to become one. He told me that was your reason for returning to the city, so that you could be made different."

"He lies," I said. "All I want is to be let go."

He shook his head and started to turn away.

"One more minute," I said.

He waited and looked back over his shoulder.

"You say your father will be angry if you help me. Just think of his disappointment when I tell him that you coupled with the wolf girl, Greta Sykes."

The barbed tip of his tail snapped the air an inch from my eyes. "That is not true," he said.

"You know it is true, and he will know it is true. Do you think there is anything that your father cannot know, any truth he cannot uncover if given a clue? Three pairs of spectacles will not make you seem any less a beast after he knows you have joined with the werewolf."

He stood there staring down at me.

"Did you have a cigarette afterward?" I asked.

He winced at this remark, and I laughed out loud.

I thought for a moment that he was going to ignore me, but then I realized he was moving away only to place the memory book down on the seat of the metallic chair. He came back to me and, with two precise swipes of his claws, severed the straps.

Sliding off the table, I reached down into my boot and retrieved the Lady Claw I had carried with me from the island. I handed it to him. "Give this to him," I said. "Tell him you found it next to the table. He will think I escaped on my own."

"Yes," he said, and I could see the concept of deception dawning in his expression.

I grabbed him by the shoulders and put my face up to

his. "Now go, quickly," I shouted. "Hurry." He left the room and, once outside, took off running.

Lifting the book from where he had laid it on the chair, I opened the cover and found the loose pages filled with rows of symbols rendered in a perfectly black ink. I had no time to sort them out just then, I had to get away from the city. The minute that Below knew of my escape, he would be after me. There was no stumbling to my run now as I headed out the door and began to retrace the path that Greta had used to bring me to the lab. I thought only of Anotine, especially those quiet, unamazing moments when we simply talked and shared the present. It was this that I was desperate to get back to again.

My greatest concern was Greta. I expected her to come bounding out of some shadowed nook of debris at any moment. It was still morning, though, and I remembered Misrix having told me that the werewolves did not usually awaken till noon. This must have been the case, because I cleared the crumbling walls of the city with no incident. When I stepped out onto the fields of Harakun, I felt a great surge of energy, thinking, "I've done it. I have the book. I have the antidote." I ran like a demon.

I covered half the distance to the tree line where I had entered the fields the previous day before I began to lose my stamina. A sharp pain had developed in my left knee, causing me to gallop awkwardly like Quismal inspired by fear. Still I kept going, heaving for air. "How many times am I going to have to dash across these damn fields," I thought to myself as the sun began to work its harsh process on me again.

Then, nearly three-quarters of the way to the cover of the trees, I turned my ankle in a hole and fell forward. The book slipped from my grasp, twirling upward as I went down. In its ascent, it opened, releasing the symbol-laden pages like a pod bursting, its white seeds flying everywhere. I gathered myself up and stood, stunned for a moment amidst the snow squall of falling paper.

Having no time to feel thwarted, I immediately set to gathering the pages together. I thought, "If I can just find that one that has the eye, the hourglass, and the circle on it, I can leave the others behind." They all appeared the same, though, as I

chased them down and added them to my stack. When I
turned to gather those that had fallen behind me, my sight
was attracted to something in the sky. At first I thought it was
a bird, but then saw that it was far too large for that. The
wingspan was enormous and it was closing fast, swooping
low over the fields. "Misrix," I said, and frantically began
searching again for the page.

I lifted three more sheets of parchment, and then, approaching a fourth, I saw it, an eye looking back at me from
the top of a column of symbols. Falling to my knees, I reached
for it, but the action of the demon's wings as he landed, blew
it away from me.

"Damn you," I said, standing, seriously preparing to fight
him. "I warned you I would tell your father about the wolf
girl."

Misrix laughed. "Cley," he said, "you're mistaken. It is me
from your own time. I finally broke through into the memory
world. I am here to take you back."

"No," I cried. "I'm not going back. I'm not finished here."

"We can't wait. My father's condition has grown worse,
and the memory world, all of it, is disintegrating."

"I must see Anotine. I promised her I would return."

"You can't. Cley, she is just a thought. You are risking
both our lives by delaying for nothing more than a spark, a
breath of air."

"Don't say that about her," I said. I could see what I had
to do then. I walked forward as if I was resigned to going.
When I drew within a foot of the demon, I balled my right
hand into a fist and putting all of my strength behind it,
punched him squarely in the jaw. He reeled backward and fell
over onto the ground. The second he went down, I scrabbled
over to where the page had blown and retrieved it. Without
checking to see what condition Misrix was in, I again made
for the tree line.

I heard his wings above me before he landed on my back.
His arm came around my throat from behind, and he tried to
subdue me by preventing me from breathing. Stopping short
in my stride, I ducked forward and he flew over me, but at
the last second, grabbed my shirt and pulled me down on top
of him. We wrestled fiercely, turning one over the other across

the ground. Finally, his superior strength won out and he sat atop me, his left hand clutching my throat.

"I can't let you stay," he said, and then brought his right hand down with great force, smashing me across the face with the back of it. As I lost consciousness, I felt myself losing Anotine, and I knew exactly what it was like to die.

We were flying low through the night sky of Misrix's mind, over the forests of the Beyond.

"I lost track of you when the island disappeared," he said. "I had to search innumerable memories in order to find you. It took hours. I thought you would both perish."

I felt very weak and completely blank.

"The antidote, did you find it?" he asked, soaring upward into the night sky.

"It's the beauty," I said. "What else? Sheer beauty."

He reached the pinnacle of his ascent, then began the downward rush into our own reality. Somewhere in the descent, I passed into a deep sleep that was mercifully dreamless.

I opened my eyes, and found myself sitting in the chair in the room that contained Below's bed. My feet were up on the bench, and I was in the same position as when Misrix had placed his hand upon my head and initiated the dreaming wind. Looking to my left, I saw the demon, hunched over his father's body, administering a dose of the beauty to the vein in the old man's neck.

My muscles were cramped from having sat in the same position for so long, and I needed Misrix to help me to my feet.

"It took four hours," he said, as he wrapped his arm and wing around me for support.

We moved slowly toward the door. The pain in my knee I had gotten from running across the fields in the memory world had followed me back across time and space and now throbbed. Leaving the room, Misrix turned back and closed the door behind us.

Once I was sitting at the table in the room I had eaten in earlier, puffing on a Hundred-To-One, a cup of shudder sitting in front of me, the demon sat down. I still felt drained, both physically and emotionally.

"I feel dead," I said, letting out a trail of smoke.

"You look it too," said Misrix. "You spent too much time in the mnemonic reality. Your coming out was like an infant leaving the womb."

"I'm empty," I said.

"Cley, I wasn't going to tell you this, but I found the cure for the sleeping disease before you did. In an earlier memory of my father's, I stumbled upon him just as he discovered that the beauty would reverse its damage. I had to come and get you, though. You've got to live your life. If there was any way I could have brought the woman out, I would have. Can you forgive me?"

"I find it truly insane," I said, "that I have searched for love my entire life, and finally, when I found it, it was in the mind of a man who I considered to be a symbol of pure evil."

"But do you forgive me?" he asked.

"There's nothing to forgive. You are the only one of the three of us who operated out of truth. Your father and I were deceitful, he toward the world, and I with myself. You were right about something else also," I said, and took a sip of shudder.

"What?" asked the demon.

"It turned out to be a love story."

30

MISRIX LEFT THE ROOM IN ORDER TO GO CHECK ON BELOW and see if there was any change in his condition. Meanwhile I sat listlessly, staring at the wall and smoking one cigarette after the other. I knew now what it was like to lose someone close to you. Granted, Ea and Arla and their children had left and gone away to the Beyond, but at least I knew they were still out there somewhere. Anotine, on the other hand, was as good as dead now. I could remember Below's memory of her, but I could never again be with her in the same way as I had. "She must think I betrayed her," was what I kept saying to myself. Although I had returned to reality in one sense, the loss I felt was like a barrier that continued to separate me from it.

Quite a long time passed, and when the pack of Hundred-To-Ones was empty, I realized that I had to begin thinking about getting back to Wenau and administering the Beauty to those trapped in the sleep. I was about to get out of my chair and go in search of Misrix when the door opened and he entered, followed by Below. To my surprise the Master no longer wore the blue pajamas, but was now dressed in a formal-looking black suit with a broad-brimmed hat on that I could have sworn had been Mayor Bataldo's. He walked upright and showed no ill effects from the long illness he had just come through.

The second he saw me, he smiled.

"Cley, I've had you on my mind quite a bit lately," he said, and laughed raucously at his own joke.

Misrix pulled the chair across from me out for him, and he took a seat.

"Excuse me for a moment, Cley," he said. He turned to Misrix. "Listen, boy, I want you to go over to the Ministry of Education, back there where I've been stockpiling the beauty. Load it on the wagon, hitch the horses to it, and bring it around. It's time to ingratiate ourselves to the good people of Wenau."

"The werewolves, Father," said Misrix.

"Oh, yes," he said. From around his neck Below removed a chain with a small thin cylinder attached to it. "Take the whistle. If they bother you, blow on it, and it will put them off."

The demon took it from him, but did not move.

"Yes?" asked the Master.

"I want you to know that Cley saved your life, sir," said the demon.

Below reached over and rubbed the fur on Misrix's forearm. "I'm aware of it," he said. "I'll never forget it."

The demon smiled, then, giving me a quick look, turned and left the room. The instant the door closed behind him, Below reached into his jacket, pulled out a pistol, and laid it on the table in front of him.

"What do you think of him?" he asked me.

"He is very special," I said. "You should have more faith in him."

"How might that be possible?" he asked.

"Why do you think you have to coerce the people of Wenau to accept him? I'm telling you, they will be frightened at first, but once he has a chance to prove himself, you won't need to force them to see his kindness. With the plan you have, you will end up making them hate him as they hate you."

"I wish I had the faith in people you have, Cley. I only have faith in power," he said with a sigh.

"And so you are going to shoot me?" I asked.

"It is a rather second-rate means of execution. I would have liked to have thought up something more diabolical in keeping with your remarkable qualities, but, as you know, I've been out of sorts lately, and my imagination needs time to rebuild."

"What will your son think when he comes back and finds me dead?" I asked.

"He will be upset for a time. Parenting is a tough business. You can't shield your children from the realities of the world forever. I tell you it makes the process of raising a son bitter-sweet, knowing the vicissitudes of life he will have to face," he said, staring at the table. A look of true sadness came over him.

"Were you aware of me in your memory?" I asked.

He nodded. "I saw you flailing around, but it was as if I was paralyzed at the bottom of a deep well. It was a struggle to focus on my memories. Things were not always clear. I really had to concentrate. My word, what an effort it took to invigorate my form on the dome and set a course that would lead you to the antidote."

"You consciously sent me back to the ruins of the city?"

"I could see that you had botched the situation on the floating island. I knew I had to help you get to a particular memory where the antidote would be more obvious. When Anotine kissed me, even though it was a memory kiss, it still carried a hint of the beauty, and this revived my will just enough for me to start the dome's engine and set a course."

"And what of Anotine?" I asked.

"She is still there, Cley. You saved her, and what's more, if I am not mistaken, she is pregnant with your memory child. Watching you interact with her was somewhat pitiful, but it offered a bit of amusement."

"She was a woman you loved and abandoned?" I asked.

"No, no, no, her memory seized while studying Scarfinati's book. She's on a ship somewhere encased in a chemical ice that can't melt. She's out there somewhere," he said, sweeping his hand in front of him. "The ship left port one year and never returned."

"That's not what Scarfinati told me," I said.

"Oh, please, Cley. You should know at your age how the imagination, how desire, influences memory. My memory of Scarfinati is a mischievous entity in my mind. You can't believe a word of what he said. These things can't always be controlled. Take the Delicate, for instance. He came to me in a nightmare when I was a child, soon after my sister's death. I've been trying to get rid of him since, but he persists. He's a symbol of something very powerful that I can't quite understand and can't, for the life of me, forget."

"There is a world of evil inside you," I said, "but I also found love there."

"One thing you've got to understand, Cley. What you experienced wasn't all me. Your presence changed things; your desire was so inextricably intertwined with my memory that it would have been hard to separate the two. What belonged to whom is difficult to say. Perhaps, for a short time, you made me better than what I really am. For that, I'd be happy to spare your life, but from past experience I know you are an incorrigible meddler. If it were anything else but Misrix's future, I would let you go."

"Promise me that you will protect the people of Wenau," I said.

"I intend to. Where would I be without them?" he said, and, taking the gun in his hand, pushed his chair back and stood. "Stand up," he said, pointing the gun at me.

I thought about leaping over the table at him, crying out for help, running for the door, but the dull ache inside me caused by my loss of Anotine canceled my will to act. "Shoot," I said.

He took aim at my chest, and I waited for him to pull the trigger, but then he started coughing violently, making him unable to aim. Holding his free hand up as if to indicate he would be with me momentarily, I could tell he was trying to utter one of his witticisms, but the words came forth in a tortured gurgling. It was obvious he was having a hard time catching his breath, and I waited, really rather bored, for the episode to pass. Only when he dropped the gun and brought both of his hands to his throat did I realize his condition was serious. He stumbled back against the wall for support, all the while making these slight wheezing noises.

I came around the table to try to help him. "What is it?" I yelled.

The door opened and Misrix entered. "Everything is ready,

Father," he said before noticing us. A moment later, he saw
what was happening and came over to Below's other side.
There was a look of intense fear on his face. "What's happening, Cley?" he screamed.

"Your father was going to shoot me, but then he started
choking. I don't know."

The Master quickly went from bad to worse, the complexion of his face turning nearly as blue as those of the spire
miners of Anamasobia, who, after years, take on the hue of
the mineral they work. The wheezing diminished, he lost consciousness, and we eased him to the floor.

"What should I do?" asked the demon.

I shook my head. Whatever was happening was a mystery
to me.

Moments later, Below's whole body suddenly relaxed. I
felt for a pulse but could find nothing. I could hardly believe
it. The great Drachton Below, the Master, was dead. His eyes
stared coldly at the ceiling, his mouth was agape, his hands
lay on his chest.

"How?" asked Misrix, tears in his eyes.

My life had just been spared by some wild fluke, but still
I felt terrible for the demon, having recently experienced an
equivalent loss. I stood up and backed away.

"What is this, Cley?" he said. "Look, there is something
in his throat."

I came back and knelt.

"There," he said, pointing with the tip of a claw.

Pulling down on Below's chin in order to open his
mouth yet wider, I bent low and peered into the dark behind
his tongue. There was something there. It appeared to be a
small flap of some kind. Then Misrix changed his position
to look over my shoulder, and the light, which had been
blocked by his head, now revealed to me the color green.
My hand immediately went to my breast pocket and found
it empty.

Misrix reached past me and, using his claws like tweezers,
snagged the edge of the flap and pulled. The veil came forth
like a long green tongue, like a trick from a children's magic
show. I couldn't believe what I was seeing. The demon started

crying again as he unfurled the piece of material until it was completely open.

"I don't understand," he said, and laid the veil across Below's face, covering his hideous expression.

I knew then that this was my miracle. Having eaten the white fruit, I kept waiting for something unusual to happen either to me or for me. I had taken for granted that my simply surviving the mnemonic ordeal had been the marvel I was waiting for. Somehow a thought had taken on physical actuality. I was sure that Anotine was partially behind it.

Misrix took the chain with the whistle from around his neck and handed it to me. "Go," he said. "The wagon is just outside. There is enough sheer beauty on it to cure a thousand Wenaus. Help your people."

"Come with me," I said. "I'll see to it that you can find a life with us."

"I can't leave now," he said. He took the spectacles off his face, dropped them on the floor, and stomped them with his hoof.

I was about to plead with him to come accompany me again, but he turned away, and yelled, "Go!" As I left the room, I looked back to see the demon kneeling over Below's corpse. He put his arms around the body and laid his head on the chest. Then his wings came up and covered them from my sight.

It took me some time to find my way out of the Ministry of Information, but eventually I wandered into a corridor that led to a door that opened on the street. There was the wagon loaded high with crates of sheer beauty, two horses harnessed to it. I climbed aboard the seat in front and lifted the reins. These beasts were somewhat more helpful than Quismal. I did little more than flick the reins, and they started off. They took me through the city, around rubble and blasted buildings, always finding a clear path through which the wagon could pass. It took no more than fifteen minutes before we had traveled through a spot in the circular wall where the masonry had been completely obliterated.

The wagon was sturdy with huge wheels for traversing ditches and mounds, and the horses were not only bright but strong and fast. Once they hit the plain, they started running, and I swore to myself that this would be absolutely my last time crossing that hellish tract of ground. I had Below's whistle ever at the ready, but I saw no sign of the werewolves. It was important I stay aware of our progress as we sped toward Wenau, but all the time my mind was on Anotine.

31

It was I who brought the serpent to paradise. There were no needles in the crates of beauty, so I guessed at a dose and administered, orally, two drops of the concentrated formula to adults and one to children. The results, as in Below's case, were remarkable. Within hours, the victims of the disease were up and walking around. By the time the sun went down, I had brought so many back from death's door that I was actually beginning to feel I deserved all of the praise that was bestowed upon me. A great euphoria swept through Wenau, partially the thrill of resurrection, partially the hallucinatory effects of the drug.

I had to warn each of the victim's families that the beauty was a serious narcotic and that their loved ones would experience visions and all manner of paranoid delusions. They accepted this as a small price to pay for a cure. I should have told them all about the brutally addictive effects also, but I couldn't. It wasn't that I forgot. I just couldn't bring myself to take responsibility for the tragedy I knew would follow.

I used less than a quarter of one of the thirty cases on the wagon and ended my rounds late in the evening by the river, drinking field beer with Jensen and Roan, their wives, and some of my other neighbors. The night was cool, and the smell of the open air, the rushing water was so fresh after the stale atmosphere of the ruins. Someone lit a fire, and we gathered around it. One of the children carried over to me a letter of thanks from the entire settlement on blue paper that had been hastily scrawled for the event.

Then Jensen quieted everyone down, and said, "Cley, we are waiting to hear of your journey."

I waved him off, and said, "Talk will only cut into my drinking."

"Now, now," said another. "We want to know."

"Is Below still alive?" asked Semla Hood.

"Below is dead," I said.

A round of applause went up, and for some reason this saddened me. They pressed me for more details, and I began to cry uncontrollably. The group went silent around me and each of them looked away in order to spare me embarrassment. I was greatly relieved when conversations broke out around the circle, and I was no longer the focus of attention.

Miley Mac's wife, Dorothea, told the woman next to her, "I never felt better then when I awoke from the sleep. The strangest thing happened. I saw a face on the wall of my bedroom. It was my brother, who had died in the destruction of the Well-Built City. Stranger yet, I had a conversation with him."

More testimonies followed hers concerning the hallucinatory effects of the drug. Most of them were positive. But that is the way the beauty works. I remember it well. The first time it shows you what you most desire, but once it has you in its grasp, your will is no longer your own.

As these tales of visions were being related, I excused myself, climbed into the wagon, and headed away from the center of the village toward my home in the woods. I can't describe to you the sense of relief I felt when I stepped across the threshold. The place was utterly quiet, and only then did it strike me how much I had been through in the past few days.

I had thought that it would be the finest feeling to again lie in my bed, but when I did, I could not fall asleep. Thoughts of Anotine rushed into my mind, and I tossed and turned with loneliness and desire. The loss of her was something I could not put behind me. Even when I finally dozed off from complete exhaustion, I had nightmares in which she came back to ask me why I had abandoned her.

The next day, I woke late, but did not get out of bed for hours. Instead of going into the forest to gather wild herbs and roots as was my routine, I lay there listlessly, staring at the ceiling, trying to remember the faces of Nunnly, Brisden, and the Doctor. Though I remembered their names and their specialties, some of the things each of them had said to me, I couldn't conjure a clear image of any one of them. This frightened me, and I crawled out of bed finally, telling myself, "Come on, Cley. You've got to get going."

I dressed and went outside into the bright light of afternoon. The very first thing I noticed was that two of the crates of beauty were gone from the wagon. I counted them again and again, but there was no mistake. This was the first theft I had ever heard of in Wenau. The drug had already begun to work its will. Right then, I should have destroyed the stockpile and gone to the market to warn my neighbors, but I didn't. The village I had worked so hard to help found had begun on a course of self-destruction. I knew I didn't have it in me to stand in the path of that boulder rolling down hill. Instead, I hefted three crates inside my home.

Whereas I had administered two drops for the other adults of the village, I prescribed four for myself. Sitting at my table, facing the window that showed a lovely scene of silver-backed leaves shifting in the wind, I tasted sheer beauty, perhaps the most bitter substance known to man. I audibly groaned as it worked its way through my system, growing like a vine around my heart and mind. Then, everything became soft and slow.

I looked up and there was Anotine, sitting across from me. She was laughing as if I had just told her a joke. Her hair was down and she wore her yellow dress.

"I missed you," I said to her.

"Don't worry, Cley, I'll be here for you now," she said. She got up and stepped around the table in order to lean down and kiss me.

Two days passed, and every time she began to dissipate, I took more drops of the bitter liquid. I ate little and only went outside to relieve myself. By the end of the second day, I noticed that there was only one crate of the beauty left on the wagon.

Occasionally the drug did not bring me Anotine, but instead Below or the Doctor or Misrix materialized to torture me with recriminations of one sort or another. One night, after having just made love to Anotine in my bed, I heard something creeping around the door of my house. The moment I leaped up, she vanished. I was suddenly frightened, thinking that someone had come to take the last of my store of the beauty. I knew that by this time, the entire village must be out of its mind, swinging between elation and craving. It was more than conceivable that someone would be willing to kill for a drop or two of the drug.

I fetched my stone knife, and creeping over to the door, swung it open quickly. There, sitting before me, was the black dog, Wood. When he saw me, he barked once, then trotted past me into the room. His ear had been torn off and there were nasty-looking wounds that had healed on his right shoulder. At first, the sight of him frightened me, as if he was a ghost. Then, he walked over to where I stood trembling, reared up on his hind legs, and threw himself against my chest. I put my arms around him and petted his fur. I had dried, salted meat in my pantry, and I gave him a huge plate of it. He sat at my feet as I opened another vial of the beauty and took five drops. Anotine returned, and I told her all about the courage of the dog. When the sunrise turned the sky red out on the horizon, she vanished, but Wood remained. As the days passed, it became evident that he had really survived our ordeal on the fields of Harakun.

Semla Hood came to visit me one afternoon just after I had taken the drops. I saw her approaching out the window, but when she knocked, I tried to pretend I wasn't in. To my horror, she was not put off by my silence, but opened the door and stepped into the house. The minute she saw me, she shook her head.

"I came to you for help, Cley, but I can see you are no better off than the others."

"I'm sorry," was the best I could do.

"That cure you brought has turned Wenau into a living hell," she said. "There is thieving and there have been two murders over that witches' brew. Men and women are acting like children, and there are children who sit all day drooling, staring at the sun."

I shook my head.

"There are a few of us who are trying to restore things to normal, but it seems impossible. You brought my husband back to me, but now I have lost him again."

"What can I do?" I said. "I'm tired."

"Well, I just wanted to tell you that Jensen Watt drowned yesterday, chasing a beautiful angel into the river."

"You will have to leave," I said to her, because I could see Anotine materializing in the kitchen. I turned away and heard the door slam behind me.

That night Wood woke me with his barking. I rolled out of bed and grabbed the stone knife. Crouching behind my chair, I waited to see if I was being robbed. There came a knocking at the door.

"Who is it?" I called.

The dog growled.

"It's me," said a deep voice.

"Go away," I said. "I have a knife."

The door suddenly burst open with so much force, I fell back onto my rear end. The demon stepped through the entrance. His eyes burned with a yellow fire, and his tail was snapping the air. I put my hands up to protect myself as he came forward. He reached down with a massive hand, and his claws passed right through the material of my shirt without cutting my chest. Lifting me off the ground, he said, "I've been watching you, Cley," and with this, backhanded me into unconsciousness for the third time.

I woke the next morning tied to the posts of my bed and saw Misrix standing by the table across the room. He was lifting the remaining vials one by one out of the crate before him and crushing them in his hands.

"It's time to wake up," he said.

The withdrawal nearly killed me. It took a solid week before I could get out of bed and move around on my own. I can't bring myself to tell you the depths to which I sank in the midst of my craving. The pain was so intense I thought my head would split open. There were entire days of shivering and sweating and endless tears. I derided the demon with the worst curses and disparagements my insane mind could conjure. I told him he was responsible for his father's death, and that he was nothing but an animal who had been tricked into thinking he was human. Through it all, Misrix's only reaction was to laugh. He made me soups out of plants he gathered in the forest while I was sleeping. Wood and he became fast friends as they watched over my return to life.

Finally the day came when he untied my hands and feet, and told me, "You are finished with it now, Cley. Don't worry about trying to find more; I have destroyed the last of it."

He led me out into the forest to a pool and made me wash. When we returned to my home, and I had dressed in fresh clothes, he said, "I have something for you."

Holding out his hand, he opened it slowly to reveal the green veil. "Don't worry," he said, laughing, "I washed it."

With the veil returned to me, I felt whole again. My body began to rejuvenate from the ravages of the beauty. My mind began to clear, and I knew I had to leave Wenau.

"Where will you go?" asked Misrix when I told him of my plan.

"I don't know. Somewhere far away from here."

"Travel with me to the Beyond," he said. "I am going back. This humanity does not suit me well. I want to lose myself in the forest again. I want to fly above the Palishize and hunt like the creature I truly am. I have thought far too much for a demon."

I pictured the Beyond, its boundless tracts of undiscovered territory. "Paradise is there," I said. "I tried to reach it once, but I failed."

"You've got to keep trying," he said.

We made our plans. Misrix flew back to the ruins of the City to gather the supplies we would need for our journey. During the days of our preparation, I wrote this testament for you, good people of Wenau. It is an explanation, a warning. It is a love story. I hope it can somehow cure the evil I had no choice but to loose upon you. Embrace your memories, but be wary. The truth lies in them.

In the small hours of the morning, I will lay these pages

on the doorstep of Semla Hood's home, and then Misrix and I and the black dog will strike out for the Beyond, where the demon hopes to forget his humanity and I hope to remember mine.

Acknowledgments

I could not have written this novel without having read two books about mnemonics by Frances A. Yates—*The Art of Memory* and *Giordano Bruno and the Hermetic Tradition*. These are truly incredible works of scholarship, and I recommend them to anyone with an imagination.

I also must thank the following individuals for their help and encouragement:

Bill Watkins, Kevin Quigley, Mike Gallagher, and Frank Keenan for reading and commenting on this manuscript in its various stages of creation.

Walter, Jean, Dylan, and Chelsea for their generous technical support.

Jennifer Brehl, editor of this book, who, amidst the baffling maze of memory, would not allow me to forget to remember.